DUCKBOY

BILL BUNN

Published by Bitingduck Press
ISBN 978-1-938463-60-0

For information contact
Bitingduck Press, LLC
Montreal • Altadena
notifications@bitingduckpress.com
http://www.bitingduckpress.com
Cover image by Dena Eaton

Publisher's Cataloging-in-Publication
Bunn, William [1963 -]

Duck Boy/by William Bunn—1st ed.—Altadena, CA: Bitingduck Press, 2012
p. cm.

ISBN 978-1-938463-60-0

[1. Young Adult—Fiction 2. Sorcery—Incantations—Fiction 3. Alchemy—Magic spells—Fiction 4. Peer pressure—Fiction] I. Title

LCCN 2012941372

To my wife, who is life, my children, who are inspiration. Special thanks to Ken Rivard, Brad Quiring, and Diana Patterson.

Whatever you can do in a dream
Or on your mind-canvas
My hands can pull—alive—from my coat pocket.
—Hafiz, "Imagination Does Not Exist," from *The Gift*
(translated by Daniel Ladinsky)

Prologue

It was surprising how average the night seemed, considering Steve Best's mom was about to disappear forever.

Steve lay on his bed, watching a cartoon on his iPod, trying to put himself in a better mood after a rousing fight with his mom.

I need to apologize.

"Helllpppp!" Her shriek splintered the silence. Had she been stabbed? The terror in her voice made his skin crawl. The gap at the bottom of his bedroom door pulsed with light.

"Noooo." A second spine-chilling howl.

A loud smash on the hardwood floor followed by a softer thump, and the line of radiation snapped into a black silence.

"Mom?" Steve shouted. "Are you all right?" He felt for his night stand and set down his iPod. "Mom?"

Standing, he groped for the door and knuckled the

bedroom light on. He opened his door into the black of the living room. He skulked across the floor to the far wall. He could hear his dad fumbling in their bedroom.

Steve's fingers found the plastic bank of switches and flipped them on.

His dad jerked through the door, blinking as his eyes adjusted to the light. A zombie. Hair a wild, balding nest perched on his head.

"What's going on?" he demanded, one hand shading his eyes from the light.

"I dunno."

In front of them both, Mom's yellow overstuffed leather chair. The chair's right arm gashed with four lines made by her fingernails. Clawmarks. A brown pond of coffee on the floor, its edges creeping into a widening circle. A ruffled notebook seemed to float in the middle of the pond, soaking in the coffee, surrounded by the shark-fin shards of a shattered mug and smashed coffee table light. Chair empty. No blood.

"What the...?" Steve breathed. The house waited in silence. No footsteps. No screams. No scuff marks on the hardwood. After a moment, Steve's dad marched into the kitchen.

"Did you hurt your mom?" he asked slowly, as he returned with a roll of paper towels.

"No," Steve answered, offended. "Of course not. You serious?"

His dad met his stare. "That was a wicked argument.

You told her to go jump in a lake."

"Dad, I didn't touch her. I would never. I can't believe you think I might have."

"Susan? Honey? Are you OK? Can you hear me?" Mr. Best returned and hurled the paper towels towards Steve. "Can you work on that, while I find Mom?"

It was a wicked argument.

Steve began applying patches of paper towel to what was now a brown lake, and went to fetch a bowl from the kitchen. He could hear his dad plunging into the basement and through the rest of the house, calling out, "Honey? Susan? Where are you?"

After hollering through the whole house, Mr. Best returned to the living room, agitated. "Susan, this isn't funny anymore. Stop it." His face was wild with dread.

Steve sopped up the coffee lake, dropping the drenched paper towel into the bowl.

"Have you seen her?" Dad squeaked.

Steve shook his head.

"You're not in on this?" Mr. Best yelped, still apparently hoping it was some kind of weird joke. But he didn't wait for an answer. He scoured the house again, searching behind furniture, peering around corners, opening doors, yelling into rooms.

Finally he seemed to give up, laughing nervously. "Your mom does these things from time to time," he attempted, eyes darting around the room.

"You could have done a better job of cleaning up," he

added, suddenly angry. He tore the towel out of Steve's hand and knelt over the stain. "Why would she do this?" he said quietly to himself as he mopped. "Why would she do this?"

Steve winced as he thought of his last words to his mom. His dad probably heard them. As they reverberated in his mind, he knew they were words that should never have been spoken. "I wish you would go away and never come back." He sunk his head into his hands and sighed.

Sorry, Mom.

After a nervous clean-up, Mr. Best flopped on the couch next to Steve. He tapped his foot on the floor, his eyes darting with every little creak and groan in the house. Every few minutes he'd holler his way through the house again, then collapse once more.

"Something's not right." He bounced suddenly off the couch.

"Geez, Dad. Take it easy."

"Sorry, Son. I should call a few of her friends." He strode to the imitation antique phone, pulled the earpiece from its cradle, and dialed.

"Chrissy? Doug Best calling. Sorry to call so late. Is Susan over at your place?" Some muffled squawking. "OK. If she does drop by, could you tell her to call home?" More squawks. "Thanks. Goodbye."

He repeated this call at least fifteen times, different numbers and names but the same outcome.

Steve closed his eyes and tried to imagine a happier

ending to the argument he'd had with his mom.

Dad appeared tormented after the phone calls. "Any ideas?" he asked Steve. "Did I check the bathrooms?"

He didn't wait for a reply and swept through the bathrooms. "Nada," he said in an outlandishly cheery voice. He returned to the living room, his face contorted with suffering. Then an anxious smile. "The cars!"

Out the front door, into the night in his PJs and bare feet. Steve could hear yells through the front door, still wide open, as his dad rummaged through the yard. Front and back. Then to the garage. A distant crash and a matching set of obscenities. Mr. Best darted back into the house, slamming the front door.

"Something's not right. This is not like her," Dad sputtered, little globes of saliva spraying as he spoke. Eyes rimmed with red. Lip twitching. "I don't know where she went," he cried.

Steve shook his head. It was official, he was drowning in guilt.

She was gone. And gone she stayed.

CHAPTER ONE

STEVE STOOD IN A short line at a checkout, staring out the mouth of the store at the banks of outlet shops and the empty corridors festooned with fountains.

And, of course, the faces. He always checked faces. The elderly man in line ahead of him, the woman selecting headphones from the wall behind him.

"Have a nice day," the clerk said to the man, her smile as plastic as the bag she handed him. The old man clasped the bag with tremulous, aged fingers and headed out aimlessly towards one of the fountains, allowing Steve to step forward with a new iPhone.

A woman browsed a display of cards set out on the tiled corridor at the front entrance.

"No way," Steve stammered to himself.

He forced his eyes into a slow blink, to cleanse his vision. And gawped again.

"Mom?" His heartbeat sounded like a drum in his ear. She continued to strum through the rack of cards. A few purchases dangled in bags from her left hand.

"How would you like to pay for your phone, sir?" droned the cashier. Steve meant to set the phone package on the counter, but he couldn't stop staring at the woman. The phone slipped from his grasp and bashed on the floor. His wallet flapped open in his other hand, as though he held a bird by its wing.

"Sir?" the cashier urged.

"Mom? Mom? Is that you?" Steve yelled, a kind of sick, sticky thrill rising in his throat. The woman turned to Steve. "Mom?" he repeated. Her eyes opened in horror as the recognition burned home.

"Um... ah." Words stalled. Crimson blazed on her cheeks. She flung her purchases and bolted.

The old man was still at the fountain, mesmerized by the fountain's jets. The woman hit him square in the back with enough force that he toppled into the water, full of spare change. Steve began to move towards the fountain.

"Sir, your phone is on the floor," the cashier huffed. Steve's open wallet dropped to the floor a few feet away from the iPhone.

"Sir?"

His mom had a head start, already slaloming through the food court tables. He chased, but his legs refused to work quickly. "Mom... Mom," he screamed down the mall. "Why did you do it? Just tell me why you left."

In an instant, the mall was awash with a sea of people. Steve bumped his way through the crowd.

By the time he arrived at the food court's tables, his mother was slamming through the mall doors to the parking lot. Steve felt a familiar lump crush his throat. He ran to the doors and yelled at the tiny sprinting figure. "You don't have to come home if you don't want to."

From some distant place, Steve heard an annoyed voice. Oh, right, he thought. This is a daydream. More like a nightmare. Except during the day. A daymare.

"Mr. Best?" The teeming crowd faded to black. Even the daymare wouldn't stay.

Mr. Pollock stood before him, frowning. His arms folded defiantly over his ample gut. A tie tied slightly too short. A white dress shirt with blue and red stripes, with a few straining buttons around his navel. A badly dressed frown with legs. And the frown was aimed at Steve.

"Mr. Best! You're traveling again." The rest of the class laughed. The Frown marched along the row of desks to Steve. "Mr. Best, you still haven't answered me! Well, Mr. Best?"

"Huh?" Steve answered in a weak voice.

"Would you answer the question, please?"

Steve scoured the faces of his ninth-grade classmates for any clues. No one wanted to help. They seemed more entertained by Mr. Pollock's tirade, more interested in what was going to happen to Steve.

"Um, I guess I wasn't listening, Mr. Pollock," Steve replied. A tired pair of words flocked his thoughts. A reminder of an old wound, these words showed up whenever he felt like a loser.

Duck Boy. Duck Boy.

"I'd like to know where you go when you take these mental vacations. Next time book a two-way ticket," the Frown said. "And book it over a holiday. It'll be cheaper."

A tingle of embarrassment burned Steve's face.

"I'm sorry, Mr. Pollock," hoping to end the attack. But the Frown hadn't finished with him.

"Get out of my classroom," snorted the teacher. "Principal's office. Now." He raised an arm and pointed dramatically toward the office and waited.

Steve collected his books and shuffled through the door.

The classroom door slammed behind him, leaving him alone in the hallway.

Alone. Finally.

He already had an appointment at the principal's office, though Mr. Pollock hadn't known it. His dad was supposed to talk to the principal to review Steve's abysmal marks. The principal and Dad. Double whammy.

Steve detoured to his locker. He spun the face of his combination lock. After a third try at the combination, it opened, and he placed everything he didn't need inside. He collected his coat, gloves, hat, and his binder—he had homework over the Christmas break.

Thank God the Christmas break starts tomorrow.

Bowing his head, he rested against the locker shelf and closed his eyes. For a few moments, he stood there avoiding the thoughts pooling in his mind.

I could drown, if I think too much.

The bell rang and classroom doors burst open. Students flooded the hallway.

Startled, Steve slipped on his coat, stuffing his tuque and gloves into the pockets, and tucked his binder under his arm. He swung the locker door shut and slid the lock into place.

The short stretch of hallway towards the school door and the outside world tempted him for a moment. The winter weather would feel tropical compared to the chill he was about to face in the principal's office. He fought the urge to leave everything and walk home.

No point in making things worse.

He crawled through the crowd toward the office. As he passed the entrance to Mr. Pollock's class, the class bully crowed his arrival.

"Hey, Duck Boy," David said in a loud voice. "Duck, Duck, Ducky!"

Steve clenched his teeth, but didn't look up. As he passed, David lunged for Steve's binder and whacked it forward. It flew from under his arm and into the crowded hallway ahead of him. The binder's rings snapped open and class notes feathered the air. A pair of girls squealed with laughter. They turned away as Steve glanced at them. The brick echoes of their laughter still hit the mark.

"Hey, you—Duck Boy!" yelled another classmate.

Steve forced his eyes down and away from his schoolmates' faces as he passed them, away from the paper, and up the hallway. Away, away. The pack of students kicked and frolicked through his notes, giddy with the thought of Christmas. David and his cronies eyed him, probably hoping Steve would frantically attempt to recapture all the paper.

I refuse to pick it up.

Instead, he stomped through his own notes, the paper crinkling and tearing as he walked over it.

Duck Boy. Duck Boy.

The nearly empty binder lined up with his foot, and in a final act of defiance, he punted it. It flew between several students, shedding a last few sheets, bashing against a stretch of lockers. It collapsed to the floor, covers partly torn, like a robin that had hit a glass window.

He stormed through the office door, stopping in front of the secretary's desk. The secretary looked up sharply, as if he had startled her, but her surprise melted into a smile when she saw him.

"Hello, Steve," she said. Membership has its privileges. Frequent fliers were greeted personally at the door. "Your dad and Mrs. Wilcox are discussing your school performance. I've got to get some photocopying done." She picked up a thick file and stepped from behind the counter. "Just wait until they finish their meeting, all right? They know you're waiting for them." As she stepped into the hallway, Steve sat down next to the principal's office. A clock whirred and clicked just above his head.

Steve felt ice close in around him as he sat. Life was

such a drag. His nickname flew circles in his thoughts.

Duck Boy. Duck Boy.

As he waited, his thoughts migrated back to his foolish duck rescue—the day he earned the name "Duck Boy."

It was in November that the pond outside the junior high school had frozen over for the first time that season. The pond looked black under the smooth polish of the first coat of ice. But the day seemed cold enough for the ice to hang on until the rest of winter arrived.

In the middle of that frozen pond sat a mallard duck, frozen to the ice. It had probably fallen asleep while the ice formed around it. When it awoke, it was frozen to the pond's surface. It flailed and screamed for freedom, but the ice wasn't listening.

As Steve stood gazing at the stranded bird, a few of his classmates gathered by the pond.

"That's hilarious," David said. "So much for the mighty duck."

"It's a dead duck," one of David's minions added. "A frozen dinner."

David bent down, found a stone and hurled it at the duck. The stone hit the ice in front of the bird and scuttled into the bird's side. The duck stopped trying to free itself from the ice for a moment and began to flap up a new panic. David carefully selected another rock from the pond's edge.

"Stop it, jerks!" Steve yelled towards his classmates. "Can't you see it's stuck? It's utterly defenseless." He rushed at David to stop his throw.

Another spectator caught Steve and pushed him to the ground and sat on him before he could reach his nemesis. "Pinhead," Steve spat in David's direction.

The rock missed.

"That duck has more happening in its brain than you do," Steve yelled with the last of his breath.

His comment earned him a slug in the gut. "Stupid animal lover." Steve fought to bring air back into his lungs. "Mind your own business."

"He's the ugly duck," David said, pointing at Steve. "So ugly that even his mom couldn't stand him."

The group laughed. "He's the Ugly Duck Boy!"

"Leave the duck alone!" Steve wheezed.

"The newspaper says there are too many ducks around, doofus," David snarled. "That duck was stupid. It got itself frozen into the pond. Survival of the fittest." David stopped talking as a fist-sized rock bashed the duck's back, and the duck stopped its fight to look up towards the bank with a dazed look.

"Nice shot," a minion remarked.

Steve heaved his captor from his body and ran, without a thought, to the pond's edge. He focused on the dazed duck, mulling his choices, and then stepped gingerly onto the new layer of ice. For a moment he stood on the pond's surface. But the ice snapped loudly, and in an instant the polished black surface around his feet burst into shards.

He stood in ankle deep water, the pond filling his new

Nike hightops. "Crap," he muttered to himself. Somehow he remembered to remove his backpack, throwing it onto the shore behind him.

Then step by soggy step he marched toward the duck, making pieces of the ice as he went.

"Look at the idiot. He thinks he's a duck," shouted someone. "He's ugly, and he can't swim." It was true. Steve couldn't swim at all, and he sure felt ugly. The four on the shore laughed hysterically and mocked.

"Why am I doing this?"

His steps broke the ice until he was up to his thighs. Once the water was too deep to use his feet to break the ice, he began to punch the pond ice with his fists.

"Get the Duck Boy! Get the loser," David commanded. The group on the shore hurled anything they could find at Steve, showering him with ice and water. Another picked up his backpack and hurled it into the pond, where it floated, sort of.

Steve hobbled on his tiptoes in frigid water almost up to his chest. The freezing water burned his ribcage, making it hard to breathe. He was still a few feet from where the frantic duck sat locked in its frozen seat. As he bobbed closer to the duck, he realized that if he wanted to free it he'd have to confront water that was over his head. And he really couldn't swim.

The school bell rang, and a few more rocks and sticks spattered around Steve and the duck before the group of students headed to school, leaving Steve, the duck, the pond, and the ice to battle it out.

Steve struggled to keep his chin above the water. The chill numbed his mind and stole his breath.

He lunged towards the duck, smashed down with his fists, hoping to crack the ice around the duck without having to attempt to swim. But the ice broke around his hands, leaving the ice around the duck intact.

Steve allowed his body to sink under the freezing pond water so he could give a strong push to where the duck sat. His head slowly dropped beneath the surface, falling into a world of black water.

He looked down. The chrome skeleton of a shopping cart shimmered under him. He looked up at the frantic, frozen mallard—its webbed feet paddled in terror, still imprisoned. Feathers flashed, were they red? and a wink of sunlight turned the ice gold. Steve stood on the cart and prepared to push himself up to the surface.

But somehow his right foot slid into a small gap in the shopping cart's metal grid. When he realized what had happened, he tried to pull his foot through. He planted his left foot on the outside of the cart and pushed, trying to muscle his foot through the cart's grate.

The last of his dry breath bubbled through his mouth. His lungs burned. He tried to spin his body, but the hole in the cart's shell wouldn't allow it. The burn in his lungs became a raging fire. He thrashed mindlessly as the pain in his lungs and leg became unbearable.

Hope left him alone in the black water. His body

stopped fighting and hung above the shopping cart, now quiet.

This is it. Dead Duck Boy.

The icy black water seemed to leak through his skin, inside, taking his last moments.

What a way to go.

As his trapped foot relaxed, the shoe loosened and dropped away, belching a bubble before see-sawing to the pond bottom. Now smaller, his foot slowly slid through the grating, and he thrashed to the water's surface.

His face broke through the pond ice and he stuffed his burning lungs with bright morning air. The terror returned. Steve floundered his way towards the shore, leaving the duck behind.

As he flailed to save his own life, a foot inadvertently broke the ice underneath the duck, freeing it from the pond's surface. Frantic wings beat around Steve's head as the bird took to the air. And the duck, probably feeling attacked, snapped at his hand. He would have hollered, except breathing and floating seemed more important.

He felt like a 1000-pound rock. Flailing arm over arm, he tried imitating a front-crawl stroke he'd seen on TV.

His TV swimming tired him, so he dropped down under the water again, trying to regain strength. He eyed the cart, which was now behind him. He bicycled his feet forward until he was standing.

"Yes," he said to himself, discovering the water was only up to his chest. "Yes, yes, yes." With each step toward the shore, terror ebbed from his mind. He stopped for a moment, freezing water up to his chest, heaving, wondering if his lungs would ever be the same again.

He realized for the first time since he entered the water that he was freezing. He reached instinctively for the house key he wore around his neck. It was gone.

"Ah, crap," Steve said angrily to himself. "Do I have to go to school LIKE THIS?" he shouted. He climbed out of the pond and noticed his missing shoe. "MY NEW SHOES!" he screamed. He kicked off the remaining Nike and hurled it into the pond. "This day sucks!"

Home or school?

He debated. His frozen thoughts moved slowly. He was probably almost a mile from home, and he had frozen feet slopping in wet socks. He had no house key. School was much closer. The choice seemed to come slowly and with great effort. His decision was a practical one, though humiliating.

Up the steps, and through the main doors of the school. His wet socks slapped on the linoleum as he walked to class, leaving a trail of small puddles.

I can barely think.

He entered the Frown's class, mid-lecture, and to the surprise of nearly everyone, plopped into his seat with a splat. The room went silent. A slow drip, drip, drip pattered onto the seat from his elbow.

Just be normal.

He smiled pleasantly, to suggest that nothing was

wrong.

The Frown, dumbfounded, joined him where he sat, inspecting him from head to toe. "Mr. Best. You are leaking in my classroom," he said slowly. Drip, drip, drip.

Steve, not quite himself, wasn't really listening. He was staring at his hands, which were an interesting shade of blue. He would have smiled, but his face felt numb.

The Frown followed Steve's stare. His scowl burst into confusion for a few moments. Then alarm. "Go see the nurse, Mr. Best," he ordered. "Now."

Though Steve couldn't remember quite how he got there, he ended up in the nurse's office, where he was given dry clothes pilfered from the lost and found. The ball-shaped nurse wrapped him in blankets and made him sit bundled until he warmed up.

The clothes. They didn't fit. They didn't match. Like his life. The shoes were size 12 at least. He wandered through the day looking homeless, which made for easy jokes. Even worse, one of the four boys videoed him stomping into the pond, and posted it to YouTube. He was the joke of the school. But the joke wasn't funny. As he thought back, he couldn't even remember if the duck was OK or not. By lunchtime, the sun had melted the ice from the pond anyhow.

The duck would probably have survived.

And it was true. The newspaper had reported that there were too many ducks in the area. Everything added up to one big disaster. To top it off, the school called his dad, who had to leave work early to pick him up.

Duck Boy. Duck Boy.

The nickname somehow stuck. Steve had only two friends at school who called him by his real name. Everyone else called him Duck Boy. And he hated it. The name echoed in his thoughts whenever he felt like a twit, whenever he felt fear.

Steve's mind resurfaced in the principal's office where he waited.

Dad's here to pick me up again. I'm in trouble again. Not much has changed.

As the secretary breezed back into the office, the main door closed behind her, popping the principal's door open a couple of inches. The two muddled voices inside the office became clear.

"I don't know how much more of this I can handle." Steve recognized his dad's tone immediately. "He was never like this. I'm not…I've given up. I don't know what to do. I'm having my own difficulties at work."

"I know you've had some difficult times recently, since your wife, um…er, disappeared, but whatever the reason, Steve is not functioning in the classroom. His work is sloppy, when he does it." That drawl belonged to the principal, Mrs. Wilcox. "He has no ability to focus on his work." The drawl paused. "If we cannot help turn him around in the month after Christmas, he'll have to repeat the grade. I'm sorry. I have no choice."

Steve felt a knot clamp around his stomach.

I won't be going to high school next year. I'll be fifteen in September and still in middle school.

"He's just having a rough time," Mr. Best pleaded. "He needs a break."

"I'm sorry, Mr. Best. I'm not in the business of giving breaks. The Board expects me to make sure each student meets the standards. It's my job. I don't like it any more than you do, but I can't bend the rules to help you or your son. It's hard to take now, but in the long run it's always best."

Doug Best jerked the door open and noticed Steve waiting. "Let's go," he sputtered.

They walked through the now-empty school corridors. A janitor was loading the last looseleaf from the floor into a recycling bin. A few straggling teachers chatted.

But Steve and his dad weren't talking. Mr. Best's pale, clamped features seemed to have scared his hair into confusion.

This disheveled man unlocked the car doors and slumped into the driver's seat. Once settled inside he heaved a sigh, reached up to his throat and loosened the knotted tie around his neck.

"Dad? Are you OK?" Steve asked.

Mr. Best folded his hands and rested them on top of the steering wheel and rested his forehead on them. His eyes closed.

"I don't know if I'm going to make it, Son." His voice was quiet, almost a whisper. "I just don't know." He dropped his hands from the steering wheel and sat up. Key into the ignition. The car choked to life in the winter air, and he wrestled it into drive.

The car's heater whirred weakly against the frosted windshield, struggling to keep a small oval of the windshield clear. Steve watched the frost for a few minutes as Dad prepared a fatherly chat. A chat always followed one of Steve's bad days.

The pattern was as predictable as peanut butter, and as tired. It wasn't as though Dad were a bad man. Just lost. Lost, like Steve. He took his wife's disappearance so personally he could barely function anymore. He wanted to do something, to make everything better, but there was nothing to be done, no words to say, no handy heroics or caped cartoon conquerors to save the day. A lecture was as good as it got.

"Listen, Steve," he began, spouting clouds of steam. "I know things haven't been easy since your mother left." He grimaced. "I'm sorry." He paused. "I meant disappeared. Your life and mine…both of us haven't done so well. But I really need you to try…you know…to get it back together."

"Dad, I heard." Steve said, cutting in. He'd heard this speech hundreds of times over the past year and a half since his mom disappeared. "If I don't improve in January, no high school."

Steve's words seemed to anger his dad. "I don't know what good talking does," he muttered. "You know what's going on better than I do." He tried to continue to talk, but his mouth fumbled and hissed steam as he began another sentence. "I… It's…you…." He shook his head in obvious frustration. "I can't deal with this anymore, Steve." His voice suddenly became a yell. "If you know what's happening, why can't you do something about it? I'm trying to hold things together here, Steve. I need you to pull your end. All you have to do is your schoolwork. That's not so much, is it?" Dad's yell rang and faded in the winter air.

"That's not too much to ask, is it?" his dad repeated in a quiet, desperate voice.

Steve didn't answer. When you're drowning it's best to save your breath.

Steve watched his father strain as black waves of emotion washed over his face. Slowly his face returned to its exhausted, frantic look. "I'm sorry, Son. I didn't mean what I just said. I had a very rough day at work. I'm taking it out on you." The hum of the car tires on the road filled the car for a few minutes. "I have another piece of news." His muscles strained and streaked like lightning bolts from his jaw down his neck. "I'm being forced to work this holiday. A bigger firm bought our company. And if I want to keep my job, I have to work this Christmas holiday."

Doug Best was a salesman. He sold fire detection and control equipment to industrial clients. A few years ago, he had loved his job. All he talked about were the things he sold—fire alarm systems, sprinkler systems, and all the related equipment. Steve loved to listen to him discuss and demonstrate the equipment. In fact, Steve felt like he knew as much as Dad did. But, something had changed. Dad didn't enjoy his job as much, especially since his wife disappeared.

"My new boss booked me for a trip to Indonesia over Christmas. I'll be selling to some companies in Indonesia that don't celebrate Christmas. I won't be in my hotel room. I'll be working every day. So, you'll have to go to your great aunt's house for the Christmas break."

It took a minute for Steve to make the connections and realize whose house he would decorate for the holiday. "What?" he exclaimed. "I can't believe you're going to do this to me. It so completely sucks. Can't I go with you on your trip?"

"I wish you could, Son." Dad shook his head and frowned.

"Did you check with Brian's family?" Steve asked desperately. Dad nodded. "They can't take me?"

"They're heading to Kicking Horse to ski for the holiday," he replied.

"They could take me."

"Steve," Dad said in a serious tone. "Do you know how broke we are?"

"No."

"There's no way around it. We'll celebrate our Christmas early, at home tonight. Then I'll drive you over to your aunt's later. I have to catch a plane to Denver about 10:30 tonight. And Steve..." Steve looked up at his dad's worn face. "I'm sorry."

It was the second Christmas since she'd disappeared. The first had been horrible. This one looked like it was only going to be awful. Only slightly better than going to school. Or the dentist.

The evening was uneventful. "I wish I could be home for Christmas Day, but this is all I can do," Dad said through a mouthful of fried rice and ginger beef. Steve and his dad exchanged their presents while picking away at boxes of cold Chinese food. There weren't any Christmas feelings to make this moment feel festive. The smiles were forced and painful, and no one attempted a "ho, ho, ho." There was nothing there worthy enough to call Christmas—just presents, tinsel, and tension.

The only Christmas sounds that played that night were the silver bells of the genuine, imitation antique telephone, which rang merrily as a call came in. Looking for any distraction he could find, Steve sprang off the couch to answer.

"Hello, Steve. This is your Great Aunt Shannon," said a warbled old voice. To Steve, her voice even smelled old. "Did your dad tell you to bring your mom's research notebook? The police returned it to you a while ago, didn't they? I think they gave it back to your father. He probably put it where it belongs—on your mom's nightstand."

"Um, I'm not sure," Steve answered, knowing exactly what she meant.

"I'll bet he forgot, the poor fellow," Aunt Shannon said. "You do remember her notebook? The one she used for research."

"Yes, I remember, Aunt Shannon," he replied.

"I'm sure you have it back by now. It's on her nightstand. Please remember that notebook for me. It's very important for my research. You forgot it the last few times you came, you know."

"What research?" Steve asked, ignoring her last remark.

"I'm going to find your mother, Deary," Aunt Shannon said. "She hasn't left you, you know. It's just an experiment gone haywire." She seemed to have no idea how much Steve didn't want to talk about it. Any time Steve remembered his mom, her disappearance, or anything related to either, it felt as though someone had taken a sharp stick and poked him in the eye.

"Whatever," he muttered.

"You'll bring some soap and some clean underwear, too, won't you? And I hope your dad asked you to behave yourself. You really should, you know."

"I'm planning on it." Steve rolled his eyes as his dad looked on.

"You know I don't like to say goodbye," said Aunt Shannon.

"Right," Steve said, as the line went dead at the other end. Goodbye, Steve thought, that's the first thing I'd like to say.

Chapter Two

The suitcase slid around in the trunk and Steve swayed wildly from side to side as Mr. Best drove their rusty blue station wagon.

"You're kinda driving like a madman, Dad," Steve commented, body-checking the door as the car rounded a corner too quickly.

"I have to be there two hours before the flight leaves," Dad complained. The car jounced to a stop at the front walk.

He looked glumly at Steve, and then at his watch. Steve slammed the car door open with a crunch into a snowbank. Dad popped the trunk. Steve got out and closed the door. The frosted passenger window whined as it opened enough so Mr. Best could speak. "I'll be back in two weeks," he said, leaning over the passenger seat. "I'd come in, but I'm late."

Steve grabbed his suitcase from the trunk, and thumped the lid closed.

"Oh my god!" he exclaimed. He returned to the open passenger window. "I forgot my backpack." The backpack held the socks and underwear he needed for his Christmas stay. Dad sighed heavily, making Steve hasten to add, "But I know where the key is and I can get it myself. See you in two weeks, Dad. Have a good trip." He tried to sound sincere as the closing passenger window moaned again. He turned to walk up the steps to the unwelcoming house.

"Steve?" Mr. Best had opened his door and was standing outside of the car. He twisted his frown into a forced smile. "Merry Christmas."

Steve nodded and raised his eyebrows. "Yeah, Merry Christmas to you, too, Dad."

His dad ducked into the driver's seat, pulled the door closed, and was gone before the steam from his words was eaten by the darkness.

The night was suddenly silent as Steve trudged up the walkway to the house. On the front door of the house hung a fluorescent orange "BOO!" In the flowerbed, a white ghost rose out of an old unkempt grave. Through the door he could hear the sounds of someone playing something like "Jingle Bells" on an organ. The organist hit several wrong keys at a time, but the music didn't slow down or stop. Steve rang the doorbell.

"Merry, scary Christmas," he muttered bitterly. He couldn't even hear the sound of the doorbell over the organ music. He rang again and sighed.

This wasn't exactly the Christmas vacation he'd

imagined—Aunt Shannon, the loony, wailing on the organ; Uncle Edward buried in some book; Steve hidden in his room. Like the last few times his father had shuffled him to her house, usually Spring Break or summer holidays. Only it was winter this time, so he wouldn't be able to easily leave the house to escape all her crazy questions.

Here comes the wacky inquisition.

Maybe his mom's notebook would keep Aunt Shannon from harassing him. He hoped so. The organist veered recklessly into another unrecognizable melody. Steve waited for the music to quiet down and rang the doorbell again. And again. Three more times. The organ music continued.

"Shannon, Shannon...." Steve could hear Uncle Edward's muffled voice shouting between the organ notes. Uncle Edward's voice faded into the blasting tones. Moments later, the organ music stopped abruptly. Steve tapped the doorbell several more times while he had the chance of being heard.

Why doesn't Uncle Edward just answer the door? It would be easier than stopping Aunt Shannon's organ music.

Several minutes later, the front door swung open. Aunt Shannon stood there with a dazed look, as if the loud notes had knocked her senseless. Green eyes, rimmed with red. Long ribbons of tears filling some of her wrinkles. Her hair bun was the tallest part of her, reaching to the middle of Steve's chest. Over her ears was a set of construction-grade ear protection—safety orange. Beside her, Uncle Edward, his pants a little too high, belted tightly over a substantial bulge. A bad comb-over: wisps of long gray hair threaded over a shiny bald pate.

"You see," Uncle Edward said triumphantly, pulling one of her earpieces away from her ear. "I told you someone was at the front door." Aunt Shannon's eyes narrowed and her mouth momentarily bent with grief. She slid the earmuffs down around her neck.

"Hello, Aunt Shannon. It's Steve."

"What is it that you want?" Aunt Shannon asked briskly. She sounded like she was addressing a door-to-door salesman, not someone she'd just invited to share Christmas with her.

"I'm Steve," Steve repeated. Aunt Shannon still didn't seem to catch on. "I'm your great nephew, remember?" Pause. Uncle Edward rolled his puppy-brown eyes but didn't utter a word to clarify the situation. "I'm supposed to stay with you for the Christmas holiday." He waited again as the information entered her ears and she processed it. "My mom left, and she's still missing."

"Oh yes." Her stern look continued. Steve didn't dare enter the house. She seemed far too fierce.

Suddenly her features exploded. "Well, what are you standing out there for? It's cold. My stars in the morning, child. Do you need an engraved invitation?" She snatched him with her boney hand and pulled him indoors. Steve sighed. The best decorations in the world couldn't turn this house into Christmas, he thought.

They won't have Netflix. I hope they have cable.

Uncle Edward had already disappeared and was probably reading his book in his chair. Aunt Shannon, with her bunned gray hair and her bone-bag body, insisted on carrying Steve's suitcase to his room. "I just look old," she snarled. "And you're my guest," she said through gritted teeth as she gripped his suitcase with both hands and horsed it up a short set of stairs to the main level of the house. At the top of the stairs, she dragged it over the lime-green shag carpet. The walls were covered in gold wallpaper veined with rivers and lakes of blood-red velvet. A violent collision of color and style.

Now I know what wrecked her mind, Steve thought, as he waited. The suitcase fell onto its side, so she shoved it with a foot into his room.

Steve's space was livable, but crowded. Coffee mugs, statues, little ornaments, and knickknacks cluttered every horizontal surface in the room. *Shanks Grill House,* read the first mug of what looked like hundreds lined up on a shelf. In front of the mugs was a row of figurines: a cowboy, a ballerina, a turtle, a puppy, and three unicorns. Steve slid his suitcase under the bed.

"I'm putting you in a room with all of my collections, so you need to be careful. My coffee mug collection is nearly priceless."

"Ah…yeah. I'll be careful," Steve replied.

The nightstand beside the bed was covered in a sea of ornaments and trinkets of any and every sort. The bed was clean and freshly made. On the pillow sat a black metal box. Steve raised it from the pillow.

It's heavier than it looks.

He turned it around, looking for some clue. A label on the outside read "Richard E. Bacon—August 19/63—June 21/79." Underneath the first line, there was a company name: Coral Smith Funeral Homes. Steve shook it. It seemed filled with sand. He dropped the box onto the bed when he realized what it was.

"Oh, geez," Steve grumbled. "Richard's ashes. Perfect."

Aunt Shannon poked her head through the open door to see how Steve was settling in. She noticed the black box lying on the bed.

"I see you met Richard," she said pleasantly.

"These aren't his ashes, are they?" he asked.

"Of course, dear," Aunt Shannon replied. "Who else's could they be?"

Steve picked up the box and offered it to his aunt. "Could you please put this somewhere else, Aunt Shannon?"

"For your information, you are sleeping in Richard's bedroom," she retorted.

"This was his bedroom?"

"This IS his bedroom," Aunt Shannon corrected. "He still sleeps here. He just takes up a little less room than he used to." She didn't make any motion to take the box out of Steve's hand.

"No, really," Steve replied firmly. "Could Richard sleep somewhere else while I sleep in his room?" Aunt Shannon paused to think. She ran her fingers gently down the outside of the box and studied them for a moment. She looked up at Steve again.

"I suppose I could put him on the couch for the next few nights. Edward won't let me put him in my workshop." She took the box from Steve's hand. "Did you bring your mother's research notebook?" she asked, changing the subject.

"Yup," Steve chirped, happy to have won the discussion of Richard's remains. "It's in my suitcase." He squatted down and pulled the suitcase from underneath his bed, extracting the notebook. Mom's notebook looked like a recycled goose. Tattered pages surrounded the coiled wire binding like a bird on a bad-feather day. Coffee-brown bubbles warped the paper, tinting the birdish book.

This is one sick chicken.

"Good work, Steve." Aunt Shannon smiled for the first time. "It looks like it's been through a bit of a tornado." She held the notebook and gently turned and flattened the first few mangled pages. "This is an important first step. We'll bring your mother back with this."

Steve smiled politely. "Sure…whatever," he said weakly.

Mom is gone.

Aunt Shannon seemed oblivious to the facts. The facts told the story. A team of this city's best detectives, their staff, and a good bit of publicity couldn't scare up any clues at all. The case had even been aired on the TV program *Unsolved Mysteries* a few months after she'd disappeared.

And now, a year and two months after the show had aired, everyone seemed to have a theory. The case hadn't moved anywhere—no witnesses, clues, anything. The police concluded that Mrs. Best had run away. At first Steve had been angry. They were wrong; Mom hadn't run away, he had told himself. She wouldn't run away. Now he wasn't so sure.

Run away? Merry Christmas.

"Steve?" Aunt Shannon called. "Steve?"

"Huh?"

"Are you all right?"

"Uh…yeah. I'm OK," Steve responded.

"We'll talk about it over cocoa in the kitchen."

"Yeah, sure…whatever."

He replaced his suitcase under the bed and flopped onto the ruffled green comforter. He didn't want to share a mug of anything with anyone. He hoped Uncle Edward and Aunt Shannon would just get on with their evening and leave him to himself. He relaxed, letting himself slip into the only place he liked to go these days—sleep.

"Steve," Aunt Shannon called. When he didn't respond, she repeated herself a little more loudly. "Steve!" Nothing. She trudged down the hall and yelled sharply into the open bedroom door. "STEVE!"

Steve almost jumped out of his skin. It took him a couple of minutes to figure out where he was and what he needed to do. Reluctantly he slid off the bed and trudged to the kitchen. He slumped into a seat at the kitchen table.

Across from him sat Uncle Edward, who was reading a book titled *How to Build Your Own House* while he sipped his cup of tea. His pudgy eyelids crinkled as he scrolled over the page of his book. Uncle Edward was wearing a plaid shirt. He always wore plaid.

"Are you planning on building a house?" Steve asked as he read the title of the book. Uncle Edward just snorted.

Aunt Shannon answered the question in her husband's place. "Edward doesn't read so he can do anything. He reads because he likes to read."

"Oh," Steve replied. Aunt Shannon set the coffee-stained notebook on the table.

"What's that?" Uncle Edward asked, jerking his nose towards the notebook. Steve wondered how he even noticed the notebook. He didn't seem to look up from his book as he read.

"It's my mom's notebook," Steve responded glumly. "Aunt Shannon thinks it might have some clues to Mom's disappearance."

"I see," Uncle Edward commented in a disgusted tone. "More hocus-pocus, huh? I wish you'd leave that stuff alone, Shannon."

A whirring microwave oven on top of the fridge dinged loudly as it finished warming Steve's hot chocolate. Uncle Edward stood, his eyes never leaving his book, and retrieved the cocoa. He slid it over the tabletop to where Steve was sitting and returned to his seat. Aunt Shannon set a full teacup beside the journal and lowered herself into a chair.

She smoothed the warped pages of the notebook gently, but the pages refused to lay flat. "I've wanted to read this for a while now." She slid a finger through the handle of her cup of tea. "Can I read it?" she asked politely. Then she schlorpped a mouthful of tea, returned the cup to its china plate, and wiped her face with the back of her hand.

"Go ahead," Steve returned. "You can keep it."

"Oh no," Aunt Shannon said with a frown. "It's far too valuable to give away so hastily. You really don't know the potential here, do you?"

"Whatever," he replied with distinct indifference.

"Regardless of how you feel, young man, I need to ask you a few questions." She paused for a moment as if to clear her mind of daily details to make room for a big thought. "Now, tell me about the night she disappeared—what happened?"

Steve shrugged. "I dunno. All I really know is that she screamed and then she was gone."

"That's it?" Aunt Shannon asked. "That's all you know?"

"Yup."

"Come on, Steve. You know more than that."

Steve sighed. This wasn't a bus worth taking. "I don't. I was almost asleep when it happened."

"I know you saw more than you think you know. You just need to jostle your thoughts a little."

"Joss—what?"

"Jostle. I suppose it's a word that's out of fashion. I just mean you need to think more carefully about that night. I know you know some important things."

"I can't help you, Aunt Shannon."

Her green eyes dimmed.

"We can't do it with an attitude like yours."

"Can we talk about something else?"

Aunt Shannon shook her head.

"I need your help here."

"Got any Christmas shopping left to do?" Steve asked as politely as he could.

"Steve?" she asked in a hurt way. "You're not much of an alchemist, are you?"

She had switched topics, so Steve decided to run with it. "Alchemist? What do you mean?"

"You don't know what an alchemist is?" Aunt Shannon asked in disbelief. "You really haven't been brought up right, have you?"

Steve didn't know how he should respond, so he didn't say anything.

"An alchemist is a person who experiments with things and tries to change things from one kind of thing to another."

Steve nodded, but inside he winced, wishing he'd stuck with the Christmas shopping topic. He'd heard many adults introduce their own speeches, and he knew he was in for one of hers. She looked for his acknowledgment of the information. He didn't offer any encouragement, but she began anyhow.

"In olden days, alchemists tried to change lead into

gold. That was the one thing most of them focused on. But alchemy isn't about gold. It's about change. And alchemy has limitless possibilities for change. Traditionally, alchemy's about taking something and transforming it into something else. I can prove that this much is true—and so could many others. But I don't think it stops there. It may be about transforming time. It might be used to change one kind of place into another. Best of all, it could even have something to do with changing human beings—are you listening, Steve?"

Steve felt a little tired and he had lost interest in Aunt Shannon's words. "Sorry, Aunt Shannon. I'm sleepy."

"Well, if you know nothing else about alchemy, you should know that it is about experiments. Your mother must have told you what she was experimenting with."

"No, she never talked about it." Steve shrugged.

"Steve, come on. You're telling me you had no idea about her experiments?"

"Nope." This time he shook his head for emphasis.

"Did she never show you her Benu stone?" Aunt Shannon asked in disbelief. "She would have had her notebook with her and her Benu stone."

"I don't know what she was doing," Steve insisted, raising his voice a little. "All I know is that she stayed up late, reading and writing in her notebook every night."

"She was researching, Steve," Aunt Shannon said, raising her voice to match his. "She stayed up late to do her research. That's what this notebook is all about." She held the book out at arm's length and began to tenderly leaf through the battered pages. "She needed her Benu stone to transform things, so it must have been close to her, too." She paused on a few of the battered pages. "Hmm. I don't recognize her work here. Unfortunately, I hadn't talked to her for several weeks before she disappeared, so I don't know what she'd gotten herself into."

Uncle Edward sipped his tea as he read his book. He hadn't even looked up once throughout the conversation. He was probably ignoring both of them.

"Steve?"

"Yeah?" Steve answered sharply. Aunt Shannon looked up quickly and frowned. "What?" he replied to her look. "I have no idea what you're talking about. Mom didn't explain any of this stuff to me. I wasn't asking, either."

"I'm all sixes and sevens," Aunt Shannon replied.

"What?" Steve asked, shaking his head.

"Sorry. That expression just means I'm confused. I thought you'd understand a little."

"Nope. None. Absolutely not."

"Ach. Your mother, she really didn't teach you what you need to…"

"Hey!" Steve cut her off.

The only one allowed to insult her is me.

"Sorry. Good point." Aunt Shannon winced. "Poorly said."

A few minutes of silence. "We have to talk about this, Steve," she pleaded. "It's absolutely essential. I know you're not happy, and you don't seem to know anything, but that's OK. Now that we're clear, our starting point is obvious."

Steve pursed his lips, "Mmmmm."

"Now, Steve," Aunt Shannon began, "just because you didn't know what your mom was doing doesn't let you off the hook. You have a responsibility to follow the footsteps of the generations before you."

"Huh?" He was genuinely confused.

Aunt Shannon shook her head sadly, but continued, "Since you're here for the holidays, you should begin to train in the family tradition."

"What do you mean?"

"I mean you come from a long line of distinguished alchemists. It's in the family, you know. You're the only one left."

"I am not the only one left. What about Brian?" Brian was Steve's cousin.

"I am sad to say that Brian does not believe in alchemy any more." Aunt Shannon spoke of him as if he were dead. "Uncle Ken and Aunt Mary gave up their faith in this science, and so Brian, being a chip off the old block, gave it up, too. And Richard." Aunt Shannon paused. "Well, Richard is not of this world anymore. He can't help me." She sighed.

"What if I don't want to do it?"

"Why wouldn't you want to do it?"

"You don't want me, Aunt Shannon. I am not good at this kind of stuff. I can't do it." Fluttering in the back of his mind were those horrible words he'd come to hate:

Duck Boy. Duck Boy.

"How do you know? Have you ever tried?"

"No, I haven't. But I'm failing Chemistry and Algebra, and practically every other subject in the entire world. I'm no good."

"You are good. You're just the person we need."

"How do you know? I only see you twice a year, once at Spring Break and once over the summer for a few days. You know nothing about me."

"I know lots about you," she insisted.

"Whatever," Steve grumbled.

"Your mother told me lots and lots about you."

"My mother. Ha! That's a joke. Do you know where she is right now?" Aunt Shannon answered the question with silence. Steve answered his own question, "She's probably in Mexico or someplace like that. She just left. She didn't want me, not to help with experiments—not for anything." Hot tears rushed to his eyes, but he wouldn't let them fall.

"That's not true, Steve." Aunt Shannon's voice was quiet. "I think she stumbled onto something big, really big. She just needs help to find her way back. You can help her."

He pushed his chair away from the table and stood. "I can't help you, Aunt Shannon. You need to face the truth. Nothing will bring her back…Nothing." He couldn't stop the tears any longer. But before anyone could see him, he fled the room, into the hallway, just out of sight. Peeking around the doorjamb, he could still see his aunt and uncle at the table.

Aunt Shannon sat quietly for a moment. Uncle Edward glanced at her. "You shouldn't be getting that boy mixed up in all your flim-flam. You're going to end up getting him or yourself hurt…again." He emphasized the last word in his sentence carefully.

Steve's tears fell silently. He mopped them up with his shirt sleeves.

Aunt Shannon smiled in a way that seemed like she, too, might cry. "Edward," she said sharply, "Stop it. Just because you've never liked alchemy doesn't mean other people should feel that way."

"Listen, you already lost Richard…." Uncle Edward continued.

"That's not fair!" Her face twisted in agony. "Are you going to make me pay for that the rest of my life?"

"He was our only son," Uncle Edward said quietly.

"I couldn't have stopped him, and you know it," Aunt Shannon said firmly.

A minute or two passed in silence. Steve wiped his eyes with his hands.

"It is going to be more difficult than I thought," she mused. "I do have a couple of tricks up my sleeve, though. I think I should introduce him to Lindsay Locket."

Uncle Edward snorted.

"What's so funny, Edward? She's a clever one, and she's catching on to my hocus-pocus quite quickly, thank you very much. For your information, she already knows how to make her Benu stone. She just needs to find it." She paused and stared into her teacup, as if looking for hints of the future. "We're going to find Steve's mother if it kills us."

"Be careful," Uncle Edward replied. "It just might."

Steve had heard enough. From the hallway he tiptoed to his room.

CHAPTER THREE

"I WANT TO GO HOME," she wept, standing on the edge of a lake. The face before her showed no emotion.

"That isn't a possibility. You belong to us now. You won't be going home again."

She continued to weep, thinking of her husband Doug and her son Steve. "They'll never know what happened."

"They don't need to know."

"What are you going to do to me?" she asked, as bravely as she could.

"I think you can guess."

She began to cry again.

It was twilight. On this night, her last.

"OK," she said at last. "I'm ready."

Deep grief wracked her body as the dissection began. And after a while, she couldn't feel anything anymore.

Chapter Four

STEVE BRUSHED HIS TEETH in front of the bathroom mirror. He didn't look very happy or healthy. His nose poked out a bit too far from his skinny face and hollow cheeks. His features shared space with several red dots of acne and freckles. His forehead was a bit too high. His teeth looked too big for his mouth. A crop of short, spiky hair, flaming red, glowed atop his head. His green eyes were rimmed with red.

There's nothing great about me.

The mirror seemed to agree. He daubed toothpaste onto a finger, and touched the red spots with the paste. This made things a little better.

His conversation with Aunt Shannon had stirred up the mud of old feelings.

It's going to be hard to fall asleep tonight.

At home, he would have watched a few SpongeBob episodes on Netflix. SpongeBob helped him forget and smile. He returned to his bedroom and pulled out his iPod, checking for open wireless connections. There were several networks in the area, but all of them were secure.

No SpongeBob tonight.

He prepared for bed quickly and slid under the covers with the bedside lamp on. On the nightstand, among the knickknacks, sat an old book. Steve picked it up. He read the title—*The Way of Alchemy*. The author, Graham Pankratz.

No doubt Aunt Shannon placed this strategically.

He could feel the clouds of negativity darken and grow, so chose to read to distract him from his thoughts.

"Books, the original iPods," he said aloud.

The book's cover was tooled leather, well used. He batted the cover open. Someone had scrawled a greeting on the inside cover: "To William Durant Pankratz, January 19, 1805."

Aunt Shannon's maiden name is Pankratz. So was my mom's.

Obviously this was some old relative, somehow tied to his family through his mother. He riffled through the book's pages, stopping at the occasional picture. There were drawings of laboratory instruments and odd symbols. Pictures of creepy people. He paused on a page with a woodcut of a dragon eating its own tail. The caption underneath the drawing read "Immortality and the Elixir of Life—the Ouroboros."

In the middle of the book there were some disgusting photographs of human body parts. Evidently these were part of the alchemist's experimentation. He thumbed through the last few pages, reading a paragraph here and there. The words seemed like an odd mix of the Bible, magic, and science. He turned to the first chapter, "Of Alchemical Philosophy," and began to skim.

One paragraph jumped from the page:

> The Benu stone is the central goal of the alchemist's work. Once successfully made, the stone is used to transform one thing into another. Traditionally, many have understood that, with this stone, lead could be transformed into gold. However, more recent alchemists have begun to experiment with the idea that the Benu stone may lead to transformations of a more general nature, not merely a transformation from lead into gold.

Somewhere in the middle of Chapter Two, his head began to nod with sleep, but by then he had a feeling for Alchemy—test tubes, experiments, fire, and water, and the hunger for change. Sleep called him as he clung to the page's words until his eyes blurred and the book fell to his chest and slipped to the floor. With his mind brimming and aflame with strange thoughts, Steve fell asleep.

In the morning he rolled out of bed, hoping to find some sugary cereal squirreled away in one of the kitchen cupboards. When he got to the kitchen, he found Aunt Shannon sitting in a chair with a cup of tea in her hand, reading Steve's mother's journal. A stranger, a girl about

Steve's age, sat beside her.

"Good morning, Steve," Aunt Shannon said. "I'd like you to meet a friend of mine. This is Lindsay Locket."

Lindsay shot Steve a cold, polite smile. She seemed smart. Maybe a tad geeky. Long golden hair framed her face, with a piercing pair of azure eyes. Braces, yes. Possibly. Hard to remember because her eyes were so distracting. He realized that his housecoat hung loosely about his shoulders and his hair was a greasy fireworks display, his face dotted with dried dots of toothpaste. In a flash, he wrapped the lapels of the housecoat together, cinching the belt tight around his waist with an impossible knot. His face glowed as red as a pimple.

"Ah… um… m-m-morning," he stuttered as he pulled open a couple of cupboard doors quickly, hiding his head behind them. "Do you have any cereal?"

"You mean breakfast cereal? No, we have porridge for breakfast. I made some for you this morning and left it on the stove there." She pointed to a battered pot blurping on the stove. "Lindsay is keen on learning the alchemist tradition, too, Steve. She can't stay very long this morning, but she just lives across the street."

"Oh." Steve's voice echoed off the back of the cupboard.

Duck Boy. Duck Boy.

"I really have to be going now, Aunt Shannon," Lindsay said smoothly. "Maybe… ah… I'll see you tomorrow."

"See you then, dear," Aunt Shannon said in an overly sweet tone. "Aren't you going to say goodbye to our guest,

Steve?"

"Bye," Steve grunted to the back of the cupboard, as Lindsay walked to the front hall.

Steve groaned quietly into a group of porcelain figurines in front of his nose. He heard the girl's feet thump gently down the short set of stairs, and the front door open and close.

Great—a surprise visit from a girl while I look like a serial killer.

He backed out of the cupboard doors and headed to the porridge pot on the stove, catching his own reflection in the pot's lid. His face ballooned and twisted in the reflection of the dented chrome lid. The lid seemed to say it all.

And porridge is such a drag.

"You didn't have to be rude," Aunt Shannon said when she returned to the kitchen. "It's quite impolite to hide from guests."

"Well, you could have warned me you planned to have company," Steve answered.

"You always need to be prepared for surprises, Steve."

Aunt Shannon crossed the kitchen to peer out a window into the morning's frosty face.

"It's sunny, but a biting frost in the air," she muttered. "Too cold for my old bones." Her gaze rose from the landscape toward the sky. "Edward, are we having trouble with our phones again?" she asked.

"Dunno," Edward replied from somewhere else in the

house.

"Someone is working on the lines again," she said thoughtfully. She stood and mused for a moment, letting the morning sun warm her hands and face.

While his aunt and uncle talked, Steve had been working his way through each of the cupboards, looking for a bowl for his porridge.

"Bowls are in that cupboard, there," Aunt Shannon said cheerily, with a finger pointed towards a bottom cupboard next to the fridge. Steve opened it and found several hundred vinyl records stacked in piles in the same cupboard. "You'll find the bowls in behind the Country and Western albums."

Records. How retro.

"All right," Steve grunted. He reached behind the stack of records—the album on the top featured a picture of a horse and a woman swinging a lasso. His hand found a small stack of bowls and pulled one out of the pile.

"Why are the bowls behind your records?" Steve asked.

"Because music is more important than food, dear. I can skip breakfast once in a while, but I simply cannot live without music. Spoons are in the fridge," Aunt Shannon added, before Steve had the time to search for them.

Steve trotted over to the refrigerator and scoured the inside for a couple of minutes before he found the spoons in the "Cheese and Butter" compartment. He resisted the temptation to ask the obvious question.

As he moved to the stove to take a small helping, Aunt

Shannon turned from the window to the stove and grabbed the porridge pot. Steve sighed and held out his bowl, and she blobbed in the entire batch, filling it to the brim.

"I really don't want that much," he objected quietly. "I'm usually not very hungry in the morning."

"You ought to be very hungry—just look at you," Aunt Shannon replied firmly. "Eat all of it. You're too skinny." She squinted. "And what are those dots on your face?"

Steve sighed.

"Don't give me any attitude, young man," Aunt Shannon said sharply. "You need to eat well, even if you don't want to be an alchemist."

He rolled his eyes and began to walk out of the kitchen, back to his room, to eat.

"Where are you going?" Aunt Shannon asked.

"I'm going to eat in my room."

"Sit down here in the kitchen," Aunt Shannon ordered. "Food belongs in the kitchen."

"Country and Western records belong next to your record player," Steve quipped.

"You'll eat in the kitchen, young man," Aunt Shannon commanded. "Sit."

Steve returned to the kitchen table to avoid any more confrontations.

"Now what do I need to do today?" Aunt Shannon asked herself. "Oh, yes. I need to call the library."

"Why don't you just tell them that you lost the books and pay for them?" Uncle Edward asked. "Sooner or later they're going to catch on."

"I'll find them, Edward," Aunt Shannon replied.

Uncle Edward sighed and returned to his book.

"I'm heading to a book sale this morning," he informed them, shaking his head while he read. "I'll see you two this afternoon."

"See you, Edward," Aunt Shannon replied. "Bundle up warmly. And don't forget your bus pass." She turned to Steve, parked behind the steaming bowl of porridge. "Now, young man, let's talk while you eat your breakfast."

Steve gave a feeble smile and limply picked up his spoon as Aunt Shannon looked on. "Got any sugar?" he asked with a grimace.

His aunt returned to the kitchen sink and opened a cupboard underneath. "There's a leak in the sink's plumbing, and that keeps the brown sugar from getting those incorrigible lumps," she explained, responding to the look on his face. "Thank you for eating your porridge and obliging an old woman, by the way," she added with a smile. "There's hope for you yet. At least you can listen to my ideas, even though you don't agree."

"Sure." Steve grimaced. It might even pass as a smile, if he was lucky.

"Did you read that book on your nightstand?" Aunt Shannon asked.

He looked up. "Um, yeah. But, that alchemy stuff is pretty weird. All those experiments with body parts, and burning stuff until it's blacker than black. It's absolutely weird." He stopped for a moment, staring at his bowl of goop. "I thought you said yesterday that alchemy would help find my mom. I don't think this stuff is going to help. For one thing, changing lead into gold is impossible. And for another, even if we could change lead into gold, it won't help my mom. If we could invent that 'elixir of life,' it would help other people but it wouldn't help us to find my mom."

He paused. Aunt Shannon looked thoughtful but didn't say anything. "Do you really think lead can become gold?" he asked, as if he was checking to see if she was still all there. The cord of thought didn't seem to reach the outlet of sanity. "I mean, a bit of lead in a beaker isn't going to change your life, is it?"

"You're partly right, Steve," Aunt Shannon answered. "You can't change lead into gold with a beaker. I do think our ancestors were wrong on that point. But I am quite sure that you *can* change things. It's not beakers and lead with a bit of some kind of tincture; that idea is for puffers."

Steve nodded and pursed his lips. Hopefully it would look as though he understood.

"Sorry, Steve. I can see you don't know what I'm talking about. Now let me see. A puffer. Hmm. A puffer is an alchemist who doesn't take alchemy seriously. In the old days, puffers spent a bit of time dabbling in an experiment or two, sending feathery puffs of smoke into the air, but they didn't commit to the cause."

"Puffers," Steve repeated, trying to move her along.

"Right. Well, if you read the old books, most of the ideas you get in those books are wrong. Some people think alchemy is an early type of chemistry. Some treat it like a type of psychology. Some think it's religious, or it's about a mystical journey. All these people were right in their way. But the most important fact about alchemy is that it's real in every way. For a few centuries, alchemy was the frontier of technology. In fact, alchemical history is a cover for genuine alchemy.

"Alchemy has always been about change. Some believe alchemy changes lead into gold. Some believe alchemy changes people. Some believe it changes locations, and of course, the big question has always been how to make that change."

Steve wanted to stop her, but he could see the fire building in her eyes. Easier to let her continue.

"Alchemists, over the years, have tried many things. They've tried secret formulas and potions, trying to cook up change one way or another. In my experiments, I've tried nearly all of those things, all the things that others have tried. Beakers, baking, boiling, burning. I haven't gotten anywhere. But then I stumbled into words."

She sighed blissfully. "Words. Now that's where alchemy works. Transformation happens with words much more than beakers. You can change a thing with words much more easily than you can with fire. I can bend words so many ways, break them, and put them back together again. And when you change a word in just the right way, you change the world." Aunt Shannon paused to make sure Steve was listening.

"This is where my work has taken me. And it works. I packed up my beakers long ago."

Steve smiled and nodded. He fought the urge to raise his hand and ask a question.

Will this be on the exam?

The thought made him smile—this time genuinely.

"You don't believe me, do you?"

Steve shook his head. "I'm sorry Aunt Shannon, I don't. I would like to, but I can't."

"Finish your porridge. I'll take you to my laboratory and show you an experiment that should prove it completely."

Steve labored through his bowl of porridge, choking most of it down.

He opened the dishwasher to put his porridge bowl away and found several socks draped in the dish racks.

Aunt Shannon noticed him open the dishwasher and watched as he pulled out the dish racks. "I guess that load is finished now. Let me get those for you." Aunt Shannon stood and went towards the dishwasher and plucked the socks from the dishwasher. "There you go. Just put your bowl in the bottom rack there."

Steve nodded and obeyed.

Aunt Shannon walked towards the fridge, opened the freezer and threw the socks she was carrying in, then turned to Steve. "Come on. Let me prove to you that alchemy works."

She nearly pushed him down the hallway to a bedroom and opened the door. Inside Steve saw her organ shoved up against one wall. On top of the organ lay a drill and various parts of a disassembled lawnmower engine. The floor was littered with boxes filled with odds and sods—pieces of things. And on the far side of the room, a crude workbench: an old door resting on several stacked plastic milk crates. On one end of the bench sat the core of the disassembled lawn mower engine. In the middle of the bench there was a big box of clocks, and next to the box of clocks, the box of Richard's remains—the same box Aunt Shannon had taken from Steve's room the night before.

"He's not supposed to be in here, but we won't tell Edward, will we?"

Steve shook his head, stifling a laugh.

Aunt Shannon turned to her bench, and from the box of clocks pulled out a single alarm clock. She pointed to the box of clocks remaining on her workbench. "Would you mind putting these out in the hallway? Otherwise the whole box might go."

Steve obligingly carried the box into the hallway, having no idea what Aunt Shannon had meant. He returned to her study and she handed him a pair of goggles. She was already wearing a scuba mask herself. "Stand over here and put the goggles on," she commanded, pointing to a place a few yards away from the workbench. The scuba mask pinched her nose, making her voice sound thin and tinny. "Stand back. You never know exactly how things might turn out. You know—be ready for a surprise."

Steve moved to the spot that she had suggested, donning the safety goggles. He had a clear view of the workbench and Aunt Shannon as she hunched over the clock.

She looked over towards Steve. Her scuba mask was fogging up from the inside. "Are you ready?" she asked. Steve nodded. "Are you watching?" Steve nodded again.

"Good. Let me touch my Benu stone." She reached towards the plastic box with the ashes of Richard Bacon inside. She looked towards Steve again. "You have to be touching your Benu stone. Otherwise it won't transform," she instructed.

She turned and focused on the clock and placed one hand on the box of Richard's ashes. With her other hand she grabbed the clock.

"Clock-clock-clock-clock-clock-clock-clock-lock-lock-lock-lock-lock-lock-lock." She spoke what sounded like chicken language to the clock and stopped. Aunt Shannon stared at the clock. Nothing happened. She let go of the clock and poked it with her hand, as if she was afraid to touch it. Steve stared at the floor and couldn't help but smile. The whole scene was so odd. On the verge of entertaining.

"OK," she said. "I think the connection was a little weak. Let me give it a go again." She turned toward him for a moment, noticing his amused look. "You're just asking for a big, fat surprise to whack you on the noggin." She wagged a finger at him. "Smarty pants. You're cruisin' for a bruisin'," she warned, turning back to her work.

"Clock-clock-clock-clock-clock-clock-clock-lock-lock-lock-lock-lock-lock-lock," she clucked her chicken language to the clock again. She stared at the clock. Still nothing.

"That did it," she shrieked. "Look out!" She jumped clear of the workbench, as if something were about to explode.

Aunt Shannon beamed as the clock began to shake and shiver on the bench top. Suddenly, Steve heard a giant ripping sound. A brilliant kaleidoscope of light exploded into the room from inside the clock. Loose paper flailed and flapped in a tornado around the room. And then it all stopped. The paper wafted its way to the ground and the room was filled with an earthy aroma—the smell of freshly turned soil.

Sliding the scuba mask to her forehead, Aunt Shannon wiped a moustache of sweat from her mouth with her sleeve. "What a stubborn clock." She looked toward Steve. "I mean you expect a clock to be stubborn, but sheesh. What a cantankerous old thing!" On the workbench sat an old padlock. It looked about as old as the alarm clock had. What was once a clock was now a lock. Steve blinked slowly. And checked again.

What just happened? This isn't possible.

Chapter Five

Steve stared at the padlock—seconds ago it had been a clock.

"It's all right, Steve. It really did happen. I can assure you of that." His aunt waited a couple of minutes for Steve to absorb her words. Then she continued, "I guess I always knew that clocks were locks, and locks were clocks. I just never realized how closely related they were." She picked up the lock from her workbench and passed it to Steve. "Unfortunately, when you turn a clock into a lock you never get a key with it."

Steve held the padlock in his hand. It felt quite heavy.

"Do you want to try?"

Steve looked up at her. He tried to mumble something, but Aunt Shannon interrupted with a laugh. "I really surprised you with that one, didn't I? I'm so glad. Get used to being surprised." She stepped back from the bench. "Come on over. I'll tell you how to do it."

Steve stepped up to the bench, goggles still on. "This

is a fairly easy transformation," Aunt Shannon explained. "So the bit of power you can get through me, as I touch my Benu stone, will let the transformation happen." She placed her hand lovingly on top of Richard's remains. "Now all you need to do is repeat the word *lock* seven times and change it into the word *clock*. It goes quite easily. Then the lock will transform back into a clock." She put her hand on Steve's shoulder. "Now you have the power. Go ahead and try."

"Lock. Lock. Lock. Lock," Steve said.

"Stop," Aunt Shannon ordered. "Don't put such a big space between your words. Let them run together more. They must run together."

"Lock-lock-lock-lock-lock-lock-lock," Steve said the words seamlessly. He counted each repetition and then switched words without hesitation. "Clock-clock-clock-clock-clock-clock-clock." He stared at the lock. An electrical shock numbed his shoulder where her hand was, and traveled down his arm toward Aunt Shannon's padlock. He wanted to let go of the lock, but Aunt Shannon used her free hand to push his arm firmly against it.

The lock began to dance under his hand. Aunt Shannon released her grip and stepped back, so he did the same. The lock seemed to flatten into a photograph of the lock. And then, with a giant tear, the photograph split in two. Light gushed through the tear as a small, powerful wind circled the workbench, whipping loose bits of organ sheet music in a circle. The light from the torn photograph brightened, making it difficult to see what was happening.

"Close your eyes, Steve," Aunt Shannon screamed above the din. He obeyed. Suddenly it stopped. He opened his eyes carefully. On the workbench lay the old alarm clock.

"Ah…" was all Steve could manage in the silence that followed. A minute passed before he mustered another word. "Wow."

Aunt Shannon leaned over the workbench to view Steve's face. "Hah!" she trumpeted. "Surprise two. Steve nothing."

"It's amazing," Steve whispered.

"It's amazing, all right," she said, matching his whisper with her voice. "But it's only the beginning. Something about experimenting makes me hungry," she announced suddenly, and declared an official coffee break. The two of them headed to the kitchen to raid the fridge.

"Steve, you saw the power—the energy level that filled the room when the clock transformed, didn't you?"

"Yeah."

"That's a lot of power for such a simple transformation. And I know that that energy must be useful for something besides turning clocks into locks. It's like a whole other power source." She sighed. "You'd think after all the years I've been working on this, I'd be a whole lot farther along. I know you're impressed. But honestly, it's the only thing I know how to do. I've messed with many different word combinations, but I can't find another. It seems kind of like it's a short circuit in the language, or something.

These words are so close together, and both are relatively common household objects, that the transformation seems almost certain. I mean when you say them out loud, it's as if one word melts into the other one, right? That kind of connection between words is extremely rare, and I know because I've been looking for years."

"So you don't know any other spells?"

"They're not spells. This isn't magic. It's more like a linguistic base to matter."

"Huh?"

"There's some kind of connection between words and matter."

"Oh," Steve replied.

"And, no, I don't."

"Huh?"

"I don't know any other word combinations." She paused and looked at the ceiling. "God knows I've tried. I've spent years of my life on this riddle."

She peered over the fridge door at Steve with a sympathetic look. "Now, I know you don't want to talk about your mom, but I think what I just showed you means you should humor me for a few minutes." She paused and watched her grand-nephew's face.

"I'm listening," Steve promised.

She smiled. "Good. Very good." She filled the kettle with cold water and settled into her seat. "So, alchemists have always been obsessed with transforming one object into another, mostly transforming an inexpensive object into an expensive one. To make money. I can't do that, but I can transform one thing into another. But what if this transformation wasn't just limited to an object? What if it were possible to transform places? You can see for yourself that there's a huge amount of power available. I doubt the power is limited just to locks and clocks.

"Of course, there's another possibility." She got up and dropped a teabag into a grungy looking teapot, then grimaced as though the thought hurt. She sighed as the kettle began to boil and poured the hot water into the pot, seemingly stalling for time. "Your mother might have fried herself by getting in the middle of that transformation somehow." She came to her senses suddenly and gaped at Steve. "I'm so sorry, Steve. I shouldn't have said it so rudely."

Steve rubbed his temples. "It's OK, Aunty. I've heard worse."

"But I think you would have found some of her remains, like ashes or something, you know." She smiled briefly, and continued. "Here's what I think happened. Your mom knew about my work, and I think that power did something that caused her disappearance, though I don't know what happened, or where, or even *when* she went. Time travel is possible, too, I'd guess. I mean, why not? Who knows what that power is and what it can do?"

"So how does the Benu stone work?"

"Good question. In the old days, alchemists thought that you added a little bit of the stone to things and the object you added it to would transform into something else, like lead into gold. Some people thought that the Benu stone was really just another word for a person's own life, so if a person underwent some intense situations, he would be refined to the point where he was transformed. Some thought it was a spiritual thing. These were old ideas." Her face brightened a little. "But my own research tells me it's not the way. It wasn't so much research, actually, as an accident. I can't really say how it is that it even happened. All I can say is that it worked. The Benu stone is some kind of important object in your own life, something that has a deep personal meaning. When I touch this object, I get power."

"How'd my mom find hers?"

"I actually don't know what your mother's was because we hadn't talked for some time. We had a bit of a spat."

"A what?" Steve asked.

"A fight."

Aunt Shannon looked sheepish, sipping at her empty teacup. "I showed her my Benu stone and how it worked. I showed her what I showed you. We talked about it, back and forth, for a few weeks, and suddenly she found hers. Then, before we ever got together to discuss it, we got into a fight. About you, actually."

"Oh."

It was all Steve could think of to say, and Aunt Shannon seemed to clam up. After a minute he drained his cold tea, left the cup on the table, and went back to his room.

This time when he tried his wireless he found an open network named "dlink," and started surfing the Internet for information on alchemy. Other than historical material, he couldn't find much about what his aunt had just showed him. He googled alchemy. Just more weird pictures, stories of strange, dead people, and a fog of contradictory ideas. Eventually he gave up on finding helpful information and played a few online games.

A sharp knock distracted him, causing the little stick-figure man on his screen to get shot in the head and explode into a red ball of blood.

Aunt Shannon opened the door a crack and stuck her head into the room. "Time to eat a little lunch and decorate for Christmas," she called cheerily.

Steve winced as he thought of what might be for lunch. But in the kitchen he found a very respectable egg salad sandwich and a glass of milk. He sat and ate his plate clean in what seemed like seconds.

"Guess you were hungry," she commented.

"Yeah, I guess," Steve grunted, still chomping. He stood to return to his room.

"Just a minute, Sonny. The plate and glass go in the dishwasher."

"Right."

"And who made the sandwich?"

"Thank you for the lovely lunch, Aunt Shannon," Steve said without enthusiasm, resorting to the script grownups sometimes forced him to use.

"Did you like it?" Aunt Shannon asked. "It's my special egg recipe."

Steve nodded his whole upper body as he gulped the last of his milk.

"We're going to get ready for Christmas now. This isn't going to be easy—we haven't decorated for Christmas here for many, many years. But since you're staying with us, we're going to have a bit of a party," she said with a wink. "I'll meet you in the living room." She headed down into the basement, leaving Steve to flop onto a psycho-colored paisley couch.

She was gone for a while, but from somewhere in the clogged bowels of the basement, Aunt Shannon produced a boxed Christmas tree layered with the dust of decades.

"We haven't used this tree since Richard left us," she blurted, suddenly near tears. "We got one of those new-fangled pretend trees, so we wouldn't hurt another Christmas tree." She sniffed and buried her nose in the puffed shoulder of her dress as she gripped the box. "It was Richard's idea. I…I don't think I can open this box. Would you?"

She looked towards Steve, holding the box suddenly like a swaddled baby. Dust caked on the front of her dress. Steve took the box from her carefully, as though he were lifting a newborn from her arms.

He gently placed the box on the floor and unfolded the cardboard flaps, flinging a garden of dust into the air. Within he found what looked like a box of giant green toilet brushes.

It took quite a while to insert each branch into the centre post of the tree. The finished product looked very much like a brush that would have been used to clean the toilet of a three-story giant.

Merry stinking Christmas.

"That does look like it always did," Aunt Shannon sighed sweetly, tears streaking through the dust on her cheeks. "Oh, Richard, I miss you."

Steve began stringing the old-fashioned Christmas lights around the tree, and after another moment of reverie, his aunt seemed to wake up.

"Now we need some ornaments." She disappeared again, returning with a box of jumbled kiddie crafts. "These are things that Richard made for our tree over the years."

There were rock-hard, marshmallow-and-toothpick snowflakes. Yellowed paper snowflakes that looked like they were cut by someone recently introduced to scissors. Strings of popcorn garland, looking very, very old. Glued noodle angels. Aunt Shannon pulled each item tenderly from the box and laid on the cushions of the couch with great care.

Steve took a few items at random, placed them on the tree.

"Oh no, dear, not there," Aunt Shannon exclaimed as he hung a crayon-colored popsicle-stick star from a thick arm of the toilet-brush tree. She pulled the decoration from his hands and set it down lower. "He could only reach about there, then."

Steve sighed quietly to himself, lifting another piece off the couch. It looked a little more sophisticated than the last ornament so, he figured, it would probably go higher on the tree. He took a wild guess and stuck the kiddie craft on the branch about chest height.

"Yes," she approved absently. "That's about right."

Pleased, he persevered. An angel made out of bent brass wire, he thought, seemed fairly advanced as a craft, so he placed it a little over head-height on the tree.

"Oh no, dear," Aunt Shannon said with a chuckle. "I helped him with that one. In fact, I did most of it myself." Her smile soured. She pointed to where he had hung the ornament. "He never did make it quite that high on the tree. He was shorter than you are."

Giving up, Steve relinquished the task of decorating the tree to his aunt, who talked to herself as she placed each thing on the branches. He couldn't hear most of what she was saying as she worked, but since TV wasn't possible, she was the most entertaining thing around.

"Time for tinsel," Aunt Shannon announced. "Start at the bottom, and please don't put any tinsel above the top ornament." The tree was heavily decorated, but the top foot and a half of the tree was bare, green toilet-brush.

"Steve, can you put on the star?" The crowning touch was offered to him. "This was my great-grandmother's once." She held a blown-glass star carefully in her hands. "It's nearly two hundred years old."

Steve set up a chair, and nervously mounted the star on the top toilet brush. A beautiful crown for an ugly tree.

When the tree was done, Aunt Shannon took a seat on the couch, a little winded. "Edward, come take a look," she shouted into the kitchen. The legs of a chair squawked as Uncle Edward got up to join them in the living room.

"Oh, oh, oh. Shannon, my dear, what have you done?" He looked at the tree in astonishment, looking years younger than he had seconds earlier. "Oh, it's a glorious thing. Wondrous." The glow lasted for another second or two. He looked as though he might shed a tear, too, but before he did, he dove into his book again and the emotion on his face evaporated. His age returned. "But he's dead now, so I wish you wouldn't remind me of him." Like a bad Christmas-light bulb, the joy that had just been there disappeared, replaced by darkness. He turned from the room and headed to the kitchen.

"Did you bring any gifts for Christmas?" Aunt Shannon asked. "Ones we can put under the tree?"

"Ahhh. Ummm. No," Steve admitted. "I completely forgot."

"Well, then, we shall go to the mall. We can't afford anything extravagant, of course, but I think we need a little something for one another under the tree. Let's go," she commanded, heading off to her room to get ready.

Steve got his coat and went to meet her in the kitchen, by the back door. It was kind of a long wait. She came back with her hair in a bun, a thick coat of overly red lipstick, and a loud polyester-print dress, apparently pleased with her efforts.

I'm going to the mall with a cartoon.

The two headed out into the weak afternoon sun. "It's warmer than it looks," Aunt Shannon said, as she opened the garage door.

Inside was a white monster. Aunt Shannon's car was old and very large—a 1966 Dodge Monaco convertible. It was in fairly good condition considering its age. Kind of like Aunt Shannon herself.

"I haven't started her in a while, so we'll hope she goes." She gingerly lowered her bony bottom into the driver's seat. Steve folded himself to fit the bench seat next to her. Too bad he couldn't remove his legs and put them in the trunk.

"How you doing, old girl?" she asked, patting the dashboard. "We need to go to the mall." She slipped the key into the ignition and turned it. The car talked back to her: "Woah, woah, woah," it said. She released the key. "I know it's cold, but you'll warm up quickly." She tried the key again, and the dragon rumbled to life.

"I'd like any old thing you can find me," Aunt Shannon announced as she backed out of the driveway. She leaned forward in her seat as she drove, so she could see over the dashboard. "It's been years since I've been Christmas shopping." She glanced quickly at Steve. "Edward and I don't usually buy one another anything. Do you know what old ladies like?"

"I don't know."

"Well, you can buy almost anything that's chocolate, but I'm sure you know that. You can buy perfume and lipstick and that sort of thing. These are the sorts of items men like to think women want. But they're really last resorts." She glanced at him quickly. "If you see something that you think I'd like, and it's not one of those things, get that."

"What about Uncle Edward?" Steve asked.

"Books, books, books," she replied quickly.

"But I don't know what he's read," Steve replied.

"It doesn't seem to matter."

"I don't know what he likes."

"He reads anything on any topic."

"Wow. That's easy."

"Yes. But I wish he'd put those books of his down."

"Does he like candy?"

"Yes. But he's fussy. The only candy I know he likes are those jellied candies shaped like fruits, like lemons and limes."

"That's what I'll try to buy him. Sounds like candy might be better for him than another book."

"Good thinking."

They circled the parking lot for quite a while before they could find a spot. Actually, there were two smaller spots, but the Monaco likely wouldn't have fit. Aunt Shannon waited for several minutes until a huge pickup truck backed out of its spot, leaving enough room for the white beast. They hurried through the cold parking lot to the mall, but just as they stepped through the doors, she stopped. "Here's some money," she said, holding out three twenty-dollar bills.

"Ah." Steve felt awkward. "I can get some of my own money, Aunt Shannon. I have enough in my bank account. And I have my bank card with me."

"Take this, just in case," she insisted, holding the money to his nose.

"OK," Steve sighed, secretly relieved.

"Meet you back here in two hours." The two of them plunged into the Christmas mob and disappeared in the currents.

Steve found the fruit-shaped candies for Edward right away. An easy score. Aunt Shannon would be more difficult, though, because, for some reason he wanted to find her something special, something that would surprise her. So he spent most of his time browsing the shops, row after row of doodads and geewgaws. Sale this, and percentage off that. One free with purchase. He was about to settle for a season of *Gilligan's Island* episodes on DVD, when he found an odd little square case in a suitcase shop. It looked about the same size as the box that contained Richard's ashes. It was multi-colored, which he knew she'd like. It was extremely square and looked like a purse. It seemed like leather, and had been reduced from $79.99, to $39.99 to $17.49, and sat on a table marked "All items $9.99." Perfect, he thought. He took it to the till and paid for it.

He felt surprisingly good and decided to shop for more.

Next he bought a little chocolate for Aunt Shannon and a massive photographic book on the Beatles for Uncle Edward—all on sale. Then he went to the bank and tried to withdraw some money. The words "Insufficient Funds" blinked on the computer screen, canceling his transaction automatically.

"Stupid bank," he said to the machine.

He wandered through the mall for the last half hour before closing, buying himself a small drink in the food court and sipping it until it was time to meet up with Aunt Shannon. He wandered to the meeting point just outside the mall entrance and waited until she emerged from the crowd, dazed and laden with bags. Though she looked directly at him, she didn't seem to recognize him. He sidled up beside her and touched her elbow. "Aunt Shannon."

Her head turned to look at him and the confusion slowly melted away. "Let's go home," she said. And home they went.

They came into the kitchen with their bags of things and set them down on the counter. Uncle Edward emerged, suddenly, from the living room, looking sheepish, his eyes rimmed with red, as though he'd been crying. He moved quickly to the kitchen table where his book lay, splayed open, spine up, like a seagull in flight. He snatched it from the table.

"I'll be reading in the bedroom," he announced and disappeared.

Aunt Shannon made a quick pot of tea for herself, while Steve made himself a hot chocolate in the microwave.

"If you don't mind my asking, how did Richard pass away?" Steve asked, as they drank tea in the kitchen.

"Oh. I don't mind. He drowned." Steve waited a few moments hoping she might explain, but she didn't.

"Ah. Oh." The ice was thin, best to tread lightly. "That must have been difficult."

"Yes." She replied. Silence.

"Um. How did he drown?"

"Oh. Yes. I'm sorry. Of course." Aunt Shannon seemed to suddenly wake up to the question he was asking.

"It was a snorkeling accident. He loved to snorkel, you know. I'm not sure what really happened. Somehow, he ended up in his bedroom drenched, on the floor, wearing snorkeling equipment. The coroner said he'd…um… drowned." Grief twisted her face. "But…how?" Her lip trembled. "How? His bedroom door was locked." Her face was torn with emotion, and the tears coursed down her cheeks. "That…" Her chest heaved up and down as she struggled to control herself.

Steve felt like he should do something, but he wasn't sure what.

After a few minutes, she managed to speak a single word, "Tissue." Steve figured it out and yanked three tissues from a box on top of the fridge, handing them to her. She dabbed her eyes and blew her nose with one, then balled the other two and pushed them up her sleeve.

"Let's wrap our gifts," she suggested. She went briefly to her lab and returned with tape, scissors, and several old rolls of wrapping paper. "You first," she said, leaving the living room to allow Steve to wrap things up. He was quick, and clumsy, but his packages were together and under the tree in a matter of minutes.

"Aunt Shannon," he called. "Your turn."

Aunt Shannon nearly pranced into the living room. "You can finish up the dishes from tea. They go in the dishwasher."

Steve nodded and suppressed a comment, and reported for duty in the kitchen. It didn't take him long to arrange the cups on the top rack of the crusty old dishwasher. How effective it would be at cleaning them, he couldn't say.

"I'm done," Aunt Shannon bellowed right after, clearly excited. "Just look," she cried as he entered the room.

"That's great," Steve replied, sticking to what he knew she wanted to hear. In reality there was a giant, badly decorated toilet brush, with several poorly wrapped, odd-shaped lumps beneath it.

"Oh, I forgot to wrap one thing. Can you pass me some wrapping paper?"

Steve grabbed a roll of paper and passed it to her.

"No, no, dear. That's completely inappropriate," she chided, after taking the roll from his hands. "It's a bit too, um, feminine, really. I'd like something with richer colors." As she spoke, Steve noticed that her hand gently covered Richard's remains.

He sighed quietly, scooped most of the rolls from the floor and placed them beside her as she knelt on the carpet.

Aunt Shannon deliberated for quite a while, finally choosing a regal-looking, mostly red paper. She carefully cut a square away from the roll and placed Richard's remains in the center of the paper. Then, slowly, fold by fold, she wrapped him up like a present. "There, Deary, don't you look festive!" she announced to the box. Out of a large tangle of ribbons and wrapping fragments, she pulled a gold-colored bow.

"Can you put him under the tree, dear?" she asked.

Steve, too tired to argue, took Richard to the toilet brush tree and placed him under the branches. Aunt Shannon followed him.

"I won't leave you there for long, Son," she said. "Just a little Christmas fun."

With the decoration complete, the trio ate supper. Then Steve retired to his room where, surfing on the Internet through a neighbor's open network, he watched a couple of his favorite TV shows.

He emerged sometime later to get a snack before bed and found Aunt Shannon sitting in the dark living room, studying the tree, which blinked and glowed like a disco. She appeared to be in some kind of trance, and didn't notice as he walked into the kitchen. Uncle Edward was sitting in the kitchen, reading deeply.

"Why'd you set up that infernal tree?" he asked abruptly.

"I didn't—I mean, I did set it up, but not because I

wanted to. I was helping Aunt Shannon."

"I don't like it, in case you're wondering," he growled.

"Sorry about that. I guess we could take it down."

"Shannon won't have it, I'm sure."

"Well, why don't you talk to her about it? She's in the living room right now."

"I know." He got up out of his chair, swatting his book onto the table. "Shannon, we've got to talk," he announced firmly as he walked from the kitchen to the living room.

"Oh, Edward," Shannon replied, ignoring his gruff tone. "Come and sit with me."

Steve shook his head and began to search the cupboards for a good snack.

There were muffled tones of discussion from the living room, but he ignored them. He was looking for something: marshmallows, chocolate chips, even raisins—he was that desperate.

With Uncle Edward out of the way, his search was detailed and undisguised. He found a bag of shredded coconut. He poured a little into his palm and ate it. Rancid. He bent over the sink and spit everything out. Sticking his mouth under the kitchen tap he ran some cold water in, swished it around violently, and spat into the sink.

He examined the package—Best before October 19, 1984.

Nice. Antique coconut.

Steve slammed the package into the garbage.

He continued his search and found a bag of raisins. He

checked the best-before date: two and half years past their expiry. But he tried one just the same.

"Hmmm." A little hard and dry, but otherwise tasty.

He took a small handful and threw them into his mouth. Hard, like gravel. Sweet, like sugar, sort of. His jaw was sore after a few handfuls, and he headed back through the kitchen to go back to his room. As he walked through the living room into the hall he noticed Aunt Shannon and Uncle Edward. They were now both staring at the tree, holding hands. It looked like they were crying together, as the shiny streaks of tears blinked different colors with the Christmas-tree lights.

"Good night," Steve called softly, as he made off with the raisins down the hallway. "See you in the morning."

There was no reply.

Chapter Six

Steve got up late the following morning. Aunt Shannon was hurrying around the kitchen, but when she saw him, she smiled. Christmas knickknacks flooded the counters: snowman salt and pepper shakers, plastic elves, a sleigh-shaped napkin holder with a full set of reindeer pulling it. A glass crèche illuminated by a colored light.

Christmas crap is here.

"Ah, the dead have risen," she quipped. Steve nodded. "I'll make you some porridge."

"Thank you," Steve mumbled. His first words of the day. "Please don't make as much for me this time."

"Of course, Deary. Uncle Edward is off this morning. He'll be back after lunch."

After finishing his porridge and placing the bowl in the dishwasher with his spoon and glass, he attempted to leave the kitchen, hoping to hide out with the Internet again.

"Ahem," she announced, clearing her throat and blocking Steve's path.

"Thank you for breakfast, Aunt Shannon."

"You're welcome." She didn't move. "Don't we have work to do?"

"Um… I don't know," Steve replied.

Aunt Shannon pointed to a kitchen chair. Steve sat down. Aunt Shannon joined him. She was working on finishing another pot of tea.

"Don't we need to find your mom?"

"I didn't know she was on my 'to do' list."

"She is now."

"I don't know what to do. You're the magic expert."

"Ah, ah, ah," she said, rebuking him. "This is alchemy, a sort of science, not magic. Most people tend to get magic and alchemy mixed up. They're nothing like one another."

"It sounds like magic."

"Magic means that a supernatural force changes things. For alchemists, things change because it's in their natures to do so."

"Oh," Steve replied, working hard to sound like he had understood what she'd just said.

"As I said to you earlier, I think your mom may have accidentally traveled somewhere."

"You mean got sucked into the vortex?"

"Perhaps."

"Wouldn't she be dead then?"

"I don't know, dear. I haven't been able to figure out whether that energy is deadly to humans or not."

"So, you think we should try to see if it is?" Steve said

incredulously. "Couldn't that kill someone again?"

Aunt Shannon pursed her lips and crossed her arms. "No one said that experiments were for cowards."

"Well, I don't have my stone."

"We need to help you find it."

"And then what?"

"Then you start to experiment, like your mother… like me."

"How 'bout I help you experiment?" Steve suggested.

Shannon looked at the ceiling as she considered his offer. "That's probably a good way to start. Sure, we could—"

A heavy knock on the door interrupted them.

"I wonder who that could be?" Aunt Shannon wondered. She set down her teacup, crossed the hallway, and trundled down the short set of stairs to the front door. Steve stayed in his seat, studying the decorations on the table. The Christmas sleigh filled with napkins was about to hit three child-shaped candles, skating on the table top in front of the sleigh.

Call the Christmas ambulance.

Aunt Shannon unlocked the deadbolt, but left the door chain in place. She pulled opened the door and peeked out through the crack.

"You again!" she said angrily. "I've told you. I'm not interested in talking to you. My experiments are my own business."

A body slammed against the door, ripping the chain out of the doorframe and whacking the door into Aunt

Shannon, knocking her to the floor.

"Stop!" she yelled at the top of her voice. The commotion drew Steve from the kitchen to the top of the stairs leading to the front door. Two men stormed through the door and slammed it closed. A thin weasel of a man stood beside a thicker man, both sporting suits. "You can't just march into my house. I don't want you here," Aunt Shannon shrieked from the floor. She slowly crawled to her knees and climbed unsteadily to her feet.

"We are not here to harm you." The thin man smiled sweetly. "Not yet, anyway." He glanced up the stairs and noticed Steve. "Oh, I see you have a guest. You must be Steve."

Steve didn't respond. An icy feeling froze his feet and began to work its way up his legs, locking him to the ground.

The thin man paused and inspected Steve carefully. "My name is… well… you can call me Mr. Gold," he decided, directing his words to Steve.

The thin man waited for Steve to speak. Steve stood, iced up, not knowing what to do. His own thoughts yelled at him.

Duck Boy. Duck Boy.

"We are alchemists, too. I want to talk to your great aunt. We want to trade alchemical secrets." Gold squeezed out another big smile. "All we want to do is talk."

"You're a thief and a scoundrel," Aunt Shannon said, spitting each word out in a righteous tone. "You coward."

Gold pretended to ignore Aunt Shannon's words and continued speaking. "If we don't talk in the next few days, you never know..." He grabbed Aunt Shannon's boney arm and squeezed it viciously in his fist, then pushed her against a wall.

Steve stood motionless. He wanted to do something—defend his Aunt.

Duck Boy. Duck Boy.

Mr. Gold held her against the wall for a moment without speaking, as winter air robbed the house of its warmth. "If you don't cooperate," he growled through gritted teeth, "something worse might happen." He released Aunt Shannon's arm.

"You bully, picking on an old woman. What kind of man are you?" Aunt Shannon yelled. Gold's calm exterior shook with rage for a moment. He raised his hand and Aunt Shannon winced as she waited for his hand to connect with her face.

"You know, Shannon, someone needs to slap you," Gold said. "If you aren't careful, it might just be me. And," he added, "it won't just be a slap." He nodded to the other man, and the two wrenched open the door and left.

"Coward," Aunt Shannon yelled towards the man as he stalked away. In seething anger, she slammed the door with such force that the house shook. A splintered piece of wood swung at the end of the door chain. Aunt Shannon swung around, intoxicated with anger.

Steve took a step backward from where he stood at the

top of the stairs, and prepared to run away to be alone until he saw some of the fire fade from her eyes.

CHAPTER SEVEN

"ARE YOU ALL RIGHT?" Steve wondered in a shaken voice from the top of the stairs.

Aunt Shannon rubbed her arm where Mr. Gold had grabbed her. She frowned, the frown slowly turning into a sob. She brought her boney hands to her face and began to blubber.

Steve looked around the room and fiddled with his hair for a moment.

Tissue! he thought triumphantly.

He darted into the kitchen and grabbed another three tissues from the box on the top of the refrigerator. Tissues extended, he slowly stepped down the front stairs to where she stood.

When he was within arm's reach, she grabbed him and clung to him as if he were a life preserver in the middle of the Atlantic. Waving the tissues behind her back like a white flag, he surrendered and returned her hug.

After a few moments she released him.

"Help me up the stairs, please," she requested. She teetered up the stairs on his arm to the kitchen, and sat down in front of her teacup.

Steve set the tissues on the table and plunked down beside her. "Whenever an old lady cries," she sniffed, "she needs a tissue or two."

Steve nodded.

"What a bunch of dunderheads," she added, as she blew her nose.

"I made the mistake of telling a reporter that I thought your mother disappeared because of an alchemical experiment gone wrong. The reporter asked me to explain a bit about what might have happened. Of course it wasn't just Edward who read the article." She turned and gestured towards the door. "Those thugs have been bothering me ever since."

"Why don't you call the police and charge them or something?" Steve asked. "You don't have to put up with that, you know."

"Well, I've tried, but it's kind of tricky. First, his name isn't Mr. Gold, so I really can't say who's doing this to me. I've tried getting the license number of his car, but his plates are all unregistered, so that's pretty much a donut. And the police don't really believe my story, like the reporter who quoted me. They're much more amused by my theory than anything else." She blew her nose fiercely. "In other words, the police won't do much about it unless something very bad happens first."

"I'm sorry I didn't do anything," Steve said. "I wanted to help but I got stuck."

"What could you do against those men?" she asked.

"I dunno."

"I don't think the two of us together could do too much. So don't worry about it." She sipped some cold tea from her cup, studying the saucer. "I'm afraid I've dragged you into this situation now, Steve. That man knew who you were, so I think you need to keep an eye out for him. Next time you see them, run. I certainly don't expect you to defend me. I'll take care of myself, but make sure you stay away from them at all costs. Don't let them threaten you or sweet-talk you." Aunt Shannon began to massage her arm again, then sipped her tea. "Ach," she cursed. "It's absolutely cold."

The two of them sat silently for several moments. "I would like to ask you," Aunt Shannon looked up towards Steve, "not to mention these hoodlums' visit, especially to your Uncle Edward."

Steve nodded. "I won't say a thing. But won't he wonder about the door?"

Shannon nodded glumly. "My glue gun will patch things."

"Just blame it on me, if you need to," Steve suggested. Shannon smiled.

"Thank you, Steve. You're a good man." She patted his hand. "Can we discuss the clock-lock thing again?" she asked suddenly.

Steve poured himself a glass of juice, while Aunt

Shannon topped up her cup with now cold tea from the teapot. She took a stiff swig.

"Sure," Steve agreed. "That sorta rocked."

"I know you think it's impressive, and I guess it is. Mr. Gold would certainly think so." Aunt Shannon pointed her cup of tea towards Steve. "But, as I told you earlier, it's not as great as it looks."

"What do you mean?"

"I first transformed clocks and locks several years ago. I really haven't been able to find a practical use for it yet." Aunt Shannon waved her cup of tea as she talked. "I can turn a clock into a lock, but so what? I have a few ideas as to what might be happening, but otherwise I'm really not sure. I haven't been able to do much else for several years. I'm stuck. I know it's important, but I can't figure out how. I need to do something with it. I think your mother may have gone beyond where I have. That may explain what happened to her. If that is the case, we need to work until we find out what she was doing and bring her back."

Steve felt some of his heart thaw, and he cringed. Somehow, the ice felt safer. But, he couldn't squelch Aunt Shannon's words and the warmth they brought.

"Do you want to give this stuff a try, Steve?" Aunt Shannon asked, with a hopeful expression. "Honestly?"

He paused. "Yes," he replied. "I think I have to."

"Great." She clapped her hands together. "Before you can begin, we need to discover your prima materia." She glanced at Steve, who must have looked lost. "I mean, discover your Benu stone."

"OK, Aunt Shannon," he interrupted. "I need to ask a bunch of stupid questions before I understand what you're talking about." Aunt Shannon nodded with a smile, so he pursued, "Here's stupid question number one: What is prima materia? Here's a bigger stupid question: What is a Benu stone? What does it do? Do I have to find somebody's ashes so I can do stuff? I hope it doesn't have anything to do with experiments using human body parts."

Aunt Shannon smiled. "I always knew you were a true adept." She stopped herself. "Oh, excuse me, I've got to stop using the jargon or explain myself, at least." She covered her mouth as if she'd burped. "I knew you'd step up to the alchemical challenge. Let me see." Aunt Shannon set her tea down to think for a moment. "Prima materia universalis, mercurius universalis, materia remota, materia tertia—they're all names for the same thing. They're old names because so many before you and me have looked for it. Prima materia is Latin for 'prime material.' In olden days, alchemists believed that this was some kind of common material, like one of the elements—say iron—something easily accessible that could be purified or perfected and made into a Benu stone. Back then, most everyone thought that if you found this element, you could refine it into a Benu stone."

She hoisted her teacup. Another sip; a slight shudder. "But I haven't answered your biggest question yet. The Benu stone... a Benu stone is the one thing that can help you transform things into other things. That's the only definition I know that matters." Her teacup clinked into its saucer as she set it down to gesture with both hands. "But this is only a working definition. To be honest, I really don't know what a Benu stone does except what you saw today. It could do other things—what those things are, I'm not sure."

"You mean travel?"

"Perhaps," she replied. "That's my best guess, based on what happened to your mother."

Steve was still baffled, so Aunt Shannon continued her explanation. "Our family alchemy, our journals and notes from seven or eight generations of alchemists, points to a different kind of prime matter. As humans, we all have many characteristics in common. There is only one prime matter, but it has many, many expressions." She paused for a moment. "This is all so complicated. Am I making any sense?"

"Sort of," Steve replied. "I'm getting some of it, I think."

"Good. That's good. Now where was I... oh yes... Um... the spiritus mundi. What will bring this prime material into existence is something special—unique to you. It's not an element. That much I've learned. Those old alchemists would have laughed if I had suggested to them that Richard is my Benu stone. But he is. And he won't work for you. You need to find something yourself that points you to the prime material in just the right way." She lifted her teacup to her mouth, closed her eyes, and tipped her head and the teacup back, draining it with an extended slurp.

"Once you have your Benu stone, you need the next big ingredient: words. Words are the second thing you need. Words are generally more flexible than most things," Aunt Shannon said. "That's why I think they hold promise." She poured herself another cup of tea and drained it in a single gulp like an alcoholic on the start of a bender, then stared at the bottom of her empty teacup as if to check whether there was anything left. "Words were here long before most everything else. And they will be here long after we go. We all use words because we want something to happen. We want him or her to do this or that." She leaned toward Steve. "If you use a word well—The Word—you can change everything for the better." She raised her eyes to meet Steve's. "I think if you use the word properly, you can change the world."

"Like the way you found clock and lock and make them change."

"Right. Absolutely right. Even without a Benu stone, the words that we believe change things. But with those words and my Benu stone, I can make the change." A shadow darkened her face, and lingered.

"So have you tried other words?"

"Oh yes." Aunt Shannon suddenly looked very tired. "Oh yes, Deary. A great many. So very many. These are the only two I've found. My entire life's work results in two words." She shook her head as if to rid herself of the depressing thought. "Although this is how these things begin. Think of electricity. It had been known to exist for at least two thousand years. It was the late 16th century before someone noticed and named it. It was another 100 years before it became useful." She smiled and closed her eyes. "Good ideas take their time."

"Does this work in other languages? I mean, have you only tried English words?"

"Oh," Aunt Shannon, said with a start. "I've never tried another language. That's good." Her eyes shone brightly. "Yes, I like that idea. Hmmm." She nodded.

"How did you ever discover it"

She smiled widely. "Happy accident. I think they call that serendipity." Her smile faded. "I started thinking this way when Richard passed away," Aunt Shannon continued. "The minister said some words as Richard's body slid into the fire—he said 'dust to dust, ashes to ashes.' And as I heard those words I wondered how they might have helped Richard's body to burn in the fire. What would have happened if the pastor said 'get up Richard… be alive!'" Tears circled Aunt Shannon's eyes, and she dabbed them with the sleeves of her blouse.

"So I started experimenting with words to revive Richard. One afternoon I was experimenting in the kitchen holding a watch and Richard and… well, you know the rest." She smiled. "It seems I can't change Richard, but he can change things." She paused to swallow. "I need you, Steve. I need you to help me. I'm stuck. I know there's something more to all of this, but I haven't been able to discover what it is."

"What can I do? Where should I start? Should I read that book in my room?"

Aunt Shannon sighed. "The book in your room won't help much with your experiments. Our kind of alchemy doesn't rely on experiments with human body parts or purifying some prime material so we can make our Benu stone. Those books talk about the wrong methods and try to do things backwards, most often.

"The only point they agree on is that change—radical change—is possible. All of them suggest you can change things. But you don't need to read those books to find that idea. Every ordinary story says the same thing—things can change. Sometimes the change is bad, sometimes good, but each story shouts that change is possible." Aunt Shannon ran her finger around the inside of her teacup and licked it. "I think we should begin somewhere else." Aunt Shannon's eyes focused on Steve, her eyes filled with a friendly fire.

"Start experimenting. Begin your great work—find your Benu stone. Learn about what you can do and what you can't. We'll work together to move on. I think the key is here in her liber mutus." She jabbed her index finger at Steve's mother's research notebook.

"Excuse me," Steve said. "You're losing me again here. What is a 'liber mutus'?"

"A 'liber mutus' is a wordless book. Latin again."

"But her book is full of words."

"But she hasn't clearly said what she was doing. She just jots down the odd thought and random insight. It doesn't spell out what we need to do to find what she was working on. So, on the big picture, it's silent—wordless, in effect. Still, I think her notebook has the clues we need to find her, even though it doesn't say how she did what she did. I think your mother was touching her Benu stone, and then she said something or did something and was transported somewhere. Somewhere nice, hopefully." But her smile seemed a little thin, her voice hollow as she spoke the last sentence.

The sharp-edged replay of his last words to his mom cut through his thoughts. "I wish you would go away and ever come back. EVER."

"I hope it's nice, too," Steve replied.

CHAPTER EIGHT

IN THE OLD DAYS, alchemists believed that to make a Benu stone you had to start with the prime material and burn it, refine it, burn it and refine it some more and purify it a few other ways."

Now that Aunt Shannon had Steve's attention, she seemed prepared to talk for days. Sitting at the kitchen table with her empty cup and cold teapot, she showed no sign of slowing down. "Mr. Gold thinks that he must build a Benu stone the old-fashioned way—he's read too many books. He hasn't lived enough. It's not about making; it's about finding. That's why books of alchemy won't help you much."

"What would my Benu stone be?"

"I don't know, really." Aunt Shannon put her finger to her lips. "It's something as dark as fear and hate that can be purified into something as light and white as truth and love."

"Sorry. Huh?"

"As near as I can figure it, your stone will be something that represents your greatest fear and your greatest hope at the same time. Like my Benu stone—my worst fear was Richard dying."

"He did die."

"Yes, he did. His death, for me, was the darkest thing I could imagine. But over time, as I worked through my pain, my darkness became light—a triumph of sorts. That's when I noticed that Richard gave me the power to work my experiments."

"Hmm." Steve thought for a moment. His forehead wrinkled as he puzzled over Aunt Shannon's words. "I'm feeling foggy. I think I need to talk about something else for a while, until my head clears a bit."

"Good idea," she replied. "Why don't we get out of the house for a while?"

"Sure." Steve added a nod to his reply.

"I've got something I've been absolutely dying to do. And I need you with me to do it."

"What do you want to do?"

"I think we should drop by the police station and read the police report. That report might remind you of what happened that night, and we'd get some clues to go along with your mother's research notes."

"Maybe we should drop by the house, too," Steve suggested. "I left my backpack at home. It's got some clean clothes I'll need. I can pick it up."

"That's a great idea, Steve," Aunt Shannon exclaimed,

obviously pleased. "We can reenact what happened the night your mother disappeared while we're there."

Aunt Shannon picked up the phone and called the police station. "Do you know who the detective was?" Aunt Shannon asked as she waited for someone to answer the phone at the station.

"Yeah, ask for a guy named Larry Garner. He was the main investigator for our case."

Aunt Shannon bowed her head to concentrate as she made the arrangements to visit the detective. She was able to make an appointment for that afternoon at one forty-five.

After a light lunch, the two of them grabbed their coats. As they walked out the front door, Aunt Shannon pointed across the street to an unkempt, split-level house. "That's where Lindsay lives—you know, that girl I introduced to you this morning. I hope you two can get to know each other better."

Steve didn't reply. It was cold, and a new blanket of snow groaned under their feet as they walked to the garage.

The two of them climbed into the old beast and started it. It coughed a little before it galumphed into a steady, lumpy rumble. Aunt Shannon eased it into reverse and pulled the car out of the shadows into the feeble afternoon sun.

Steve and Aunt Shannon walked into the police station five minutes before the appointment was scheduled to begin. They announced their arrival to the constable at the desk. The constable made a short phone call and informed Detective Larry Garner of their arrival, then led them through a large room cluttered with cubicles, desks, and busy people to a man seated at a desk in the far corner, next to a window. Larry Garner, an overweight, middle-aged man, stood to greet them as they approached.

"Hello there. You must be Shannon Pankratz-Bacon."

"And you must be Detective Garner," Aunt Shannon replied.

"Most people call me Larry." He shook her hand and then noticed Steve. "Hello, Steve."

"Hello, Mr. Garner," Steve replied.

"You said you wanted to discuss the disappearance of Mrs. Best. You are family, right?"

"I'm family. I'm Susan's aunt." Aunt Shannon smiled sweetly. "Actually, I want to see the file on your investigation."

"If that's what you came to see me about, I'm afraid you're wasting your time. That information is confidential," Larry replied. "It's not for public viewing. It's for police purposes only."

"Young man," Aunt Shannon said firmly, "I need to see that file. I want to help your case."

"I'm sorry," Larry replied, "tell me what you know, and let me put the pieces of the puzzle together. That's my job."

"Very funny," Aunt Shannon replied dryly. "What do you think will happen if I read the file? Are you worried I'll solve the case before you do? I'm an old lady. I'm certainly not going to hurt anyone, am I?"

Larry shrugged. "You might."

Aunt Shannon rolled her eyes. "Besides, you haven't got a case." Aunt Shannon paused. Larry rolled his eyes. "You have no motive, no method, no idea what happened to her, do you?" Larry's polite smile flattened into an unhappy line as she spoke. Aunt Shannon continued. "You can't be any worse off than you already are. I'm just a little old lady, Detective. Humor me. Besides, there's nothing in that file that Steve couldn't tell me." Steve grinned widely at Larry and nodded.

"All right, all right. I haven't got the time to banter about it all day. I'll be right back." Larry crossed the room and retrieved the file from a row of filing cabinets and returned to the desk. "Have a seat." Aunt Shannon sat in his desk chair. "Steve, you can borrow that chair there." Larry Garner pointed to a chair next to his desk. Steve nodded and pulled the chair close to Aunt Shannon. "I only have one rule about this file. If you break my rule, you'll never see this file again: do not, under any circumstances, remove this file or any part of it from this building. If you do, I will charge you with theft and obstruction of justice and anything else I can conjure up. You can view it at my desk, and when you are finished, leave it here." He pulled a coat from a rack beside the window and turned to leave.

"Hey, Clueless." Steve and Aunt Shannon turned to see a square-jawed police officer standing across from Larry's desk. The police officer turned to Aunt Shannon and Steve and pointed at Larry. "You know why we call him Clueless, don't you?"

She forced a smile. "I have no idea."

"Clueless hasn't cracked a case here in three years," said the officer, smirking. "He's good at writing parking tickets, though."

Larry attempted to ignore the comments. "I'm making a call or two and I'll be back in an hour or so," he announced.

"Take your time," Aunt Shannon retorted.

"Going to have tea with another suspect, eh?" said the burly officer.

"It's a concept I like to call work," snapped Larry. "I'm not sure you've heard of it."

"Ooh, that hurt, Larry."

Larry turned to Steve and Aunt Shannon. "See you two later."

"See you," Aunt Shannon replied. As soon as Larry left, Aunt Shannon whirled around to face the desk and opened the thick file.

The detective who had insulted Larry grinned at Steve and his great aunt and returned to his own desk.

The file held several pictures of the living room furniture where Mrs. Best had been sitting the night she disappeared.

"These pictures were taken after the coffee mess was cleaned up, eh?" Aunt Shannon asked.

"Yeah, I guess so," Steve answered noncommittally.

Aunt Shannon shot him an exasperated look.

"What?" Steve felt defensive, although he knew what her look was asking of him. He held out his hand for a picture, and she placed one into his hand. He felt a dull ache, one that had taken a holiday for the past few hours, return with a vengeance. He glanced at the picture quickly and returned it to her.

"Yup. I cleaned it up right away," Steve replied.

"There was coffee all the way around the front of the chair, wasn't there?"

"Uh-huh."

"And the book was lying face down in the middle of the coffee?"

"Yup."

"Which way were the words facing?"

Steve hesitated briefly, expecting a trap. "What do you mean?"

"When the book was on the floor, if you sat in the chair and picked up the book, would the words be right side up or upside down?"

"I don't know…Um…Let's see." Steve thought back to that night. Everything was clear as a photograph in his mind. "I guess if you were sitting in the chair and you lifted her book out of the coffee, the words would have been right side up."

"Good." Aunt Shannon, nodding absently. "Were there other coffee stains in the house?"

"Nope. Just the puddle in front of Mom's chair."

"The mug was lying on the floor between the chair and

the coffee table?"

"I guess so."

"Don't guess," Aunt Shannon said sharply. "This is terribly important."

"Um, yeah," Steve mumbled.

"Perfect, just perfect," Aunt Shannon purred to herself.

"What's so perfect?"

"All the signs suggest that your mother was sitting in the chair when she disappeared."

"How do you know?"

"The mug was between the coffee table and the chair which means she was holding it in her left hand. Right?" Steve nodded. "And that's the hand she always used to drink her coffee."

"Yup."

"If she was holding her cup in her left hand when she dropped it, she would probably have been sitting in her chair. That's the reasonable explanation." Aunt Shannon paused. "Even her book fell into the coffee as if she had been sitting in her chair."

"What are you talking about?"

Aunt Shannon lifted the case file off the desk and held it in her hands like a book. "If I'm reading this and I drop it here, how would it land?"

"Either face up, with the words up, or face down with the words…" His brow grew heavy with thought. "Right, I see what you're saying. The way I found the book means she was likely sitting in the chair when she dropped it."

"Right," Aunt Shannon exclaimed triumphantly.

"But so what!" Steve countered. "So she sat in the chair. That's pretty obvious."

"When she dropped the coffee, she was sitting in the chair and the coffee fell around the front of the chair in a wide puddle. She would have likely stepped in the coffee and tracked it around the floor."

"I see. So you're saying she was sitting in the chair with her coffee and her book, and she dropped her coffee, and she didn't get up." Steve looked at the ceiling for a moment. "She was sitting in the chair and she vanished right in the chair?" he asked.

"I think she was sitting in her chair, probably with her Benu stone, when she did something that caused her to zap into another time or space—something like that. She disappeared right out of her chair. She probably surprised herself, dropped her coffee and poof! She was gone."

"Hmm," Steve mused.

"It's just a good guess."

"Let me tell you another guess." He held up a report from the same file. "It makes sense, for 'normal' people." He tapped the report with a finger. "She sets the scene up for a big disappearance and she takes off—she just leaves. That's what the police say happened. If you read the file you'd see that a few people thought they saw her in Montreal. That's a theory, too."

"Yes, that's a theory," Aunt Shannon admitted. "She did always want to start a singing career. But all the evidence seems to indicate that she was sitting in her chair when she disappeared." Steve didn't look up from the floor. "Steve, you're an important witness to your mother's character. You lived with her for twelve years before she disappeared. So let me ask you something. Was she the kind of person who would leave you the way you think she did?"

"Well...Um..." Silence.

"Steve?"

"Not really, no."

"She isn't that kind of woman, Steve. She's not that sort of mother, is she? She would never leave you. She wouldn't have left your dad either. I know that for certain. She loves you very much. She's just had a wee accident, that's all." Aunt Shannon closed the file on the desk. "I think we should drop by the house and look for more clues." Steve nodded without saying anything. "You do remember where the house key is hidden?" Again, Steve nodded. "Well then, let's go."

Aunt Shannon riffled through the entire file's contents carefully and reorganized it. When she was done, she left it exactly where Larry had commanded and headed to the car. The afternoon sun had dropped below the horizon, leaving a frozen twilight to grow into night.

The house looked dark and cold as Steve and his great aunt pulled up in front. A light layer of new snow dusted the yard and roof of the house. A tight lump grew in his throat as he gazed up the walk.

"Let's go," Aunt Shannon suggested. "There's no use

dawdling." Steve found the hidden key and opened the front door. The door swung open to a stifling silence.

"In we go," she said cheerfully. Aunt Shannon led the way inside to the living room. She turned on a couple of lights.

"Do you remember how it was that night she disappeared?" Aunt Shannon asked. She peered at Steve. "I want to set it up exactly the way it was."

"Yeah, sure," Steve responded. Steve shuffled into the kitchen and got a mug out of a cupboard. He sauntered back to the living room and turned toward Aunt Shannon as he set the cup down on the floor beside his mother's chair. "This is where the mug was, except it was broken."

"Was your mom's chair at this angle that night?"

Steve shrugged. "Sure."

Aunt Shannon reached into her purse and pulled out a handful of snapshots and studied them. She had taken the pictures from Larry's file.

"That's not exactly where it was, Steve," Aunt Shannon corrected with a gentle edge in her voice. "It should be at more of an angle and about a foot closer to the window—like this." She pushed the chair towards the window and angled it. She glanced again at the pictures. "That's better, see?" She turned a picture towards him. Steve recognized the pictures immediately.

"We weren't supposed to take anything from the file, Aunty," Steve moaned. "Detective Garner is going to notice what you took."

"We need these photos for our experiments, Steve," Aunt Shannon explained with a smile. "Besides, I'll tell him it was I who took the pictures. He won't blame you. Do you think he's going to throw an old lady in the slammer? Come on. Help me set this scene up." Steve sighed and began to help.

Aunt Shannon seemed pleased. "Here are a couple of pictures. You set up the coffee table and the bookshelf the way they were, and I'll get settled into the chair. Pretend I'm your mom, and arrange things exactly as you remember them." The two of them set up the room as close as they could to the pictures and what Steve could remember. Steve flopped onto the couch and stretched out.

"I want to sit as she would have that night." She settled into the chair. "Now, how did she usually sit in this chair?"

"She usually sat with her legs crossed and her notebook in her lap."

Aunt Shannon slowly, gingerly crossed her legs and set the notebook in her lap. "How do I look?"

"That's pretty close," Steve confirmed.

"Could you get me Richard, Steve? He's on the floor next to my purse." Steve retrieved the festively wrapped box of ashes and set it on the coffee table beside her. "Thank you. I think I'm ready." Aunt Shannon lifted her glasses and slid them into place. "That's better. Now let me see." She flipped through Susan's notebook until she found the last coffee-stained scribbles. Steve slouched and dropped into the couch behind him.

His aunt seemed to fall into a trance as she studied the book. "Oh, right," she said under her breath. "I forgot to look that word up before I came here. `Extravasation.' What word could that be?" she asked herself. "I haven't seen that one before." She looked up at Steve from over top of her reading glasses. "Steve, dear, could you get me a dictionary? I need to look up a word. And get your backpack. You were going to get it, weren't you? I'm just going to see if I can understand where your mom was working and then we'll go. I'll probably be just a few minutes."

Steve sighed, rolled off the couch and walked to the bookshelf to pull the big dictionary from its corner. But the dictionary wasn't in its usual place. He headed to his bedroom to get his own dictionary. Aunt Shannon was deep in thought, but held out a hand when he returned to the living room.

"Thank you, Steve," she said absently.

"Do you need anything else?" he asked.

"Not that I can think of, Deary," Aunt Shannon replied absently as she paged through the dictionary. "Now where is it… c…d…e … ex…ext. There we go."

"All right. I'm going to get my backpack," Steve declared.

"You go right ahead, Deary."

Steve ducked into his room. His backpack was sitting on the bed, right where he had left it. Turning his back to the bed, he flopped backward onto it and stared at the ceiling. The room felt like a solid block of ice.

Aunt Shannon screamed, "Steeeeeeeeeve." A bright

bluish-white radiance overwhelmed the room through the open door. A red glow and finally a bright white. Steve jumped from his bed and sprinted into the living room.

Paper swirled frantically around the room, pushed by some kind of wind. Two notebooks lay on the floor in front of his mother's chair. One was Aunt Shannon's research notes. The other was his mom's notebook, lying on the floor in a crumpled heap, like it had so long ago. The room smelled like earthy soil on a spring day. Paper wafted slowly to the floor. Aunt Shannon was gone.

CHAPTER NINE

"AUNT SHANNON!" STEVE SCREECHED. "That's a pretty sick joke. Don't play around like this."

Silence. Steve searched frantically behind furniture. Nothing. Then he broadened his search to include the rest of the house. He even used the pull-down ladder to check the attic. Front door. Her car waited in the dim darkness of the new night. He ran and reran his search pattern around the house. Terror fed a growing frenzy. Finally, he caved into a frightened, heaving heap on the couch and waited in silence. The cold slap of truth stunned him: Aunt Shannon was gone.

He stared at the chair where Aunt Shannon had been sitting only moments earlier. Jittery nerves on high alert, he half expected that she would jump out from behind something and scare him into the next life. But she didn't. As the pool of terror subsided, he replayed the scene. "The light," he said aloud, just to put something besides breath into the air. The light reminded him of the clock's transformation into the lock. "Maybe this is possible," he whispered to himself.

"Ha, ha," he said aloud, sitting straight up. "Yes. Of course."

Maybe Mom never abandoned me. Maybe it was really an accident.

He slumped back down on the couch.

I have no way to bring either of them back. I can't help them.

"How am I going to get back to Aunt Shannon's?" he asked himself. He jumped up from the couch and grabbed the phone, dialing Aunt Shannon and Uncle Edward's number. The phone rang and rang and rang. Finally, the ringing was interrupted by a sound of Uncle Edward fumbling with the phone.

After a clunky succession of whacks and popping sounds, he heard a voice. "Hello?" It was Uncle Edward.

"Uncle Edward?"

"Steve?" Uncle Edward asked. "Is that you?"

"Yeah, Uncle Edward. It's me."

"What's the matter? You sound upset."

Steve would have been surprised at Uncle Edward's awareness, had he not been so distressed about Aunt Shannon's disappearance. "She just disappeared, Uncle Edward. I don't know what to do."

There was a long pause on the other end of the phone. "Who disappeared, Steve?"

"Aunt Shannon!"

"Aunt Shannon disappears from time to time. There's

nothing unusual about that."

"She didn't just take off, Uncle Edward. She really disappeared. She vanished. She was trying that alchemy stuff, and she ended up going somewhere—I don't know where." Steve excitedly related the past few moments to Uncle Edward.

"That sounds odd," Uncle Edward's voice stiffened. He sniffed loudly into the receiver, and his voice turned cold. "I told her to quit monkeying with that junk." His voice warmed. "Oh, Shannon. What have you done?"

"I'm stuck here with the car. Now that Aunt Shannon's gone, I have no way of getting home with the car. Can you take a bus or a taxi down here to pick it up?"

"Oh heavens, no," Uncle Edward exclaimed. "I don't have a driver's license. Shannon always does the driving."

"She's gone, Uncle Edward!" Steve nearly shrieked. "The same thing happened to her as to my mom."

"I'm sure she's fine. I hope she's fine. Oh dear. Well, Hmm." Uncle Edward sniffled. "You'd better drive it home. Oh dear. You do have the keys, don't you?"

Steve scanned the coffee table beside where Aunt Shannon had been sitting. A glinting heap of metal sparkled on the floor under the reading lamp, next to the two research notebooks. "Yes, I do," he admitted, "but I don't have a driver's license."

"Drive carefully, then. Shannon loves that old heap."

"I said I don't have my driver's license."

"Oh dear, oh dear, oh dear. Steve, I can't come to get

you." His voice raised in its intensity and pitch.

"Uncle Edward?" Steve asked after a few seconds of silence.

"Oh dear. Well then, you'd better drive."

"What happens if I get caught?"

"Tell the officer you have an emergency," Uncle Edward snapped. "Oh, Shannon," he repeated mournfully, and began to sob as he slammed the phone down.

I could always take the bus, thought Steve.

No, wait. I left my money at Aunt Shannon's house. No wallet, no money, no bus pass. No bus.

He walked towards the chair and scooped the car keys off of the floor. Then he took careful mental notes of the room and its arrangement in case he needed to recreate it all again. He collected the pictures that had whirled their way all around the room and shoved them back into Aunt Shannon's purse. The two notebooks he stuffed into his backpack, on top of his socks and underwear.

Then, standing by the front door, he took a deep breath and let it out slowly. He looked around once more, opened the front door, closed and locked it, and plunged into the frozen night, taking Aunt Shannon's purse and the photographs with him. With his free hand, he opened the driver's side door and looked back at the house.

He wedged himself between the steering wheel and the driver's seat. He rested his forehead on the top of the steering wheel as he fished for the seat adjustment, first with his right hand, and then his left. Left again.

"There," he announced to himself. He swung his feet in and pushed the driver's seat back, and released the adjustment.

"The brakes. Gas pedal. Shifter." He grasped the steering wheel with both hands. "I can do this, I think." After his review, he stepped out of the car to study the evening's surroundings. Satisfied that no one had noticed him, he hopped back into the driver's seat and turned the key in the ignition. The engine roared then howled as he held the ignition key forward too long. When he released the key, the howling stopped and the engine chugged calmly.

"Sorry." He sat for a moment or two, took a deep breath and shifted the transmission into 'D.' "Here we go." With a lurch, and some wild swerving, he was off.

Uncle Edward sat inside the house reading a book when Steve galumphed over the curb and part of the lawn, pulling into the driveway.

"Hello," Steve said. He dropped the keys on the kitchen counter, with Aunt Shannon's purse.

Uncle Edward was reading a book entitled *Hamster Breeding for Amateurs*, but he frowned, and his eyes were red as if he might have been crying. "I told her she could get hurt playing around with that hocus-pocus. Would she listen to me? Not a chance." His eyes never left the page, as if his eyes were caged by the words.

"How are we going to help her, Uncle Edward?"

"We're not going to help her," Uncle Edward retorted. "We're not getting mixed up in that stuff. She got herself into this trouble, and she can get herself out."

"Do you know what happened to her?"

"I have no clue," Uncle Edward responded. "And I don't want to find out, either."

"What...Um... So we won't do anything?"

"Right," Uncle Edward snapped. "Don't try to change things. When you try to change things, accidents like this happen."

"I put Aunt Shannon's purse and keys and stuff on the kitchen counter," Steve announced.

"Fine," Uncle Edward grunted. Steve returned to the kitchen and plucked the photos from Aunt Shannon's purse. He stacked both the notebooks together, with the pictures, and carried them with his backpack to his bedroom.

He flopped on the bed, dropping the photos and notebooks on the bed beside him.

He replayed the events in his mind. Retrieving Richard. Finding a dictionary. Lying on his bed. The scream. The bright light, colors shifting. Gone.

Replay. Replay. And again.

"What am I missing?" he asked himself. He slapped the palm of his hand on his forehead. "She disappeared. The light." Steve sputtered. "The light was just like when the clock turned into the lock. All the paper in the living room looked like it had been blown around... just like when the clock turned into a lock." He picked up the book from the nightstand and flipped the cover open and closed as he thought. "Aunt Shannon disappeared with the same kind of power we used to turn a clock into a lock." He thought for a minute more as he flipped the book cover open and closed. "Yeah. That's for certain… it was the same thing." Steve examined the book his hands were playing with. He thought about his mother's notebook lying on the floor in front of the chair after Aunt Shannon disappeared. "Holy Moses," he yelled, and sat up on the edge of the bed.

Richard was gone.

Steve sat straight up as he concentrated on his insight, driving his fists into his temples. A careful review again, looking in his memories to see if Richard remained after the incident. "No," he said to himself, with a shake of his head. Her Benu stone went with her. He finished flipping the book's cover and sat it down on his lap.

What else was missing?

Suddenly, an electric jolt shot through his mind and jumped out of his mouth. "The dictionary!" Steve yowled.

"Are you all right, Steve?" Uncle Edward hollered down the hall.

"Sorry. I'm great… I'm all right," Steve responded, toning down his excitement in the hope that Uncle Edward wouldn't suspect anything. The Benu stone and the dictionary—both of them gone. Steve lay back down and lifted the book from his lap and put it over his head, like a hat.

"I wonder what it means?" he asked himself.

He imagined the two things—Richard and the

dictionary—and began to picture them.

"Yes," He muttered to himself. "The dictionary and a Benu stone. That's what did it." His eyes sprang open. "The big dictionary was missing, too," he exclaimed.

The same thing happened to Mom.

A burning warmth tingled through his chest with the thought. "The dictionary. Maybe the dictionary and a Benu stone are another short circuit, like the lock-clock thing. Maybe it's just like touching the positive and negative on a battery at the same time."

"Young man. Do you need assistance?" Uncle Edward trumpeted down the hall.

"Fine. I'm good," Steve replied.

"I need a Benu stone and a dictionary," he said to himself. The book he had been holding was about alchemy, and Steve found the table of contents and scanned it for chapters about the Benu stone. Nothing. "I guess the other question is whether or not it kills. But there weren't any ashes or anything. Plus, the lock-clock power doesn't kill. So maybe."

He leapt to his feet, and grabbing his backpack, let it dangle upside down over the bed to dump the underwear and socks into a pile. Then he slid the pictures and notebooks collection inside, and his iPod, just in case.

"My experiment kit," he said to himself.

As he stood there, the phone rang. It rang and rang.

"You'd better get that," Uncle Edward shouted down the hall, as another ring jangled the air.

They don't have voicemail, I bet.

"Steve, answer the phone!" Steve trotted to the phone.

"Hello, Steve speaking."

"Ah, hello. Shannon Pankratz-Bacon, please?"

"Um," Steve paused awkwardly as he tried to come up with an answer. "Um, I'm sorry, she's not here."

Not here, he thought, that's an understatement.

"When will she be back?" the voice asked.

"She's gone for a while, I'm afraid."

"Steve?"

"Yeah."

"I met you Tuesday morning in your great aunt's kitchen. This is Lindsay."

"Hi," he replied. "Hey, you're an alchemist, right?" Steve demanded, cutting out the normal pleasantries.

"Yeah. Kind of. Actually, I'm learning some stuff with your aunt." Silence. "Could you give her a message for me?"

"Ahh... sure," Steve replied.

"Could you tell her that she's being watched again?"

"Pardon me?"

"She was being watched a few months back, by two men, usually. And they're watching her house again. They've been there all day."

Steve recalled the pictures Aunt Shannon had removed from the file at the police station, now in his backpack.

"Do they look like policemen?"

"No. They're wearing suits. Take a look for yourself." Steve walked over to a window with the phone and gazed through a gap between the curtains. A luxury car, charcoal gray, sat idling on the icy street with the exhaust congregating in frigid clouds behind it.

"I see them," Steve agreed. "You're right, they don't look like policemen."

"I wonder what they want?" Lindsay asked.

Steve thought they were related to Mr. Gold and his group. He knew what they wanted, but he didn't say anything to Lindsay. "Good question."

"Where did Shannon go?"

"Ah, I'm not sure," Steve answered truthfully. "She didn't say, either."

"That's like your aunt," Lindsay answered.

The phone he was talking on was a rotary-dial antique. *No call display. I can't call her back.*

Another abrupt topic change. "So you know a lot about alchemy? Do you know how to make your Benu stone?" Steve blurted.

"Um… wow." Silence. "Sort of," she replied. "I mean, I know how I'm supposed to find it, but I haven't done it yet," Lindsay answered. "Though you should be asking your aunt to answer these questions, not me."

"We should talk about a few things," Steve suggested.

"Ahh. Maybe. I really just need to talk to Shannon," Lindsay suggested. "When will she be home?"

Steve looked around the living room and what he could see of the kitchen for a clock. Just an artsy clock without a dial or numbers hung against the gold and red living room wallpaper.

How are you supposed to read that? Um…6 ish.

"Oh. Right. How about seven?" Silence. "I mean, she'll be home at seven, yeah seven. And she was hoping to talk to you, I think," Steve lied.

"All right then. Why don't I drop by at seven-thirty."

"Sounds great," Steve exclaimed. "I'll see you then." He hung up the phone.

"Who was that?" Uncle Edward asked from his chair in the living room.

"Lindsay, Aunt Shannon's friend."

"Oh. I see." Uncle Edward didn't seem to be interested in the details at all, so Steve spun around to head back to his room. As he turned, the phone rang again.

"Hello?"

"Hello, is Steve there?" asked a gruff male voice.

"Steve's speaking."

"This is Detective Garner." Without giving Steve a chance to speak, he jumped into the point of his call. "I'm disappointed by your actions," he said roughly. "You took most of the pictures from my file here. That's illegal, as well as a breach of my trust. I'm surprised you'd take advantage of your time at the station like this. I'm going to have to speak to Great Aunt Shannon about what you've done. Put her on the phone, Steve."

Duck Boy. Duck Boy.

"I wish I could," Steve said. "I think this is all just a misunderstanding. It's not what you think it is."

"It's pretty clear what it is from my end. You're obstructing my investigation by removing those pictures. You're supposed to help me, not get in my way. Will she be home tonight?"

"I don't think so..."

"You're playing games with me, Steve. She's probably there right now. I'm coming over to pick up those pictures. I'll be there at seven-thirty. If your aunt isn't there, or if you aren't there, mark my words: removing pictures from a police file constitutes theft of police property. You took advantage of my generosity." The phone line went dead.

"Who was that?" Uncle Edward asked, his voice seeming like an echo.

Steve hesitated briefly, but decided Uncle Edward wouldn't care one way or another. "That was Detective Garner, the officer assigned to my mom's case."

"Oh, I see." Sure enough, Uncle Edward didn't seem interested in what the call was about. "Steve, can you cook?" Uncle Edward asked suddenly.

"Yeah," Steve replied. "I can do basic stuff."

"Can you cook some supper for me?"

"Um ... sure... I guess. Can't you cook, Uncle Edward?"

Uncle Edward turned red and gazed at the floor. "No," he replied sheepishly.

"But I've seen you reading cookbooks before," Steve insisted.

Uncle Edward nodded. "I've read quite a few cookbooks."

"OK," Steve sighed. "I'll cook."

Uncle Edward glanced at his watch. "Can you make some supper now?"

"I'll see what I can do."

Steve headed to the kitchen to throw supper together.

Putting together a shoddy supper again.

The refrigerator pickings looked sparse. Steve found some leftover meat loaf from the night before, but there didn't seem to be any vegetables to go with it.

"Uncle Edward," Steve called. "Where could I find some potatoes and stuff?"

Uncle Edward called the answer from where he sat. "We have a root cellar down in the basement. I think there are potatoes and carrots in there—a big sack of each."

Steve jogged to the basement door at the end of the kitchen. He always found Aunt Shannon and Uncle Edward's basement a bit spooky. When he tugged on a worn string and pulled the switch of the first light, a weak yellow glow shone into the basement. Piles of old boxes, furniture, and odds and ends covered the floor from top to bottom.

Classic hoarding behavior.

Between the bric-a-brac were skinny paths cutting deep into the basement's bowels. Steve sighed, shoved his fear aside, and walked down the remaining stairs to a narrow path between a few old bicycles, a lamp, an antique radio, a few dusty, stacked cases of empty bottles, and a collection of clowns wrapped in clear plastic bags. A sea of shadows, made darker with the pale glow of the weak bulb.

Chapter Ten

After hiking through canyons of junk, he found the door to the root cellar at the back of the basement. As he put his hand on the door, the weak bulb dangling at the top of the stairs sputtered.

Tink.

And went out.

"Ah geez. It figures," Steve muttered. His heart leapt a bit at the light bulb's poor timing. He began to edge his way back towards the stairs when he heard a loud crashing sound on the floor above him. Several pairs of heavy feet entered the kitchen.

"What's going on here?" Steve heard Uncle Edward's angry voice. Steve couldn't hear the muffled reply, but Uncle Edward responded to the voice with another loud protest. "I have no idea what happened to her!"

A second later he heard scuffling feet. "Ouch! That hurts!" Uncle Edward roared. It sounded like he was being roughed up. "I don't know where Steve is either," he yelled defiantly. "He went outside a few minutes ago. I don't know where he went. He doesn't know anything anyway." The discussion stopped for a moment, and then Uncle Edward let out howls of pain.

The feet sounded as if they were leaving the kitchen and moving through the house. Several heavy objects crashed to the floor. The feet moved again. The floor rattled as breakable things shattered and scattered over Steve's head. The people upstairs were wrecking the place. Amidst the sounds of devastation, he could hear Uncle Edward's voice, tinny and thin, echoing through the heating ducts.

"Wait, don't do that," Uncle Edward yelled. "Stop… please stop." He sounded as if he were sobbing.

Steve quickly realized, as he listened to the noises, that the intruders were likely looking for something in the house.

They'd better not find me.

"Where are the pictures from the file?" yelled a menacing voice.

"I don't know," Uncle Edward sniffed.

"We'll find them, if we have to tear your house down."

There were more smashing sounds and loud thumps as the intruders stormed through the house. Suddenly the loud noises stopped.

"We got the pictures," snarled the voice triumphantly. "Now where is the boy?"

Hide and seek.

Steve quietly opened the door to the root cellar. A

bright bulb clicked to life automatically, revealing an earthy room. He stepped inside and closed the door. The bulb extinguished again. The door controlled the light.

He heard the basement door open, then someone flicking the lightswitch up and down a few times. "I need a light here," a man hollered. After some commotion, a single pair of feet descended the basement stairs.

Steve froze.

Duck Boy. Duck Boy.

He carefully reached up to the root cellar ceiling and groped for the light bulb. As quietly as he could, he began to unscrew it from the light socket. The bulb complained with a squeak as he turned it in its socket. But the noise of the intruder stumbling around in the basement covered the squeak of the bulb. Under the root cellar door, a yolk of unsteady light leaked through.

Flashlight.

The intruder stopped abruptly, and the basement became instantly silent. For a brief second the bulb squeaked into the silence.

"If that's you, kid," shouted the intruder, "I'm going to get you. You'll wish you never met me."

The sound of his own heartbeat pounded like a drum in his ears. Steve left the bulb and backed into the cellar as far as he could go. He felt a big sack beside him and slunk behind it, crouching. He groped for the mouth of the sack; it brimmed with potatoes. He grabbed a potato in each hand as weapons in case he needed them.

Potato self-defense.

He heard piles topple and smash as the intruder scoured the basement, cursing as he went. The intruder reached the back wall and felt his way along the wall to the root cellar. Steve's heart stopped as he heard the intruder's heavy hand fumble over the outside of the door. Muttering quietly to himself, the intruder pulled the root cellar door open. The bulb jumped to life.

The bright light bonged like alarm bells in Steve's head. From his corner behind the potatoes, he glimpsed the face of the intruder. It was one of the men who had threatened Aunt Shannon.

The light surprised the intruder, and he stared at the bulb for a brief moment. Steve closed his eyes. The light bulb flickered and fell out of the socket, smashing on the root cellar floor. "Dude," the man yelled. "This basement is creepy."

Another set of heavy feet pounded part way down the basement stairs. "We gotta go," it said. "Move it."

"He ain't here," the seeker declared.

"We'll keep watching the place, in case he comes back."

He slammed the root cellar door, deafening Steve for a moment or two. The man bumbled and cursed through the piles of stuff in the basement to the steps. Steve stayed hunched behind the sack of potatoes. He heard some more yelling and the scuffling of feet. Something smashed. It sounded like a window. And then the house fell silent. He slowly released his grip on the potatoes he had in each hand, letting them fall to the cement floor.

Duck Boy. Duck Boy.

Steve didn't move for quite a while. He groped until he found the bag of carrots, picked one out and brushed off some dirt. He took up his position behind the potato sack and began to gnaw on the carrot.

"I am such a loser," he lectured himself. Any grown-up would have been scolding him now too, he was sure. "Aunt Shannon needed my help, and I froze. Uncle Edward needed my help, and I hid."

He sat in the back of the root cellar, cold and silent. Finally, after hearing nothing for several minutes, he groped his way through the tangle of strewn belongings across the basement to the bottom of the stairs.

He stopped to tune his ear to the silence, listening for the slightest pin-drop. Fairly certain that he was the only one in the house, he tiptoed up the basement steps to the kitchen. A frozen draft of air surged into the basement under the door. He pushed it open slowly and entered the dim light of the kitchen.

The house sat in frigid darkness except for a weak wedge of light coming from inside the refrigerator. The glow of winter wafted through the upstairs windows, the only light in the whole house. He resisted the temptation to turn on a light, thinking that the house might still be watched and the light would signal his presence.

As he glanced around, he realized they had gone. The back door of the house lay in a bed of splinters on the floor.

The cupboards and fridge door hung open, the contents of both hurled across the counters and floor—Country records, eggs, burst sacks of flour, sugar, dishes, cutlery. Elves, snowmen, Santas, skaters, and sleighs seasoned the destruction. The fridge hummed, sighed, and hummed again as it worked with the winter air to cool the house. Out of habit, Steve guided the fridge door closed.

"A flashlight." Steve stooped over one of the drawers on the floor and retrieved it. The evening light wasn't bright enough for a close inspection. He clicked it on, being careful to keep the beam away from the windows.

Two or three cupboard doors were pulled completely off their hinges. He stepped carefully around the objects on the floor and made his way around the house, looking for Uncle Edward. He stopped by his room.

His room was a wreck, too. The shelves of knick-knacks lay in a smashed sea on the floor. The bed listed on its side with fatal knife slashes exposing its stuffing; the bookcase lay face down. His suitcase knifed, things strewn around the room in clumps and heaps. Socks and gonch like confetti around the room.

He stepped through the wreckage of the upstairs rooms again. "Uncle Edward," Steve called quietly. "Uncle Edward?" No reply.

A new thrill of panic made him shiver.

I'm alone now.

An icy draft cut through the thin warmth remaining in the house. Back in his room, he pushed the bed from its side; it fell on its legs back down to the floor with a heavy thud. He sat down on the bed's edge to examine the carnage of his room.

"Aw, man!" Steve exclaimed after discovering the shards of his iPod.

The pictures that Aunt Shannon had removed from the police file were missing and so were all the alchemy books from Steve's bookcase and nightstand. By some miracle, both notebooks were buried under the carnage.

"My backpack's still OK," he noticed aloud, holding it up, inspecting it with the light from the flashlight. He returned the notebooks carefully to the inner pocket.

Maybe my underwear scared them away. The gonch who stole Christmas.

"Oh geez," Steve muttered, "Larry." He jogged to the living room to check the clock.

7:15 ish.

Christmas had been thoroughly smashed in the living room. Toilet-brush limbs strewn across the room, sprinkled generously with shoddy crafts. "Awwww," he groaned. In the middle of the shag carpet was Aunt Shannon's blown glass tree star. Smashed to smithereens. The meager Christmas he had hoped for bashed into oblivion.

He grabbed his coat, gloves, and hat, knowing that he couldn't stay in the house.

Back door.

He shambled back to the kitchen. In the weak winter light, he noticed something he'd missed earlier—a piece of paper. On the kitchen table sat a note made from letters cut out of a magazine.

Steve picked it up.

Don't be hero. Uncle dead if you try to save him or use police to help. Stay put. Will contact you

"Woah. Seriously."

The stove clock read 7:21.

Lindsay.

He dropped the ransom note on the counter, zipped his coat, donned his gloves and hat, swung his backpack onto his shoulder and sneaked out the back door.

To make sure he wasn't followed, he headed up the alleyway for two blocks before crossing the street and heading back down the opposite alleyway to Lindsay's back door.

Good thing Aunt Shannon showed me her house.

Lindsay's house was another below-average split-level in this average neighborhood. Steve knocked on the back door and waited. A daddish-looking adult answered the door—probably Lindsay's father.

"Hello, sir. My name is Steve. I'd like to speak with Lindsay, please."

The man smiled warmly. "Come on in," he said, scanning Steve from his face to his feet. "My name is Walter." He extended his hand and Steve shook it. He headed up a short set of stairs and spoke firmly into a hallway. "Lindsay, there's a Steve here to see you."

He could hear her protests to his arrival as he removed his hat and gloves, stuffing them into a coat pocket. With his hands he quickly smoothed out his hair.

"What's he doing here? I'm supposed to meet him at Shannon's," she complained, turning from the hall toward the front door.

"No. He's at the back door," Walter repeated.

She appeared shortly and took one long suspicious look at Steve. "What happened?" she exclaimed. "You look awful."

Steve hadn't noticed his appearance. He scanned himself quickly. "Oh jeez, sorry about that." He bent over to clean dust, flour and some crusted eggshell off one of his knees. "I guess I should do this outside," he apologized as he watched the eggshells flake from his pants to the floor.

"Don't bother trying to clean up," Lindsay suggested. "You're too far gone for that. Where's Shannon?"

Steve looked startled. "Um…I'm not sure. She's not back yet."

Lindsay's brow wrinkled into a questioning look. "Then why are you here?"

"Um, it's kind of a long story. I'd really like to talk to you about it."

"Sure. I'm supposed to see you at Shannon's around now, OK?"

"Um, no," Steve stated flatly. "I need your help. Now."

Lindsay's brow furrowed. "You look kind of freaked out."

Lindsay's reply was cut short as her father passed her with his coat on.

"Goodnight, dear," he said as he passed by. He pointed to Steve. "Ian, here, won't be staying for very long, will he?"

"No he won't, Dad. Goodnight," Lindsay replied with an emotionless voice.

Walter looked towards Steve. "Nice to meet you, Ian."

"Nice to meet you, too." Steve replied. Walter flashed a smile at him and stepped through the front door and whisked it closed behind him.

"Go ahead… speak," Lindsay commanded.

"Actually, is there some place we could talk privately?"

"It's private here."

"What if your mom overhears?"

"My mom doesn't live here."

"Oh. Um, do you have any brothers or sisters?"

"Nope."

"OK, then." Steve paused for a moment fumbling for a way to start the whole conversation. "It's kind of a long story," he repeated. "But I'm in trouble. And you said you knew how to make a Benu stone."

Lindsay's eyes narrowed, but she didn't answer.

"Have you made one?"

Lindsay still didn't answer.

"I need to make one soon," Steve insisted. "Aunt Shannon told me you know how to do the Great Work, you know, make the Benu stone and everything." Steve looked up at Lindsay.

"You're not making any sense," Lindsay stated in a very unimpressed tone.

"Can I come in and sit down? This really is a very long story."

Lindsay sighed. "All right." She motioned for him to come up the stairs. Steve dusted the debris and dust from his body, and followed her into the living room. She sat in a single chair, so he took the couch.

Forget the how-are-yous.

"Have you seen her change a clock into a lock and back into a clock again?"

Lindsay stayed quiet.

"I know it's a secret," Steve answered. He knew by the way that she didn't answer she had seen Aunt Shannon's demonstration. "I've seen it, too." Lindsay raised her eyebrows without saying anything. "If she let you see her experiment, then I know she trusts you. And if she trusts you, then I can trust you."

"You can trust me."

"Good," Steve replied. "I should apologize first. I lied to you on the phone this afternoon. Aunt Shannon is gone, like I said, but she's not coming back."

"What?" Lindsay shrieked. "What do you mean? Where did she go?"

Steve explained Aunt Shannon's disappearance and how it had happened. As he explained, he recalled that the police were going to call for a visit.

He interrupted his story to Lindsay to check the time:

7:35.

"Can we shut the light off in the living room? I want to see what's going on back at the house."

Lindsay gazed at him with another weird look.

"Please," Steve pleaded.

Lindsay got out of her chair and turned out the lights. The two of them headed to the main window and opened the curtain to gaze at Aunt Shannon's house. They waited a couple of minutes in silence. A police cruiser rolled up the street and stopped in front of the house. As the police car stopped, one of the policemen opened his door, turning on the interior light of the car. Steve recognized Larry right away. There was another police officer with him.

As they watched, Steve continued to explain the afternoon's events, culminating in the abduction of his Great Uncle Edward.

Larry banged on the front door of the house repeatedly, with no response from inside. Garner motioned towards the police cruiser for the other police officer to join him at the house. He left the front step to walk around the side of the house. It wouldn't take him long to discover the devastation.

A couple of minutes passed. Steve and Lindsay saw a light go on somewhere inside the house, probably the kitchen. Suddenly one of the policemen ran frantically around the corner of the house to the patrol car, yanked the car door open, and ripped the radio microphone from the dashboard. He spoke for a few minutes into the microphone and then threw it on the seat, slammed the car door, and ran back around the side of the house.

Steve slumped down onto a couch. "I'm in deep trouble now," he moaned.

Chapter Eleven

A faint sound of sirens seeded the air and began to grow. In a dramatic sweep, several police cars appeared in front of Steve's aunt and uncle's house, screeching to a halt. The frozen air crackled with the sound of radio messages bristling through bad speakers. As he and Lindsay surveyed the spread of the investigation, Steve began to tell the full story of the last couple of days.

"I'm really not a bad person. I screw up, but I'm not a bad person," Steve finished. The guilt he had carried since his mother disappeared hatched into a sense of criminality.

Lindsay's look softened. "I believe you," she said. Steve was silent. Police buzzed around the yard and through the house in a frenzy of investigation. "Aunt Shannon has been harassed and watched for months by some people who wanted the details of her latest experiments."

"You mentioned that," Steve interrupted impatiently. "And I met them today, too."

Lindsay ignored his tone and turned towards him.

"Didn't your mom disappear last year?"

"Yeah," he admitted quietly. "She disappeared the same way."

"Aunt Shannon told me that your mom was gone. For a while, your mom and Shannon were working together on a new kind of alchemy. When your mom vanished, somebody heard about it, and they assumed it was something to do with her experiments. They were right, of course. I read the newspaper clippings about her disappearance, but what really happened?"

After closing the curtains, Lindsay took a seat again. Steve found the darkness of the room somehow comforting, so he began to relate the story of his mother's disappearance.

Then he returned to the kidnapping of Uncle Edward. "I don't understand how the kidnappers knew so much. They weren't looking for Aunt Shannon, so they must have known she was gone. And they knew I was at home. They even knew about the pictures in the police file that Aunt Shannon took from the file. How did they know? I told these things to Uncle Edward, and that's all. Oh, and Larry knew, too." His forehead furrowed as he scrutinized the day's events in his mind. "I'm sure Uncle Edward never said anything. So either Detective Garner said something or someone overheard my conversations."

"Maybe someone heard your conversations," Lindsay suggested.

"How?"

She shrugged. "I dunno. Bugs, phones, or something."

Steve stopped to consider for a minute. "That's possible. Aunt Shannon noticed some guy working on the phone lines my first morning at her place." He slumped his head into his hands. "The worst part is this. Now I'm stuck—can't go back to that house, or my own house. I've got nowhere to go. And I have no money."

"You should stay downstairs tonight, Steve," Lindsay suggested.

"But what about your dad? He didn't want me to stay very long. He wouldn't let me stay."

"Nah. My dad wouldn't want you to stay, but where would you go if you leave here?"

Steve shrugged. "I dunno."

"My dad only pretends to care, anyway."

"What do you mean?" Steve quizzed.

"My dad doesn't really care," she repeated. "He only cares about himself, which means nothing else matters." She stopped for a moment. "My parents split a year ago. My dad left my mom to 'find himself,' whatever that means."

"I'm sorry to hear that," Steve interjected.

"Ah, it doesn't matter. He's never around. You saw him leave, and he probably won't be back until tomorrow morning. He doesn't really want me around, but the lawyers said he had to take me for the Christmas holidays. My mom wanted to go out and find herself this Christmas."

"That's a drag," Steve replied. "Christmas sure can suck."

"Yeah, it can. I'm sure glad I could hang out with Shannon. She's pretty wacky, but she sure is great. I don't have any friends here yet."

Lindsay began to pepper Steve with questions, probing each disappearance with careful scrutiny. She ended another long discussion by asking a big question. "What can we do?"

"I have no idea," Steve replied.

"So we need to figure this out."

"Right, exactly. Except I have no idea how to experiment, or how to find my Benu stone."

Lindsay gave him a warm smile. "You did come to the right person. I think we should make our Benu stones first. Have you done any experimenting before?"

"Nope."

"I'll get my notebook. Then we can start. When we experiment, we need to write down what we do and how we do it so we don't forget." She left the couch and jogged upstairs for a moment, returning with two notebooks. She handed him one with a chewed pen clipped to the cover.

"All right. Let's go," Steve exclaimed as he grabbed the book.

She flipped through her worn notebook looking for a specific page. "Here's how Shannon says to make a Benu stone." Lindsay looked up from the notebook pages at Steve. "Have you ever seen a picture of the Ouroboros?"

Steve flashed a smile. "Yeah. Isn't that the picture where the dragon is eating its own tail? I saw a picture of it in one of Aunt Shannon's books. But I don't understand it."

"It eats its own tail to satisfy its hunger. As it eats it grows, as it grows it eats. It never gets bigger, never smaller. Old alchemists believed that the Ouroboros was a picture of matter—of molecules and atoms. Aunt Shannon believes that the Ouroboros is a picture of language—words and letters. So as we experiment, we use words to transform things."

"The way the clock changes to a lock?" Steve asked, checking to make sure he understood. "She just says words as she touches her Benu stone."

"Right."

Lindsay looked down at her notebook again, squinting to read her own writing. "The Great Work… You know, making a Benu stone… isn't so much a matter of making the stone, it is a matter of finding that stone."

"Right," Steve agreed.

"And the stone is not a stone."

"Exactly. The stone that isn't a stone."

"It's called a Benu stone, but it might be a picture, a coin—something else. Or," Lindsay smiled, "a box of ashes from a cremation. Of course, it might be a stone, too. But we're probably looking for something other than a stone.

"And the thing you need to find is the thing that is your stumbling stone—your deepest fear—and the Pearl of Great Price—your greatest hope." Lindsay studied Steve.

"OK, I'm afraid of dying," Steve declared.

"Umm. Not sure about that one. I thought that would

be my biggest fear, too. But Aunt Shannon told me it probably isn't. So I don't think that's your greatest fear, but let's pretend it is. You look for something in your life that reminds you most of your own death. Then, you must look at your fear through that object and change your own self until it becomes your greatest source of joy—in other words, life."

"OK. If you say so." Steve knitted his eyebrows.

"I don't know if she showed you her wordless book. There are only colored pages. The book tells the same secret. You start with black—the blackest black there is. And you move through white, yellow, and finally to red. Fear is black; joy is red." Lindsay stopped and flipped ahead a couple of pages in her notebook, and then back one. "You know, Shannon never did tell me what the rest of the colors were all about. But they work in there somehow." Lindsay peered up from her notebook.

"So, what's your greatest fear?" Steve asked.

"I don't want to talk about it, actually."

"Fair enough," he agreed with a nod.

"So now, we should both spend some time thinking, trying to discover our greatest fear. Then we can begin to look for our Benu stones."

Steve sat back in his chair. Lindsay stood and approached the window, watching the crime scene through a small gap in the curtains. His mind rolled through everything he was afraid of. None of the fears he could imagine were great enough to stand out from any other fear.

As he thought, police processed the crime scene. When they finished, they bordered the property with yellow crime scene tape. A fresh patrol car parked across the street as the others left, one by one.

"A police car is watching Shannon's now," Lindsay observed. "It's going to be tricky if you have to get back into your aunt's house."

"It might be a problem getting back into my own house if I need to get anything done, too. I'll bet they're over there by now. What am I going to do?"

"I think I should set up your sleeping quarters downstairs in the furnace room. My dad never goes in there, and you'll be safe."

"Are you sure?"

Lindsay nodded seriously, still studying Shannon's house.

"OK. Actually, now that you mention it, I'm beat." Steve followed Lindsay downstairs.

She tossed him a sleeping bag and rolled a cot into a narrow little room beside the furnace and the hot water heater.

"'Night, Lindsay. Sorry for the trouble."

Lindsay smiled. "No problem. Stay in this room until I come and get you in the morning, all right?"

"Sure." Steve managed a smile. "And thanks."

Chapter Twelve

THE MORNING CAME QUICKLY somehow. Steve woke and opened his eyes as the furnace motor clunked to begin its work. For a moment he forgot where he was. The room was absolutely dark, except for a small glow from the furnace front as the gas flames ignited.

What time is it?

His empty stomach barked with hunger.

"Keep it down," he replied.

His heart warmed as he thought of Lindsay. He slipped out of the sleeping bag, sat up on the edge of the cot, and pulled a string attached to a dim bulb. He opened the door and peeked outside of his room. A dull morning light glowed through a small basement window. The day looked overcast, possibly stormy.

Steve heard a set of feet come down the stairs. He pulled himself back inside the furnace room and clicked off the light. The footsteps came closer.

Duck Boy. Duck Boy.

"Hello, Steve. Are you up yet?" It was Lindsay's voice, talking at a normal volume.

Steve opened the door to the furnace room and stepped into the family room. Lindsay smiled and passed him a bowl of cereal with milk already in it.

"Thanks," he said. He sat in a chair and scooped the cereal hungrily into his mouth.

"You're a criminal now," Lindsay said. She took a newspaper out from underneath her arm and unfolded it to reveal the headline: "Nephew Wanted for Questioning in Great Aunt and Uncle's Disappearance." Steve's vision blurred as he stared at the headline. He blinked hard to bring the letters back into focus.

"You're spilling your cereal," Lindsay said with a laugh. "You don't happen to have your aunt and uncle in the furnace room with you, do you?"

Steve couldn't reply.

"Woah. This is some deep doo-doo," he exclaimed. A smaller headline read "Son Played Role in Mother's Disappearance." Another small headline read "Boy Steals Evidence."

Steve set the bowl of cereal down and scanned the newspaper, devouring every word. After he'd finished reading about himself, he returned the newspaper to Lindsay and picked up the bowl of cereal, now mush, and began to eat. After a few mouthfuls, he stopped and considered Lindsay's smiling face. "I can't believe it. I'd have to be some kind of evil genius to pull off all that stuff."

"It makes sense that you're the prime suspect. But just looking at you now, how could anyone possibly think that you would be capable of doing something like this?"

"Thanks, I think," Steve said hoarsely. "It's funny, kinda. Except I'm in some serious trouble here." He thought of what his dad would say after returning from his trip. "I can't possibly imagine a worse Christmas."

He pulled the paper from Lindsay's hand and balanced it on a knee next to his cereal bowl. As he resumed eating, he scanned the stories again. "Oh no!" Steve dumped his spoon back in the cereal bowl. "That's the clincher. I was pretty stupid." He slapped his forehead with his free hand. "I touched the ransom note." He slumped back into his chair and covered his head with his hands.

Under the headline, Steve's picture displayed. His hair a tornado of confusion. Only one of his two eyes was looking at the camera. Head oddly angled to the left. Wearing pajamas? Yes. Pajamas. It was a photo taken of him when he and his dad had gone to report his mother missing.

"You what?"

"The kidnappers left a ransom note behind. I picked it up and read it and then left it behind. They found my fingerprints on it. It says so right here." Steve twisted his finger into part of the newspaper story.

"But they don't have your fingerprints on file, do they?" Lindsay asked.

"They sure do," Steve muttered. "They took my fingerprints when my mother disappeared, so when they dusted the inside of our house for fingerprints they could tell whose was whose."

Lindsay let out a low whistle. "Touching the ransom note wasn't a bright move."

Steve winced. "No, not smart at all."

"Are you going to straighten things out with the police?"

"I don't think I can. The ransom note said that if I talk to the police they'd kill Uncle Edward. Besides, Detective Garner will never believe anything I say now. He thinks I'm the one responsible for taking the pictures from the file, along with making people disappear and trashing houses. My picture makes me look like a baby killer. And they mention accomplices. Doesn't that make you a criminal, too?"

"You're right." Lindsay sighed. "You're the inside guy for the kidnappers. I'm an accessory to kidnapping because I'm letting you hide at my dad's house."

"Yeah. If you're right and they did tap the phones, the gang would have heard everything Aunt Shannon and I said on the phone for the last few days." He paused as his thoughts gathered into a new insight. "I just thought of something. If they were listening to the phone conversations, then these guys will know about you, too, because we talked on the phone earlier tonight. You can bet that they'll find out where you live and pay you a visit."

"Geez. I never thought about that." A look of surprise crossed her face. "You're right. And they'll know that I know how to make a Benu stone, too."

"So we're both in the same boat," Steve suggested glumly.

"We're in the same boat," Lindsay agreed. "We need to find our Benu stones today and start experimenting. Get your notebook and let's move."

"Is your dad upstairs?"

"Nah, he's not even home yet from last night."

"Wow, he likes to party."

"Yeah, he sure does," Lindsay scowled. "I think I know what my fear is," she added. "So we should begin to look for my stone first. We'll look for yours afterwards because we might have to go to your house and stuff."

Steve nodded. "So where do you want to begin?"

"I'm going to go collect a bunch of things and do the clock-lock test. Come on upstairs. We'll experiment in the living room."

"Can I get a bit more to eat?" Steve asked cautiously.

"Sure. The fridge is all yours."

Steve packed up his things, stuffing his coat, hat, and gloves into his backpack. Backpack in hand, he followed her up the stairs, to the main floor, toward the kitchen. Steve made a beeline for the refrigerator as Lindsay headed down the hall to her room.

Steve could hear Lindsay walking through the house dropping things into a cardboard box. As soon as he'd found some reasonably fresh ingredients and thrown together a ham sandwich, he made his way to the living room, munching. Lindsay arrived a few minutes later with a box loaded with items.

"I found a few things to experiment with. We can speed things up if you hand each of the things to me. I'll try them. If they don't work, I'll pass them back to you." She looked up from the box of objects and met Steve's eyes. "Keep track of which objects I've tested. I don't have the time to experiment any more than I need to. We don't have time to waste."

"Umphkay," Steve said, the sandwich in his mouth garbling his words. She took a seat in an armchair. In one hand she held a clock. Steve handed her a belt.

"Clock-clock-clock-clock-clock-clock-clock-lock-lock-lock-lock-lock-lock-lock," Lindsay spoke firmly to the belt. Nothing happened. She checked her grip and tried the words again:"Clock-clock-clock-clock-clock-clock-clock-lock-lock-lock-lock-lock-lock-lock."

Still nothing. She passed the belt back to Steve. He passed her a silver dollar. She spoke the words while touching the coin. Nothing. She gripped the coin in her fist and retried the experiment a second time.

"Why are you doing each experiment twice?" Steve asked.

"I want to be sure everything is just right," Lindsay replied. "I want to make sure my connections are good. We can't afford to make a slight mistake and accidentally miss finding it."

"Good point."

The two worked steadily for more than an hour. Steve

passed her every object she had in the box. She experimented with each thing and passed it back. Steve passed all kinds of objects to Lindsay—mugs, stuffed animals, Christmas decorations. Nothing worked.

"Let's take a break," Steve suggested after they'd finished the last object. "You've been working pretty hard."

Lindsay nodded tiredly. She seemed worn out by the experiments. They chatted a bit and then looked over at Aunt Shannon's house. A patrol car sat dutifully out front. Lindsay got up and walked through the house, replacing old objects to their proper locations, and finding new ones to test.

"If I had time to think more about this experiment, I'd have a better idea of what to look for. But since we're in a hurry, I have to count on luck a little more." She passed Steve the new box of things and they began their experimentation again. He picked a small doll out of the box and passed it to Lindsay. So it began.

An hour and a half later they were both exhausted and still hadn't found what they were looking for. "Did you miss anything?" Lindsay asked angrily.

The tone of Lindsay's words jolted Steve out of his tired daze. "I've been careful," he said quietly. "You experimented with everything in this box."

Lindsay's features relaxed quickly. "Sorry, Steve. I'm just frustrated." She took the last object—a plastic dollhouse—tossed it into the box, then slumped forward with her head in her hands, looking discouraged. "This isn't easy. I've tested everything I could think of. I can't think of another thing to try."

Steve's part in the experiments had given him a few clues as to things she might be looking for. "Why don't I look around for some stuff? I might see something you missed."

"All right," Lindsay agreed. Steve looked around the house and collected a few things that they hadn't tested. Steve brought them into the living room where Lindsay sat resting.

"Are you ready?"

"Yup, give me the first thing," Lindsay requested. She resumed her grip on the clock. Steve handed her an empty bottle. Lindsay snorted a laugh when she saw it. She tried it, but like the rest of the things they had tried, it didn't work. Steve went to take the bottle from her hand and replace it with something else. But Lindsay wouldn't let go of the bottle.

"You know," she said thoughtfully, "I was thinking that the object had to be a 'special' thing to me. But it might just be an ordinary thing, too. If a thing represents my greatest fear, I probably wouldn't like it, right? It could be just any old thing?"

"I suppose so," Steve shrugged.

"I'll be right back." She disappeared for a moment and returned with a key in her hand. She held it overhead triumphantly. She bounced into the armchair with a new energy. "I'm going to try this." She grabbed the clock and squeezed the key with her fingers.

"Clock-clock-clock-clock-clock-clock-clock-lock-lock-lock-lock-lock-lock-lock." Lindsay stared at the clock. The clock sat quietly for a moment and then began to shake in her hand. She opened her hand wide, like the clock had somehow shocked her. The clock dropped onto the floor. Lindsay and Steve heard a giant ripping sound. The room filled with a brilliant kaleidoscope of light. A tight vortex of wind swirled around the room. And then it all stopped. A pleasant earthy smell filled the room as Lindsay and Steve sat together silently, struck dumb by their success.

CHAPTER THIRTEEN

"IT WORKED," LINDSAY WHISPERED hoarsely.

"Unbelievable." Steve shook his head.

"One down, one to go," Lindsay sighed with a grin.

Steve returned the smile. "I'm still amazed that this actually works."

Lindsay gave him a puzzled look. "What do you mean? You just saw what happened, didn't you?"

"Yeah. I saw it. I don't mean to say that I don't believe in this kind of thing. It's just that I was brought up to believe that things like this weren't possible. That's what I learned in school. That's what my dad tells me at home. That's what Larry says. If you listen to those people long enough, this alchemy stuff is a big surprise."

Lindsay's puzzled look gave way to an understanding smile. "Shannon always said that we ought to be surprised that life rumbles along as normally as it does. She was always surprised that she wasn't surprised. She told me once that she was surprised at how many miracles it took to give someone a boring life."

"Yeah. That's true—I'm beginning to see her point. You get so used to those little miracles that you take them for granted."

"We really should leave and work on your stone."

"I think we need to go to my house."

"Great, then that's where we'll go."

"I'm a little nervous. The police will probably be watching my place. I don't know how we'll get in."

"That's a good point." Lindsay added, "You might be recognized on the street, too—your picture was in the paper."

"Right, I forgot about that. What should I do?"

"Just wear a hat to cover your hair and use one of my dad's coats instead of your regular one. That should fool the general population."

"What if there is a police car in front of my house?" Steve asked again.

"Let's worry about that when we get there. Do you have your house key?"

Steve patted his pocket. "Yup."

"Then let's get going. I'm going to write a note to my dad so he knows where I am—not that he'll care." She sighed.

The two of them cleaned up the objects Steve had selected for Lindsay's experiments and prepared to leave. Steve slid into a long wool overcoat belonging to Mr. Locket. It was far too big, but it did alter his look fairly well. He wore one of Mr. Locket's hats, too, pulled low over his brow to cover his hair and shade part of his face. His own gloves and hat he removed from his backpack and pushed into the coat pockets. Then Steve placed his notebook in his backpack, alongside Aunt Shannon's and his mother's, and slid the pack onto his shoulders. "This might not be so bad…" he started to say, but his words were cut short by a loud bang.

The front door to the house swung open and Walter Locket walked in.

"Hello Lindsay, I'm back. How's my little girl?"

The two teens froze in the living room. Lindsay grabbed Steve's sleeve and whispered harshly into his ear, "Hide quickly. My dad will get really mad if he knows you're here. He'll think… well… just hide, OK?"

Steve whipped his head around the room looking for possible places to hide. He selected some heavy drapery that shrouded the far corner of the picture window in the living room.

"Hello, Dad," Lindsay called in a honey-sweet voice as Steve headed for his hiding spot. "How was your night?"

Mr. Locket jogged up the stairs. "Why, you're in a pleasant mood today." He smiled vacantly towards her and headed into the kitchen to open the fridge. "I am absolutely starved." He poked through the contents of the fridge. "Did you eat all the ham, Lindsay?"

"Umm. Yeah. I guess so."

"You should know so. You ate almost all of it." He

looked up from behind the fridge door. "I thought you hated ham."

"Most of the time I do, but today I was in a weird mood," Lindsay said with a weak smile. Steve's heart pounded as he listened to the exchange.

"Hmm. Teenagers."

Mr. Locket pulled a few bits of food onto a plate and headed into the living room. He flopped onto the couch right beside the drapery where Steve was hiding. Still wearing Walter's coat and hat, Steve felt like a furnace. He carefully slid his hand up beside his body and removed the hat, quietly stuffing it into a pocket of the coat.

Lindsay stood nervously surveying the whole scene.

"Did you have something to say?" Mr. Locket inquired. "You have a weird look on your face."

"Umm, do I?" Lindsay returned hesitantly.

"Are you feeling all right?" Mr. Locket asked. "If you're feeling all right, I'd like you to go out for a while. I'm having a friend over. You look like you were going somewhere, anyway." Lindsay glanced down, noticing that she had her coat on, too.

"I'm meeting a friend at the BUS TERMINAL," Lindsay said, emphasizing the last two words. "I might be a bit late coming back from the BUS TERMINAL because I don't know when he—I mean she—is going to arrive."

"That's fine, dear. You go along and have a good time. Here's twenty bucks. You can leave now, and don't come back until, say, eight tonight, OK?"

Lindsay nodded.

"Thanks, my little Sweetums," he replied.

He thumbed through his wallet, chose a couple of bills, and extended them towards her. Lindsay crossed the room and pocketed the cash. "Here's an extra five for the girl I love," he added, poking out another bill. "I'm planning to have a few friends over for a party tonight, around ten of them. Just so you know. Please don't make a scene like you did the last time."

Lindsay felt the blood rush from her face. "Yeah, I promise." She shot an eye at the drapery.

"See you," her dad said, clearly hinting that he wanted her to leave. Lindsay gave no response, but hovered where she stood. Her father stood where he was and pointed to the door. "Get out," he said firmly. "Go."

She sighed, swallowed around what looked like a big lump in her throat, descended the stairs, and walked out the door.

Steve panicked silently as he heard the door shut behind Lindsay.

Duck Boy. Duck Boy.

He leaned over carefully and looked out the window. Lindsay was standing just below the window. When she saw him she waved frantically. She mouthed a couple of words at him. They looked like the words he had heard—"Bus Terminal." He nodded, trying not to disturb the curtains. She jumped in the air a few times and pointed to the street. A look of terror crossed her eyes, and she ran out of Steve's view—towards the bus stop, he supposed.

He turned back towards the living room and retreated from his view of the window. Walter was chatting on the phone.

"Hello, Alice. No, no, I'm fine. I just got home. Yes, I want to see you again, too. That's why I'm calling. My kid's away this afternoon, and she won't be coming back until tonight. Yes, exactly, why don't you come over? A few of the people you met yesterday will be over later tonight. Sure, I'll see you then. I love you, too."

Walter made several more phone calls to arrange for his evening get-together. He wasn't leaving the room any time soon. When he finally hung up, he stood silently for a moment, and Steve noticed a change in his friend's father's mood. Something had eclipsed Walter's sunny demeanor all of a sudden. The older man sighed heavily and again picked up the phone.

"Hello, honey, it's Walter. Listen. I wanted to know if you could do me a favor." He paused, listening to a tinny, hostile sounding jabber pouring from the phone's earpiece. "I don't really want to argue about that right now. Can we save that for another time? Could you help me out? I'm really busy here this Christmas with work and everything. Could you take Lindsay for the second week of Christmas break? No. I know we said I should have her for the entire holiday, but my work plans have changed. I'm absolutely stuck." He paused again as the tone on the other end seemed to go ballistic and shrill. "You won't, huh? Geez, I wish I knew what to do. No, I won't call again. Bye."

Steve peeked out from behind the heavy drapery through a sheer fabric curtain. He could see the dim outline of the room and Walter. Walter stretched out on the couch and closed his eyes. Steve scanned the room for exit locations. From where he was hiding, the closest exit was the front door. No chance of sneaking past. He stood there for what seemed like hours. Sweat drizzled down his forehead, stinging his eyes. His underarms—well, enough said.

After what seemed like hours, the doorbell rang.

Walter rolled off the couch and headed to the doorway. "Hi! Come on in." He led a woman into the living room by the hand. She shed her coat, dropping it on the floor. The two of them fell onto the couch in an embrace and began chatting.

"Could we have something to eat? I'm absolutely famished," said the woman.

"Let's check out the kitchen," Walter suggested.

He stood and pulled her off the couch towards the kitchen. Steve's heart pounded as the two of them left the room.

This might be my break.

He stepped from behind the curtain and moved behind the couch towards the inner wall.

"Did you see the paper?" the woman asked as she stepped back into the living room. Steve dropped flat on the floor between the couch and the wall. He felt his heart pound wildly in his throat as he lay face down on the carpet.

"The police are looking for a kid who hurt some old people across the street from here. It was in the paper. A couple of people disappeared, and they think he's involved."

"Really?" Walter responded from the kitchen.

She walked over to the living room window and pulled aside the sheer curtain. "I think that's it. That must be the place. It has all the police tape strung across the property."

Walter joined her at the window. "I didn't notice that when I came home."

"Did you know them?"

"Yeah. Sort of. A wacky old couple live there."

"Did you ever meet the nephew?"

"No," Walter replied, showing little interest in the story. "But did you find my cigarettes last night?"

"Yeah," she replied. "They were in my coat."

"Let's finish that sandwich then, shall we?"

"I am under your control," she quipped. They both returned to the kitchen to finish their meal. Steve let himself breathe again. He moved slowly to his knees and carefully peered over the couch. The living room was empty once again.

He inhaled deeply and stood, moving quickly to the edge of the kitchen entrance. He'd have to cross the entrance to get to the front door. He carefully scanned the edge of the kitchen to see which direction the two were facing. They were wrapped around each other in a deep embrace. He pulled the hat out of his pocket and pulled it over his head. Then he made a run for it. He passed the door to the kitchen quickly and headed down the short set of stairs to the front door.

"Is that you, Lindsay?" asked Walter. Steve froze on the steps. "I didn't hear you come in. Did you forget something?"

Steve forced his legs into motion again. He opened the back door, slammed it behind him and ran, crossing the lawn quickly to the alley.

He was five houses away before he turned around to see what had happened behind him. Thankfully, the house seemed uninterested in his exit. Steve slowed his pace and waited near the bus stop, fishing his bus pass out of his backpack.

As he waited, his hammering heart quieted enough that he detected the heavy silence that surrounded him. A lead-colored evening sky threatened to smother the earth. A few lonely snowflakes wafted to the ground. But the sky stewed and brewed, looking as though it might deliver a lot more than these few flakes.

No time to waste.

The bus squealed to a stop, the doors flopped open. A quick flash from his wallet to show his pass.

"Just a minute there son, can I see that pass again?" The bus driver asked firmly.

"Sure," Steve squeaked.

Duck Boy. Duck Boy.

His hand shook as he tugged the bus pass out of its wallet sleeve and handed it to the driver.

"Cold, are you?" the bus driver commented.

"Yeah," Steve replied. He glanced towards the closed bus doors.

Would they open if I hit them hard enough?

The driver looked over his glasses, holding Steve's pass close to his forehead and passed it back.

"I'm afraid I'm going to have to ask you to pay," the bus driver declared.

Steve blinked several times, surprised by the bus driver's request.

"Your pass is valid on school days only, not on weekends and holidays."

Steve nodded without speaking. He stirred his hand in his pocket, searching for change with his fingers. He didn't have enough, but he had a lot of small change. He dropped it into the fare box, and it jingled impressively.

"Thank you," the bus driver said.

"Transfer, please," Steve requested, just in case he needed another bus ride.

"Merry Christmas," the man said again, holding a transfer up for Steve.

"Yeah. Merry Christmas to you, too." Steve turned to face a thin crowd of passengers, none of whom showed any interest in him. Most heads were idly contemplating the advertisements lining the inside of the bus, or staring blankly out the window.

The bus jerked and rolled toward the terminal. In the middle of the journey, the winter sky tore open and began to hurl everything it held. Snow gathered quickly on the ground. Small drifts covered the street and sidewalk in a few short minutes.

This is going to be a wicked storm, Steve thought, eyeing the wall of falling snow.

He stepped out of the bus at the terminal and headed inside to meet Lindsay. He scanned the terminal's waiting area for any sign of her. Nothing. He strode towards the coffee shop, thinking she might have purchased something to help her pass the time. She wasn't there either. He took off his hat and gloves and shoved them into his pockets. As he crossed the main floor towards the army of waiting buses, he passed a rack of payphones. One of them began to ring. Steve ignored it as he scanned the buses through the glass doors. Someone beside him decided to answer the phone. Steve looked over towards the phones.

The man who answered the phone had a funny look on his face. He nodded and looked around the bank of phones towards various people who stood around the building. When the man saw Steve, he motioned him to come over to the phone.

"It sounds like the guy on the phone is describing you. Is your name Steve Best?" Steve nodded, confused. "I think the phone's for you," he said. He passed the phone to Steve and walked away. Steve held the phone up to his ear.

"Hello?"

"We have your girlfriend, too," said a hoarse voice. It sounded like Mr. Gold's voice. "She was going to meet you at the bus terminal, and we gave her a ride."

Steve felt his temper and terror rise. "What do you want?" he said angrily. "We haven't done anything."

"We want you," said the hoarse voice. "You know everything. You know how to make the stone; you know how to make things disappear."

"How would that help you?" Steve asked. "It hasn't helped anyone yet."

"That's our business, not yours."

Steve backed away from the phone and panned the terminal, looking for someone who stood out. He saw three men in sunglasses. Mr. Gold, talking on a cell phone, and two others. Mr. Gold stopped walking, and the two gray suits strolled casually towards him.

Duck Boy. Duck Boy.

Steve's eyes met the eyes of the man talking on the cell phone.

"Hello, Steve," said Mr. Gold's hoarse voice. "We don't want to hurt you."

Fight or flight? Flight.

Steve dropped the receiver and headed for the glass doors and into a sea of buses. The two men ambling towards him broke into a run. Steve crossed a bus's path as it shot out past the terminal's doors. It locked its brakes and slid over the snow, swerving to avoid him. The bus slid sideways and lurched to a stop as an angry middle-aged bus driver cursed at Steve, struggling to bring the bus to a controlled halt.

Snow licked Steve's face as he dodged between people and vehicles. Spirals of snow slicked the pavement with a coat of white. Steve rounded the front of a bus and headed towards its back end on the far side. The two men weren't far behind, except they were wearing shoes that didn't hold well in the world of ice and snow, so they skated over the snow-covered road toward Steve. Steve rounded the back end of the bus and turned around and grabbed the bus's bumper. By this time, the bus driver had opened her fresh-air window to shout expletives at the two bumbling henchmen and to sound her horn to make sure they understood how she felt.

The blowing snow gave Steve a small advantage. The two men had difficulty spotting which direction he had gone. They finally noticed his footprints and set off towards the end of the bus. The angry bus driver hammered the gas pedal and sent a cloud of black diesel exhaust and the roar of the engine into the storm.

Steve hung on to the bumper and skied behind the bus onto the street. Fortunately, the street was amply coated with snow. He slipped past his aggressors. The two men seemed bewildered. They inspected the bus as it passed them. They saw Steve hanging from the bus's bumper. He gave them a small wave.

"Hey!" one of them yelled. The other skated back toward the terminal.

Chapter Fourteen

Steve surfed the snow-slick streets for several blocks, breathing fresh diesel fumes as they belched from the exhaust.

Gold's on his way by now.

When the bus turned onto King Street, Steve released the bumper and jogged up the sidewalk. A narrow corridor between two old buildings offered discreet shelter, so he ducked into it.

There was just enough space for him to stand.

I need my Benu stone before I can help anyone do anything. If my stone is anywhere in this world, it'll be at home.

He hunkered between the two buildings in his oversized dad-style coat, enjoying the blowing snow and empty streets. The violence of the storm seemed somehow protective—almost inviting.

Only a few moments passed before the charcoal Lincoln Continental slithered by. He knew they would catch up to the bus he had hitched a ride from very soon. They'd backtrack quickly once they discovered he wasn't in tow. It was time to move.

Steve crossed the street and headed up a few short blocks to Queen Street. The wind stiffened and whipped the snow into white sheets. He turned up the collar of the coat to help repel the cold. He found his school, and went to stand by the bus stop. The school seemed like a shell—dark and hollow. Steve shivered when he saw it.

A few minutes later a bus slowly rolled up to the bus stop. Steve had already decided to take the bus so he could warm up on the way to his house. He climbed on the bus, showed the driver his transfer stub and took a seat near the back door. He was the only rider.

His eyes scanned the advertising as he waited for motion. The bus roared away from the stop and hummed along the route. Steve looked towards the front of the bus and met the bus driver's eyes in the rear-view mirror. The bus driver was staring at him carefully, but when their eyes met, turned away from the mirror immediately.

Uh, oh. Duck Boy.

He heard the driver mumble something into his radio. Instinctively, Steve stood and pulled the bell cord to let the driver know he wanted out at the next stop. He was less than halfway home but he didn't want to chance getting caught.

Steve stepped to the back doors of the bus and waited for them to open. He waited as the bus sat in the storm, but the doors wouldn't open.

"Open the doors, please," he asked the driver.

He looked up towards the front of the bus; the driver was again staring at him in the mirror and jabbering away quietly into the radio's handset.

"Can you open the doors, please?" Steve repeated. The bus driver shrank into his seat while looking over his shoulder.

Steve's mind scrambled for a few seconds. He slid into a seat next to a big window and lifted up on the handle at the bottom labeled "Emergency Release Lever." The window popped open and Steve jumped from the bus window into a white blur of snow.

Steve walked past the front of the bus. The driver fixed his eyes on Steve while he yammered into the radio microphone.

"I'd better head in a direction I don't plan to take," Steve said, thinking out loud.

He turned down a street close to where the bus had stopped and slowly rounded the corner, hoping that the bus driver had seen him move. He crossed the street and walked down the alleyway. At the end of the block, he crossed the street, checking for the bus.

If I can't see it, it can't see me.

The bus still sat at the stop: he could see the headlights flicker weakly in the snow. Beside the bus there was a police car with its blue and red lights flashing. Heading into the alley on the opposite side of the street, Steve ran towards home.

The storm will cover my tracks, too.

Through the snow,he ran. Through the angry columns of snow. He knew where to go, more from his memory of how streets connected than by sight: the storm only let him see a step in front of his path.

The rest of the world had taken refuge indoors. From time to time a warm yellow glow from a house teased him with the idea of home.

Did I leave the bus and police behind?

He wasn't sure.

After forty-five minutes of battling the storm, Steve finally entered the back alley that ran behind his house. He walked up to the back fence and peered through a missing fence board, to comb the yard for cops or robbers.

No one seemed to be around, though it was difficult to tell for certain because of the snowfall. The house seemed empty, haunted by nothing. Steve opened the back gate, pulling it open with all his strength. The falling snow had piled around the bottom of the gate making it difficult to open. Steve carefully shut the gate behind him, making sure it latched.

As he stepped closer to the house he noticed that the back door wasn't closed properly. When he reached the back door, he saw that the frame was splintered near the lock. Snow had drifted in the kitchen through the partially open door. Steve studied the snow around the door for any recent footprints—there were none except for his own. Obviously the break-in had taken place some time ago.

He stepped into the kitchen carefully and quietly. The house moaned as icy wind blew through the open door. The narrow snowdrift led the way into the kitchen, flattening into a light coat over most of the kitchen floor. Steve again noticed no footprints, so he figured no one had been in the house recently. He kicked some of the snowdrift out of the house and closed the back door. The wind blew it open again, so he closed it firmly and slid one of the chairs from the kitchen table against it to keep it closed.

The Bests' house had been thoroughly wrecked, too. The kitchen was destroyed and lay in pieces: food, dry goods, and fragmented dishes lay across the smooth linoleum. Steve tuned his ear to the house noises, straining to hear anything that sounded out of place. He felt the toothed edges of fear close in around him and squeeze.

Duck Boy. Duck Boy.

"Stay here," he ordered, speaking to himself. The urge to run, at that moment, was overwhelming—to run away from his house, his problems, his life. He forced himself to stand still in the kitchen.

Steve imagined the house bathed in a warm yellow light, and conjured his mother sitting in the living room in her chair. His dad, laughing along with the laugh track of some lame TV rerun. The warmth of memory helped to loosen his feet. Steve stepped through the kitchen towards the living room. He removed both of his gloves and jammed them in his pockets. Through the sheer curtains in the front window he could see the red glow of car taillights.

He watched for a while as the storm slowly revealed the shape of the vehicle: it was probably a police cruiser. Steve was certain that the officers wouldn't bother checking on the house unless they saw movement. It meant he had to work in the dark.

He edged his way down the hallway, stepping over bits of things plundered or pitched by the intruders. The fragments, as he stepped around them, chipped away at the control he held over his fear. He worked hard to remember a golden summer night with his mom and dad sitting on the porch swing, teasing each other over a glass of lemonade.

His room. Though his room was bathed in the late night darkness, he could tell from misplaced shadows on the wall that his own room was a disaster. There were several huge holes in the drywall where someone's foot or fist had gone through the wall looking for anything hidden there. It was going to be difficult, especially in the flat darkness of the house in this storm, to find anything to experiment with at all.

Instinctively, Steve went over to where his desk lay on the floor. Each drawer had been removed and turned upside down. The contents lay scattered all over the floor. Steve felt a lump build in the back of his throat. Hot tears of anger dribbled down his cheeks as he met the dark piles of mayhem. He knelt in the rubble and, on his hands and knees, began to crawl over and search the drawers' contents. The house was barely warmer than the outside. Steve could still see the ghost of his breath hovering in the dark air. He scrambled through the objects on the floor until he found his alarm clock. He gripped it firmly in his left hand as he searched for other objects with his right. He found a photo album, filled with family shots.

"Clock-clock-clock-clock-clock-clock-clock-lock-lock-lock-lock-lock-lock-lock," he whispered into the darkness. Nothing. He repeated the transforming words. Still nothing. He tossed the photo album to the far corner of his room, near his overturned bed and slashed mattress.

Steve's hand patted the floor sifting through debris looking for another object to test. He had a small idea of what he was looking for. He found a small die-cast car and experimented with it. Nothing. He crawled around on the floor experimenting with anything he could find for what felt like hours. Finally, he decided to take a break.

He stopped and walked into his dad's bedroom to check on the police car. It still sat there. He could barely see the car with the blowing snow, but the car's marker lights somehow burned holes through the storm.

After his short tour through the house, he returned to his room, dropped to his knees and began his search and experiment again. Item after item.

What else could it be?

He stood and wiped his sweaty forehead. The room was cold, but Steve's body burned with energy. He took off his hat, put the hat in the pocket. He glanced over to the far corner of his room. A mirrored plaque hung over his bed.

His mother had given it to him a few years ago. He crossed the room to read the familiar words: *Fear thou not, for I am with thee.*

He remembered the day she had given it to him. It had been hers when she was a little girl. That day when she had placed that plaque in his hands his mind had connected with all that his life had been and all that his life was going to be. For a short moment, when he held it that first time, he could see everything.

Steve knew in an instant what was his greatest fear. His mind buzzed with excitement as he removed the plaque from the wall and held it in his hand.

"Clock-clock-clock-clock-clock-clock-clock-lock-lock-lock-lock-lock-lock-lock." The little alarm clock shook in his hand. He felt his arms go numb and vibrate as if he were gripping a high-voltage wire. The energy throbbed from the hand holding the mirrored plaque to the hand holding the clock.

The power. There's so much power.

The clock flattened into what looked like a transparent piece of paper, a picture of a clock. Despite Steve's best efforts the clock dropped from his hand onto the floor. A giant ripping sound filled the room, followed by a brilliant kaleidoscope of light. A tight vortex of wind swirled around room. And then it all stopped. That familiar earthy smell filled the now-warm room as Steve stood staring at the dark floor. He bent into the darkness and groped the floor and found a metal lump. He lifted it into the storm's weak shimmer—it was a lock.

The light.

Steve rushed to his dad's room to check on the police car. The police lights now flashed. He couldn't make out whether the doors to the car were open or whether either police officer still sat in the car. But they'd seen the light thrown from the clock as it transformed, and they knew someone was in the house.

Steve ran for the back door. He needed to find some place where he had access to a dictionary. There weren't any left at his house—both had disappeared, one with his mom, the other with Aunt Shannon. He tore through the kitchen and tripped over a burst bag of flour, and the plaque dropped out of his hands and slid across the darkness and debris covering the floor. Steve scrambled up and chased it down. His hands fumbled through the wreckage on the floor.

He heard someone's fist pounding on the front door, which probably meant that someone was coming around the back to make sure he couldn't escape through the back door. His hands felt the smooth polish of the glass plaque. He scooped it up and headed back into the depths of the house.

The attic. I can get out from one of the attic windows.

He grabbed the spring-loaded ladder from underneath the attic entrance and pulled it down—it unfolded automatically. Up the ladder he moved, pushing the attic cover away from the opening. He crawled inside, pulled the ladder up into place behind him, and slid the cover back into place. The mirrored surface of the plaque shimmered faintly with the storm's pale glow.

I'd better put this in my bag if I'm making a run for it.

He placed it inside and tied the mouth of his backpack closed, then re-shouldered the pack.

Where do I go now?

One of the attic dormer windows—his escape. He inspected it, opened the latch. But he didn't want to be on the roof when the police constables were still in the front yard. They would catch him too easily. He had to make sure they were inside the house.

He waited noiselessly, listening for clues to where they were. He could hear nothing but the muffled howling of the winter wind. He returned to the window and cracked it open, and a knife of frigid air jabbed his hands. He heard a set of feet on the floor below him. He backed away from the window.

Suddenly he felt an arm in a heavy wool coat grab him around the neck, lifting him off the floor.

"You will want to come with us, if you want to see your uncle and your girlfriend alive again. Mr. Gold wants to see you," said a hoarse whisper. The arm was thick and steely—no chance of escape. It clamped down on his throat, making Steve gasp for breath. Down below, there were sounds of police officers scuffling through the house.

"Let me get my Benu stone," Steve rasped. "I will come with you after I get it."

The man loosened his grip on Steve's throat and that was all Steve needed. He slid under the man's arm and ran towards the window, slammed it open, and dove onto the snowy roof. He tobogganed over the snow-covered shingles and off the roof, tumbling on a snowdrift under the eaves on the front lawn.

He struggled to his feet in the deep snow. Then he ran for all he was worth. He heard some kind of commotion behind him, but he didn't bother to check it out. He just ran.

Up the street and down another alley. It took him a minute or two of careful looking to get his bearings again. The storm was burying all that was familiar, and it took a good hard look to find anything recognizable.

He ran for about two blocks. It was hard to say for sure because the blowing snow boxed him in on all sides like a prison cell. His fear of being captured kept him running into the snowy maze, with no way to know where he was going.

Steve ran for half an hour, ignoring his draining energy. He hadn't had anything to eat for hours. He slowed to a walk and began to trudge through the snow.

His thoughts labored as if they were stuck in a storm, too. The white pixels were merciless, shapes and faces appearing to him as he trudged. His mother's face appeared and winked and blew away. Aunt Shannon, looking around nervously, drifted before him. Then a worried, stressed man. Dad.

Snow blustered down the collar of his coat and stung him with sparks of cold pain. As he trudged, he lost his sense of direction entirely. He couldn't see a fence, a house, or a light. He tripped over a wire cable, strung around some kind of park or parking lot.

I've heard of people dying in storms like this.

Steve focused and cursed the wire as he stood, kicking it with snow-filled shoes. His feet were so numb with cold that he couldn't feel the pain from kicking the post. Sleep. Sleep was all he wanted. He stood and trudged on. His coat hung open and he staggered on through the storm, not knowing or caring where he was.

"How do I find another transformation?" His head felt light, like it was slowly turning. "Lob blob. Gag bag. Ring gring." he said to himself, his mind trying to pair words that might work the same way as lock and clock. "Snow knows?"

Steve watched his thoughts fly apart and lose their direction.

Very entertaining.

Steve almost laughed aloud.

Pieces don't make any sense.

It was about that time that he realized he was in trouble. In a lucid moment he realized his body was very cold and that he probably had hypothermia, or was close to it. He couldn't see any lights from any buildings or cars. There were no buildings or landmarks, just snow. Snow on the ground, snow in the air—snow everywhere. With his last remaining bits of consciousness, Steve did up his coat, pulled Walter's hat out of his pocket and put it on his head, and donned his gloves.

He wandered without sense for quite a while, until he almost hit the side of the some kind of building. He was no more than a few feet away from it before he could see it at all. As he moved closer to the building, he recognized it. The odd brickwork on the outside meant he had somehow found his school. He put a gloved hand on the wall and began to walk around the outside.

Not much time.

He found a window he could reach, and smashed it with a gloved hand. It shattered. He almost climbed through the window.

The shards.

Around the edges were sharp glass teeth. He pulled a few out, so he could enter the building without cutting himself and bleeding to death.

He lay on the floor, frozen and exhausted. The occasional gust of snow through the shattered window melted on his face.

Chapter Fifteen

He may have dozed. Or slept. He came to some time later, feeling a little more like himself. He rolled from his side and crawled further away from the window.

I need heat.

The radiator at the back of the room nearly scalded his fingers when he touched it. He lay on his side with his back against it. Another little nap. When he awoke again, he felt much better.

The brightness of his walk in the snow made the shadows of the schoolhouse extremely dark. It was quiet, too.

He could hear the wind moaning outside, begging him to step into the storm again. Sometimes snow whispered and rattled against the windows. He walked hesitantly up the hallway. His footsteps echoed up the corridor. All the classroom doors were closed.

He walked to Mr. Pollock's room and opened the door, stepped inside, and closed the door behind him. His stomach growled, echoing inside. He checked the clock above the chalkboard: 2:15 a.m.

Steve removed his backpack, pulled his notebook and plaque from inside. Stepping through the shadowed shapes of desks, he moved towards the classroom's windows to catch some of the storm's pale light on his notepad. He struggled to angle the pages in just the right way. The handwriting looked like chicken scratches, unreadable.

A fist of wind rattled the windows. The hiss of snow against the glass grew louder. The storm wanted in. But the school defied the winter storm.

Though the shadows wouldn't let him read, he wrote. He recorded, as best he could, the experiment he conducted that led him to discovering his Benu stone. He set his notebook with the others in his bag and swung it onto his shoulders. He held the plaque and moved towards the front of the classroom.

Steve stepped up to Mr. Pollock's desk. He swept his arm over the top of the desk to clear the desktop entirely, pushing the items on the desk onto the floor, including the picture of Mr. Pollock's wife. Steve grinned.

Sorry, Frown. Owed you.

He moved behind the desk and sat in Mr. Pollock's chair. He placed the plaque down on the center of the desk. The plaque's blue-mirrored face winked with the pale glow of the storm. His heart began to hammer in his chest as though it would break through.

Steve swiveled the chair around to face the bookcase.

Mr. Pollock kept a large dictionary in his shelves, and a pocket one.

"Pocket dictionary, please and thank you," he said to the shelves.

He selected the dictionary from the middle shelf and placed it carefully on the desk. He then swung his backpack to the desktop and slipped the large dictionary inside.

Might need backup.

Steve replayed the transformation he had caused earlier at his house, and remembered that he had a hard time holding the clock as he changed it into the lock. So, to be cautious, he removed his Benu stone from the center of the desk and placed it in his bag, too. Then, gingerly, the pocket dictionary, too.

This might be the last thing I ever see.

The blue of the storm bathed the room in shadow and a cold glow.

How depressing.

"Dad," he said to the silence, "I'm going to try to help us." Not that his dad would ever hear those words.

He looked around the classroom slowly, for perhaps the last time. He looped the strap of his backpack firmly around his left arm. After a deep breath, he plunged his hands into his backpack, grabbing the plaque and the dictionary at the same time.

A powerful numbing shot up both arms and into his body, causing him to yelp. He struggled with the numb feeling, fighting to keep a hold on his plaque and the dictionary. A blinding spiral of light exploded in the dark classroom. Steve could see everything with absolute clarity. The room seemed to flatten into a photograph. The photograph shrank and shrank until it was the size of a regular snapshot. The wind blew papers and dust around the classroom, but Steve only watched the wind—he couldn't hear or feel it. Finally, the picture of the classroom began to fall, like a photograph, landing on the ground where he was standing. When it hit the ground, it vanished.

CHAPTER SIXTEEN

STEVE STOOD IN ANOTHER place.

"It worked," he whispered, while exhaling. Then inhaled.

Breathing is good.

The sky radiated a subdued gray light, like an early morning sky an hour before the sun rises. Steve stood on some kind of surface; he was still holding his plaque and the dictionary inside of his backpack. He let go of both items, allowing them to fall to the bottom of the pack, and slipped it onto his back. His arms still felt odd, as if they had lost circulation. Darts of feeling shot up his arms as he regained control of his hands.

This place was neither warm nor cold. The sun was just coming up or going down, so it was neither light nor dark. It wasn't snowing. In fact, it hadn't snowed.

Is this another time zone?

Steve had left night behind at the school. He left winter as well, it seemed. He didn't feel as if he were outdoors anymore: this place was too warm. Though it didn't feel like indoors either: it wasn't quite warm enough. No sound—no birds, no traffic, no planes. No breeze, though the air carried an earthy, primal smell, like the smell of freshly turned soil in the spring.

He scanned the horizon, looking for a recognizable object that might clue him as to where he was, but he could see nothing familiar. No buildings. He couldn't even really see what he was standing on. He bent down to feel the surface. His fingers slid over a completely smooth surface—like linoleum or a marble floor, perfectly smooth and dark.

The weak lighting prevented Steve from putting a name to the color of the ground. Perhaps black. The land looked flat, as though it stretched on for miles, like some great plain.

This place feels empty.

He took a step, carefully, setting down a foot in front of him.

Maybe this is all mud, or water.

But it held. He took another step. And another. His feet clicked on the ground as on a hard floor. So he began to walk.

Am I the only human here?

He fought the urge to yell a "hello," to see if anyone would answer.

But that might bring on more trouble than I can handle.

Each step he took tick-tacked loudly in this place.

"Hello, Whole One," said a voice behind him.

Steve whirled around to find a sort of a mask, depicting a hollow human face, floating in front of him. He couldn't tell if it was male or female, old or young, beautiful or ugly.

Steve shivered at the sight of this hovering mask of a face. "Um… hello."

I'm dreaming. Maybe I did die.

"What is it you seek?"

"Where am I?"

"There are many names for this place. There are too many names for this place, I couldn't begin to tell you, nor could you begin to understand." The mask paused. "You are a Whole One," said the mask as if the words "whole one" somehow explained Steve's lack of ability to comprehend. Steve decided to change the subject.

"Who are you?" he asked.

"I am the face of this world. I am the only thing permitted to share recognizable wholeness to communicate with visitors to our world."

"Am I dead?" Steve asked, genuinely concerned.

"No, you are not, which is why I am here."

"What world is this?"

"I cannot say. It is a world of so much. I cannot begin to describe it. I suppose you could call it a world of pieces."

"The World of Pieces? What do you mean? Where is this?"

"It is here, Whole One," replied the mask.

This isn't planet Earth any more.

"When you say `whole one,' do you mean human?"

Steve asked.

"I mean whatever you are, if you are anything at all."

"I see. Do you have any other whole ones here?"

"Yes. I should think so. We have everything here."

"What do you mean you have everything? I haven't seen a single thing here."

"Oh, you haven't? Speak the name of something out loud," the mask commanded.

Steve glared at the mask and said, "Car."

With a whoosh a ghostly image of a car appeared in front of him. Steve could tell it was a car, but not what kind of car. It was just some vague kind of a car.

"Whole one," Steve said. A picture of Steve appeared. Steve stood staring at a ghostly image of himself.

"I'd like you to follow me," said the mask. "You look tired, so we would like to offer you some hospitality—perhaps a meal."

"I'm looking for my mother and my Great Aunt Shannon. I'm not sure I have time for hospitality."

"You must refresh yourself. You look tired and hungry," said the mask, sweetly.

Steve felt his tiredness hit him suddenly, like a tsunami. He wanted to sleep. The thought of a meal caused him to salivate.

"Why don't we make you a meal—a feast for a Whole One," the mask said. Steve nodded timidly to hide his enthusiasm. He balanced his thoughts between a meal and his quest to find Aunt Shannon and his mom. The meal felt morc important at this particular moment.

"Where is my mother?" Steve asked suddenly.

"What is a mother?" questioned the mask.

Steve struggled to frame the question so the mask might understand. "I guess you would say that a mother is a whole one who gives birth to other whole ones."

"Ah, we do have a mother here," said the mask. A ghostly image of a motherly figure appeared. It wasn't Steve's mom. It just somehow seemed like everyone's mom, and no one's mom.

"Is my mom here?" Steve asked emphatically.

"We have fingers and toes, lips, fingernails, tissue and lipstick. Your mother couldn't be here."

"But you said you have everything. You must have my mom here, too," Steve asserted. "She came here a couple of years ago. My great aunt is here, too."

The face seemed to grimace. "We have teeth, nostrils, earlobes, and ankles. Bits and bytes, baskets and gaskets, atoms and molecules—glorious, perfect pieces." As it spoke a lump seemed to rise out of the ground just ahead of them.

"What are you talking about?" Steve asked.

"I'm not talking about anything—we're just using words, stringing letters together—one letter, then another one, and then another one."

The mask turned towards an opening in what looked like an elaborate, lavish tent. Steve followed. Inside the opening was a palatial dining room with a very long wooden table. The table was covered with food. Steve walked over to the food and grabbed at a grape he saw before him. His hand reached the grape and closed around it. But his fingers passed right through it. His fingers were grasping at the air; the grapes wouldn't feed him—they were ghosts of real grapes.

"You cannot eat this food yet," said the mask. "We must perfect you first."

"It's not real food."

"It's not real food, because you aren't a part of this world yet. You are an imperfect collection of imprints—a Whole One. This world contains the seeds of what might be, pieces that can be put together, arranged in any way that might suit us. We have found our perfection, not by embracing generalizations, nor by finding universal truths, but by breaking things apart."

"Sorry. Don't follow," Steve snipped, testing to see how this entity handled his tone.

"Whole Ones, like you," continued the mask, "are the only things that struggle with what is right and wrong. You are the only things that suffer the pain of whole existence. Your smaller parts do not suffer as your whole self does. Your skin cannot feel disappointment. Your eyeball doesn't want a mother. Your foot doesn't ask why it exists." The mask paused. "You see, your molecules can't be right or wrong. They just are. And perfectly so."

"But you can't do anything if you're in pieces," Steve argued, his hunger flavoring his words.

"Your talent is perfect until you use it, as a glass of water is most perfect before it's sipped. Perfection exists only as we are about to use our pieces to do something. If we actually succeed, we lose the perfection in the trying."

The mask's smooth silver voice brought out Steve's tiredness. He stared impatiently at the food.

"You can be perfect if you come and live with us."

"What will happen to me if I live with you?"

"You will be perfect. Your mother's disappearance won't bother you anymore. You won't have to face the police if you stay here. You won't have to go to school any more."

Steve felt sleepy. "How do you know about my mother?"

"I know everything about you, Steve," the mask replied, tenderly. "I can see everything that you ought to be. And I can see what's left over. Do you want to eat? What you see before you is the perfect food. Look at it. Do you see anything wrong with it?" Steve moved closer and tried to grab some bread. His fingers cut through the loaf and came out the other side. Ghost bread. Ghost food. The whole spread shimmered just as ghostly illusion should. His stomach growled audibly.

It figures. I'm haunted by food.

Steve moved over to a couch sitting against the wall and tried to sit on it but fell right through it and onto the ground.

The ghosts of furniture and food.

"Perfection has no truck with the imperfect. It will not let you touch it until you are clean. It is everything that a couch ought to be. If you were as perfect as that couch, you could sit on it, and likewise you could eat the food set before you." Steve's mind felt as numb as it had when he'd been lost in the snowstorm. He nodded as the face continued its hypnotic conversation.

"You shall be perfect. You shall always be about to be, and no part of you shall be capable of failure. Only Whole Ones fail. You shall live with us in the World of Pieces."

"I see," Steve said with blank eyes and a monotone voice.

"Do you want to join us? Do you want to eat? Do you want to sleep?"

Steve smiled a deep, sleepy smile and nodded.

"You only need let us help you attain perfection and you shall have it all. What you know can be stored in perfection—zeros and ones—clean, brittle, and bright. What you are can break down into primary pieces and then secondary ones, and so on and so on, until you achieve perfection—no more pain, no fear, nothing." The mask smiled. "If you join us, you shall know everything in its perfection. And you won't need to go to school to learn it."

Steve looked up with glazed eyes. "I'm tired of fighting," he admitted. "I work so hard to keep everything together. My world is already shattered in pieces. I might as well look like what I am. I don't think I can make it." Steve's speech slurred as his mind and body grew heavy. He felt as though he could never get up off the floor, and he didn't care. "I have nothing to live for. My life is already gone to pieces." A new thought slowly curled into his thinking: "I know my mother's here. You said she isn't, but I know she is." He stared at the mask and waited until his eyes focused. "Can I live with my mother?"

"Yes," said the mask softly.

"Then, I will live here with my mom," Steve said carelessly. His head slumped down towards his chest. He fell asleep.

He woke up slightly as he felt himself being lifted from the floor. His body floated out of the room and out the door of the tent. A few yards in front of the tent curved the shore of some kind of big lake or ocean. The force carried him right to the edge of the ocean and stood him up on his feet.

He heard the mask's gentle voice say, "Raise your arms." Without doing anything himself, Steve's arms went up automatically. Skinny arms dangling in the huge sleeves of a coat that wasn't his.

"Now, we will perfect your little finger."

His sleepy eyes looked around. He watched his own hand. A force of some kind, not visible, pulled the pinky finger off his left hand. He didn't feel anything.

Chapter Seventeen

As the little finger on Steve's left hand separated from the rest of his body, it didn't hurt. In fact, it felt rather soothing. The finger floated in front of him and then it separated at the two finger joints into smaller pieces. The fingertip split into the fingernail and surrounding flesh. And so it went until the pieces of his finger became so small they were no more than a fog of bits hanging in the air.

Finger smoke.

Some sharp thought poked Steve's thinking and forced him awake.

"Wait. Stop!" Steve shouted as loudly as he could.

The mask suddenly reappeared with a blink in front of him. "We are helping you become perfect," it said in a soothing tone.

"I don't want or need that kind of perfection. Give me my finger back."

"I'm sorry, but it is already a part of our world. It can

never come back to you." Suddenly the force that was supporting Steve left him, and he collapsed on the ground.

"Where are my mom and great aunt?" he yelled as he picked himself up.

"They have become part of our world," answered the mask.

"Let them out!"

"I cannot, but you can go and live with them."

"I won't live with them. You have to let them go."

"You are merely a Whole One. Against our entire world, what can you do? You have no idea what to call us, or what we are. Yet we know you, and what you are. You are just a collection of parts, borrowed from what we are. We are perfect. You are not."

Steve didn't know how to respond. He stared at the mask. "I want my finger back. What did you do with it?"

"You gave us your finger," replied the mask. "You gave us your finger of your own free will. You told us that you wanted to `live here with your mom,' didn't you? You promised us the rest of you, too. You belong to us now."

Duck Boy. Duck Boy.

Steve backed away from the mask, frightened by its power and the realization that he had given his life away. "I want my finger back," he said in a squeaky voice.

"I cannot give it to you." The mask's smile didn't fade, but it suddenly looked vacant and empty. "It is now more perfect than you could ever be."

Duck Boy. Duck Boy.

Steve wanted to be strong. He wanted to demand that the mask give his finger back, but he couldn't.

"You must give us the rest of you, now," stated the mask. "Your life now belongs to our world."

"It does not. My life belongs to me," Steve said quietly.

"It belongs to us. You gave it to us," insisted the mask.

"I didn't give it to you," Steve protested, unable to meet the mask's vacant eyes. "You misunderstood what I said."

"A word spoken in our world is as good as the deed. You belong to us. Your life is ours. You must join the ocean of pieces you see before you."

"I won't give myself to you. You said words weren't really words —they're just shapes in a row," Steve said quietly, as firmly as he could. "So what I said couldn't mean anything anyway."

"You are whole, and you spoke whole words—you do not speak letters, as I do. It is not a matter of giving or keeping yourself. You already gave it to us, so your life is ours," declared the mask with an empty smile. "You belong to us now."

Steve panicked and swung his backpack from his shoulders onto his arm, grabbing his mother's plaque. He plunged his hand into the bag to grab the dictionary but accidentally touched his own notebook instead.

The mask didn't betray any emotion.

Steve felt the electrical numbness work up his arms and into his entire body. He fought the urge to release his notebook and his plaque. The landscape flattened into a picture and hc was surrounded by a whirlwind of light. The picture grew smaller and smaller until it was the size of a small snapshot. The whirlwind of light began to fade and the picture floated lightly to the ground, disappearing into nothing.

"He's in the bedroom," a voice yelled. A herd of heavy feet trampled up the hallway of his house to where Steve was standing, dazed and disoriented. It took Steve several seconds to figure out that he was in his own house. "Put your hands in the air where we can see 'em," bellowed a man's voice.

Steve pulled his hands out of his backpack and lifted them into the air. The bag slid up his arm to his shoulder as his arms raised. Two officers entered the room with their guns drawn, pointed at Steve. One of them slid her gun back into her holster and pulled out a set of handcuffs.

"Cuff him."

She wrenched Steve's hands from the air and pushed them behind his back, removing the backpack from his right hand and setting it on a table nearby. She pushed the sleeves of his heavy coat away from his hands to expose his wrists. Then she locked his hands together behind his back with a pair of handcuffs. "You have the right to remain silent. Anything you say can be held against you in a court of law..."

"Could you make sure my backpack goes with us, please," Steve asked as sweetly as he could, knowing that this kind of request could be refused. He tilted his head in the direction of the backpack.

The other constable flicked on the lights in Steve's bedroom and inspected Steve's bag. She opened the backpack and pulled out Steve's notebook with the two others, the mirror plaque, an alarm clock, and dictionary and rummaged through the remaining items, smiling as she pulled out a pair of underwear.

Oops. Duck Boy.

"They're clean," she laughed to the arresting officer.

"The underwear or the backpack?" asked the other officer.

"Both," she said. "We'll bring it for you. It is the Christmas season, after all. Though you are some kind of sicko."

They pulled Steve's hat and gloves from his coat pockets, after patting him down and removing everything they could find, and wrapped him up for the journey to the police station. Then all three headed into the winter white to the police car.

"Good thing we left the lights goin'," yelled the female officer into the wind. "We'd a never found the car without 'em."

She was right. The storm had swallowed the car entirely. The only thing that stood against the winter blast was the lights. They loaded Steve into the police cruiser. After a little trouble pulling out of the growing snowbank and onto the road, they headed back to the station as the winter storm buffeted the car.

"What time is it?" Steve asked. The woman officer glanced at her wristwatch.

"It's a little after three-thirty," she said.

After a slow and slippery ride, the car bumped over the curb and came to rest in a growing bank of snow outside the station. The two officers led Steve into the police building downtown; one of them carried his backpack for him. Inside, they removed his gloves and hat, the handcuffs.

"We don't need his fingerprints," the woman said. "We got 'em on file already, from when his mom left." She didn't bother to correct herself.

Steve glanced down at his hands, as he remembered.

No pinky.

He felt the space where his baby finger had been. His finger still felt like it was there, but it wasn't.

So it wasn't a dream.

"Do you want a lawyer present?" the policewoman asked, almost monotone. "Anything you say in the interrogation room can be used as evidence against you. A lawyer makes sure that you don't say anything that will get you in trouble," she explained.

"I don't need a lawyer," Steve returned quickly.

The policewoman shrugged. "I'll probably need someone to OK this, since you're a minor, but if that's your decision, we'll proceed."

"I'd like to proceed," Steve affirmed. The woman nodded and handed him some paperwork to sign. When she was done, she clacked the handcuffs back on his wrists—this time in front of his body—and led him, still wrapped in his coat, with his backpack, hat, gloves, to an interrogation room. She handed his bag to a man who was waiting outside the interrogation room and led Steve inside.

The interrogation room was more like a prison cell with a table and chairs. The room was scarred with abuse—holes in the wall, bruised and dented furniture, the chairs and table all bolted securely to the floor. Steve sat for a long time, waiting for someone to show up. His backpack was still outside. So he just sat awkwardly with his hands, handcuffed, in his lap.

An hour later Detective Larry walked into the room, his eyes dopey with sleep, his mouth set in an angry line. In his hand he carried Steve's backpack. He opened it and tossed it onto the table. Then he slammed the door; the sound echoed in Steve's ear. After he knocked on the backside of the door, Steve heard the scraping sound of some kind of lock fixing it in place.

"Hello, Steve," he snarled. "Thought you could outsmart us, huh?" He paused, assessing Steve's state and mood. "I'm going to ask you some questions, and you had better give me some answers. Do you want a lawyer present? Have you made your one call?"

"I don't want a lawyer."

"What you tell me can be held against you—you know that."

"Yes, I do."

"Where are your aunt and uncle?" Larry pursued.

"What have you done with them?"

"I don't know where they are," Steve protested. Larry's eyes narrowed into furious little slits at Steve's words. "Is this being recorded?" Steve asked.

"Yes. All interrogations are recorded."

"I'm going to explain some things to you, and I think you'll find them hard to believe."

"Try me."

"This situation is not what it appears to be."

"Oh, really?" Sarcasm seemed to wake Larry up.

"My mom and Aunt Shannon weren't kidnapped," Steve declared. "They were accidentally transported to another world." The attitude of the interview heated Steve up to fire-point inside his winter coat.

Larry laughed out loud. "Oh, that's rich. Pure gold. Magicians, right? Magic wands? Muggles. Don't tell me. Wait." He slapped his hand on his forehead. "Voldemort did it."

Larry stopped laughing suddenly and focused on Steve. "You don't have any idea how serious this situation is, do you? You are implicated in a very serious crime. You could spend a good number of years in a detention center. Or worse. I could get your case moved to an adult court." He paused and moved close to Steve. "Do not mess with me."

"I'm not lying to you," Steve said in a quiet, but frustrated tone. "You really don't understand what's going on here."

"You can't expect me to believe you, Steve," Larry roared. "You're just a two-bit punk. And you're upsetting me. I am finding myself getting very angry."

"It's the truth," Steve insisted clearly.

"You liar. What kind of yank do you think I am?" Larry growled, as he pounded his fist on the table in anger. "I've heard a lot of stories in my career, but this tops them all."

Steve felt his own anger rising. A fist of anger smashed through his icy fear, but he didn't speak.

"You're stupid. You're an absolute idiot. I can see why your mother left—she couldn't stand you."

Steve couldn't take any more. "Shut up!"

Larry looked up at Steve with a thin grin.

"Let me show you something that will make your day, Detective Garner."

Larry nodded, with a sardonic smile.

"Could you pass me my backpack?" Steve asked.

Larry pawed through the bag's contents, pulling out three notebooks, the dictionary, the sturdy alarm clock, and Steve's plaque, putting them on the table with a knot of socks and underwear. With a casual eye he inspected it until he was satisfied that there was no direct threat. Then he slid everything towards Steve.

"You're not listening to me, are you?" Steve asked, indignantly.

"What do you think I am—an idiot? Have you forgotten to take your medication? Or, maybe your teenage hormones have addled your brain," he snarled.

"Can you unlock my hands?" Steve asked angrily. "Let me show you what this stuff can do. The room's already locked, so I won't escapc."

"You're an idiot, kid," Larry retorted. Anger surged in Steve, and he fought to control it.

"Just let me try something, will you?"

"Actually, you'll have to do it with the handcuffs, because I'm not going to undo them. You'd better get used to the feeling of cuffs. I have a feeling you'll be wearing them often." He folded his arms and stood defiantly against the wall. "Impress me."

Steve raised his hands to hug the things on the table, and slid them close enough to where he was sitting that he could reach them more easily.

"What did you do to your hand?" Larry asked.

Steve had forgotten his injury, but he ignored Larry's question. He slid one hand through the strap of his backpack, placing the three notebooks, the tiny tough-looking alarm clock, and his Benu stone inside the bag's open mouth one at a time. And, finally, the underwear and socks.

"Where are you going?" Larry quipped with a laugh. "You look like you're packing things up and leaving."

"I am leaving," Steve said matter-of-factly.

"Whatever," Larry said in a bored tone.

Steve shook his head. He reached out and grabbed the plaque and the dictionary, one in each hand. The familiar warm, numbing electrical feeling rubberized each arm. The whirlwind of light started moving slowly around him.

Steve watched Larry's eyes grow large. The policeman

stood up where he sat, falling backward over the battered back of the chair. He crawled backward over the floor toward the far wall. Steve found himself smiling.

"Help!" Larry screamed.

A wind blew around the interrogation room, the file flew open and pages of the case circled madly around the room in a tornado-shaped funnel. Larry's face twisted with dread, as he thrashed against the wall, trying to dig his way out of the room, thrashing against it. Fear froze his features with a look Steve had never seen before—on anyone's face. Steve was enjoying the moment so much that he took a while to notice that the detective was fumbling for his gun. Larry eventually worked it out of his holster and fired wildly into the mayhem.

Steve ducked. The room grew flat, like a picture, and the picture shrunk to a small size. Steve checked himself for holes. The shots had apparently missed. The picture fell slowly to the ground and dissolved into nothing.

He was back in the World of Pieces. This time, however, the landscape wasn't flat. He found himself in a valley of huge mountains, all dark, like polished glass. The sky was still filled with that before-dawn kind of light. He looked around nervously, waiting for the mask to appear.

He let go of the dictionary but continued to grip his Benu stone. With his free hand he wiggled his hand until he held the handcuffs firmly.

"Lock-lock-lock-lock-lock-lock-lock-clock-clock-clock-clock-clock-clock-clock." The tornado of light surrounded him and in another moment, two tiny clocks tumbled to the ground, joined by a chain.

He dropped his plaque back into his backpack. The handcuffs—now two small, tough-looking clocks—glinted on the ground. He couldn't resist picking them up, tossing the clocks in his bag, too.

Now, where does a Duck Boy go in this world?

This time the mask didn't appear; instead it was the face of his Aunt Shannon. Her face came together with a giant whoosh, ahead of him, blocking his progress.

"So you returned," said the face with a snarl, and the voice was Aunt Shannon's, too, but the face said words he knew he'd never hear from his aunt. "You disobedient child. You will listen to me. You gave them your life, Steve. They own you now. Give yourself up."

Steve stepped towards the face of Aunt Shannon. "Do not go this way. You are standing on the rim of the Ocean of Pieces."

Steve weighed the words of this apparition carefully.

The mask wants me away from the ocean.

Duck Boy. Duck Boy.

Steve fought the urge to leave. To get out. He hated water at the best of times, but this wasn't even real water. It was worse.

But the mask. It was hiding something—something lurked behind it. Steve knew somehow that he had to face whatever was behind the mask. He bowed his head to summon strength.

Steve looked up and took a step towards the mask. Aunt Shannon's face growled and transformed into the face of a wolf and snapped at him.

Steve stepped back to avoid the snap but then pushed himself forward—toward the face. "You cannot hurt me," Steve shouted to the wolf image. "You're a ghost." He walked towards the wolf's snarl and passed right through the face. The wolf's face disintegrated and reformed in front of him. Steve realized that the mask was trying to defend something.

If I walk toward the mask, I'll find what it's trying to keep me away from.

His new plan offered him courage, and he picked up his step. The wolf mask morphed into a decomposing human skull. He walked through the skull. As he continued to walk, a host of ghostly images began moving towards him and over him. The faces of classmates, teachers like Mr. Pollock, his relatives, interspersed with body parts, horrible scenes, disgusting manifestations, furniture, and familiar things hurtled at him at incredible speeds. It became difficult to see as these ghostly images swept past him in a blizzard.

"It's just a blizzard," he told himself. Though he didn't want to, he kept his eyes open, making sure he faced the onslaught directly.

He walked slowly and occasionally stopped and closed his eyes to shut out the haunting torrent of images. When he regained his composure and his courage, he would open his eyes and continue on again.

Suddenly, the ghostly images disappeared. Steve found himself alone, standing a few feet away from place similar to the scene in his last visit—the Ocean of Pieces. It looked different this time. Waves broke out in no particular pattern, like something or someone was swimming in the middle of it. He walked over to the edge and knelt down, sweeping his hand through what looked like water. It wasn't water: it was nothing but a ghostly puddle.

This is the ocean, Steve thought. So what do I do now?

My Benu stone.

He pulled it out of his backpack and held it out towards the Ocean of Pieces. The plaque shimmered in his hand. Nothing happened. Steve waved it over the surface of the ocean, being careful not to drop it. Nothing.

Steve replaced his Benu stone in his bag and sat down cross-legged at the edge to think about what might work, and what this place offered him. He remembered how he had traveled here, and how the mask had shown him how to speak a word and the object would appear.

Words… it's words that make this world work, he thought. Maybe this is a place of words.

He clutched his Benu stone and spoke to the ocean: "Gold." He let go of his Benu stone, let it slide back into the depths of his backpack. What looked like mist rose from the ocean and traveled over to where he was standing, formed a cloud and dropped like a rock before him. He bent towards it and his hand passed through the chunk of gold—it was the spirit of gold.

He thought a bit. And as an experiment, he pulled out his Benu stone again, held it in one hand, and reached for the gold with the other. He bent forward and picked up the chunk of gold. This time it looked and felt real enough. He picked it up and threw it back into the ocean. The gold puffed as it hit the ocean's surface and burst into a small cloud of fragments disappearing beneath the surface. After a little more thought, he came up with his next experiment.

"Aunt Shannon," Steve yelled at the ocean. Aunt Shannon seemed like the best choice in the situation. He had no idea what he might expect. From nether regions of the ocean, mist came together and hundreds of women of all ages materialized over the water's surface and began to float toward the shore. They lined up along the shore in a perfect line.

Crap!

The people weren't alive. They were just hollow shells—houses without occupants. Benu stone in hand, he pushed the closest body back into the ocean, and when it hit the surface it vaporized. The dog poo woofed into a small cloud and dove back into the ocean..

"Be more specific?" Steve whispered to himself. "Shannon Riley Pankratz, born 1929 in London, England," he screamed into the boiling waters. The rest of the group of women evaporated into mist and retracted into the ocean. A single form assembled and congealed in front of him. It was his Great Aunt Shannon.

She had a vacant look on her face. Steve inspected her form for damage. Her body seemed perfectly fine. Like the others, she had no life in her, and as she stood there he wondered what he needed to do. He reached out to touch his great aunt, and his hand moved through her arm as if she were a cloud.

"Oh, yeah," Steve muttered to himself. He stuck his hand into his backpack and touched his stone. Reached out for Aunt Shannon again, and this time her arm became flesh. But, her skin was cold and clammy—lifeless.

"Aunt Shannon," Steve called, addressing the empty body of his great aunt. The ocean behind her rumbled, as if an earthquake had hit it. Her eyes looked empty. Aunt Shannon's body had returned, but her life hadn't.

"OK," Steve muttered to himself, "step one worked. What would step two be?"

Steve couldn't think of how to wake her up. His own Benu stone didn't seem to be working. Aunt Shannon's body stood motionless as Steve tried different combinations of things to try to wake her up, but nothing worked.

The ocean behind her began to rock frantically, boiling as if something were about to explode from within its surface. The ground beneath his feet began to shake as if something huge were about to rise out of the ocean. Steve panicked. He lost his focus and abandoned the experiment, wondering what might be happening next.

Duck Boy. Duck Boy.

Aunt Shannon stood motionless and lifeless on the

edge of the ocean as it raged behind her. Fear overcame Steve and he turned from the ocean and began to run.

Steve ran for cover, but there was nowhere to go. He looked back towards the ocean. Aunt Shannon's body stood at attention, alone.

He was thinking about returning to his great aunt's side when the ocean's surface broke open and several items spouted out from within the depths. In a pang of terror, he plunged his hands into his bag and grabbed his notebook and the plaque.

Aunt Shannon and the rest of that world flattened into a picture. She looked lonely as she stood there. The picture shrunk and floated to the floor. He was at his house again. He ran to a window and searched the front street.

The cops aren't here. I wonder if the guy is still in the attic.

As he looked out a window, he noticed that the snowstorm was beginning to subside. He replaced the plaque and his notebook in the backpack. The interior house glowed with a sick morning light, reflecting off the snow. But Steve didn't notice. Though his winter coat still hung over his shoulders, he felt a deep frost.

Duck Boy. Duck Boy.

He gasped for air to recapture the breath that fear had squeezed out of him. The image of Aunt Shannon's empty body, standing all alone. Another failure.

What a loser. I'm a total wimp.

Depressed, he went to his room quietly and lay down to think. On the verge of sleep, Steve decided that before he ended up in another difficult situation, he should record all of his previous experiments. So he sat down and scribbled them all out quickly, using the frail morning light for illumination.

Once he finished recording his experiments, a sick feeling knotted his gut. He had left his great aunt in danger and had run for safety. His anger simmered as he considered how he'd just acted.

I'm tired of being a loser.

His anger with himself pushed the feelings of fatigue and panic outside the perimeter.

I'm going back to rescue her.

He shoved his hands angrily into his backpack, grabbing the dictionary with one hand and his plaque with the other. The light enveloped him and whisked him back to the World of Pieces.

When Steve returned, the landscape was transforming and changing every few seconds. He watched rolling hills grow and cut into the air as they transformed into sharp peaks, and then retract to the earth and turn to plains.

"Aunt Shannon," Steve screamed into the ocean across the landscape. Nothing. "Shannon Riley Pankratz who was born January 19th, 1929, in London, England."

Nothing.

Maybe I have to speak into the ocean. How am I going to find my way back there?

"Mask!" Steve shouted hoping that the mask would reappear in front of him and lead him to the ocean. This time, nothing—no mask appeared. Steve hoped that the Ocean of Pieces couldn't be very far, so he struck in a direction that seemed right. Wherever he stepped, the shifting landscape became still, supporting his foot. But shifting shapes prevented him from gaining any sense of where he was. He walked a fair distance, but there seemed no end to the landscape; it went on forever. Nothing seemed to be the way it was when he found Aunt Shannon.

"How could I have been such a wimp?" Steve growled to himself. "I'll probably never find her again." He sat on the ground, drowning in self-pity.

The landscape had the feeling of a shopping mall without the stores. The waving horizon looked kind of funky. And as long as the mask stayed away, there weren't any annoying salespeople, either.

It just needs some Muzak, something to liven up the dead air in here.

Steve lay on the ground and set his head down on a soft part of the bag. As he shut his eyes, his mind moved from his surroundings back to his own troubles.

If I had to live here, it'd be OK. It isn't ugly, and it isn't pretty, kind of like most neighborhoods. I'd just have to get the ground to stay in one place.

"It'd be OK," he said aloud. "Not like I'd be missed much."

Duck Boy. Duck Boy.

As he heard those mocking words echo in his mind, Steve turned his thoughts in another direction.

I'm still probably the only one who can bring Aunt Shannon home.

He sat up abruptly.

"Why am I ready to fall asleep here again? When I fell asleep the last time, I lost my little finger."

Steve jumped up and snatched his backpack.

This is no time to sleep.

He ambled for several minutes through the shifting landscape when he heard grumbling and rumbling, like a giant case of indigestion. He listened carefully to determine where the noise was coming from and turned toward it, walking for what felt like a half hour without getting any closer. Suddenly the entire horizon burst into flame.

He jumped back a few feet from the closest flames.

Run, Duck Boy.

There was something not quite right about the fire. For one thing, there was no smoke and no smell.

Not this time.

Steve forced himself to step closer and closer to the flames. He reached towards the fire and swept his hand through the flame. There was no heat. He knelt down and felt the edge of the ground near the base of the flame. The land dropped away into the fire. "Thc Ocean of Pieces," Steve exclaimed.

Time to get to work.

"Shannon Riley Pankratz, born 1929 in London, England," he yelled into the fire.

The soldier-like body of Aunt Shannon materialized on

the shore of the fiery ocean in front of him.

"Aunt Shannon," Steve called. Her eyes refused to jump to life. Holding his Benu stone, he grabbed one of her hands as it hung limply at her side and shook it to wake her up. Nothing. She just stared vacantly. Though she still seemed like just a shell, she was otherwise unhurt. Steve paused for a moment to think.

"My Benu stone won't wake her up," he exclaimed. "But hers might." He thought for several moments, recalling as many specific details from Richard's life as he could. He remembered Richard's funeral, so many years ago.

Steve stepped towards the flames and yelled into the fire. "Richard Ezra Bacon, who was born August 19, 1963." A flame licked the edge of the ocean and deposited a little box, wrapped for Christmas. Steve picked up the box as he held his stone with his other hand.

Steve turned with Richard in his hand and touched Aunt Shannon's hand to the outside of the box. Her eyes fluttered as if she were about to faint. Then she looked around the landscape. When she saw the fire behind her she jumped back, knocking Steve to the ground. She whirled around with a wild look in her eyes.

"Oh my goodness!" she yelled, almost losing her balance. "What are you doing here, Steve?"

"I was looking for you," exclaimed Steve, overjoyed at their reunion. He jumped to his feet and gave her a huge hug.

The ocean behind her began to rock and rage as if

something were about to rise from within its surface. "We'd better move away from here," Aunt Shannon stated firmly. "It sounds like it's waking up."

She surveyed the landscape around them and her happiness flattened into a grim determination. She grabbed Steve's arm. "Now we're both trapped here," she sighed. "They'll take me apart again. It's only a matter of time."

"I can get out of here," Steve grinned. "My notebook takes me out."

Aunt Shannon processed Steve's words carefully. "The dictionary brings you to this world?"

"Right."

"And your notebook takes you out of this place?"

"Yes."

"I never thought of that. Of course!" Aunt Shannon eyes exploded with fire. The two of them heard a deep growl. The growl was so low that it shook the ground they were standing on.

"Steve, get out of here," Aunt Shannon ordered. "I'm stuck here, even though I have my Benu stone. I can't leave." She turned towards Steve. "Thank you for coming to visit me. I love you."

"You're going to get out of here," Steve exclaimed.

"I can only keep them away for so long, but they will take me to pieces again."

"But I have your notebook here, too," Steve said excitedly. He opened his backpack again and passed her notebook to her. A look of complete joy spread from one side of Aunt Shannon's face to the other. "This will take you to your house, Aunt Shannon," Steve explained. Aunt Shannon's look of joy transformed to a look of understanding. "You stay at your place, and I'll come over and meet you there in an hour or so," Steve suggested. He passed her notebook and let her get a good grasp of it.

As soon as she touched it she was enveloped in light, and she disappeared. Steve checked the ground to be sure she hadn't left anything behind. Then he reached into the bag with both hands and grabbed his plaque and the notebook.

Chapter Eighteen

The light whisked him back to his house again. The cool air of the house felt good on his skin. He bundled himself into his coat, reached into his pocket, fit his hat and gloves over his head and hands. The house still lay in ruins, and he hopscotched through the mess to the back door and out the back alley.

The storm was breaking up. The morning light spilled across the snow. Steve could make out enough of the surrounding landscape to travel safely.

The bus should be here any minute.

He headed to the main road, slogging though the deep, heaped snow. The road had been plowed in the night, but there was still a slick surface of snow on the road. He walked down the bus route in the rut of plowed snow in the middle of the road. Out of money, Steve walked past the bus stop and aimed instead for a curve in the road up ahead. He knew the bus would need to slow down at the curve. He took up a position in front of a parked car, ducking down behind the front end, and waited.

The cold didn't hold anything back as he waited. It found all the holes in his clothing and froze him to the core. Finally, an old bus shunted and slowed in front of Steve as it lurched around the corner. Steve slipped in behind the bus and grabbed the rear bumper.

Bumper surfing.

The smell of diesel was thick and filled his nose. But Steve didn't mind. It was a cold way to travel, but it was safer than riding on the inside of the bus. His heart burned bright, fired by his first success.

Steve slipped and skidded over the snowy roads, dragged by the bus. He transferred to the bumper of another bus in the downtown core and made it most of the way to Aunt Shannon's.

He sneaked down the alley behind Lindsay's house and entered the yard, peering over her fence towards Aunt Shannon's house. The house looked clear and quiet. The patrol car that had been watching the house was gone, the police tape blown down and woven into the banks of snow.

I won't have to sneak into the house.

Leaving Lindsay's yard, he crossed the street and stood on the snow-covered sidewalk in front of Aunt Shannon's, scanning the house for any kind of activity. Aunt Shannon's pale face appeared in the living room window. She waved him in.

Steve ran carefully under the police barrier and around the back of the house. The back door had been lifted from where it lay on the floor and propped into its frame. He slid the back door away from its resting place, slipped inside, and wedged it back into the opening as best he could. He turned toward the wreckage of the kitchen. Aunt Shannon stood at the far entrance to the kitchen, her eyes red with tears.

Aunt Shannon moved toward him. He ran towards her, avoiding the piles of debris, and they met and squeezed each other in a fierce hug.

"You're back!" Steve muttered. "You're back home!"

"I'm glad to see you, too. What happened to our house, Steve?" Aunt Shannon asked, then broke into a sob.

Tissue.

He scoured the kitchen wreckage until he located a box of tissues, and retrieved a couple.

Aunt Shannon surveyed the destruction of the living room, her ruined furniture, upset bookshelf, and smashed ornaments. "Tissue?" Steve offered. She nodded and took them from his hand.

The two of them walked into the living room. They set the couch back on its feet and placed the slashed cushions in their places.

"Have a seat, Aunt Shannon. This is a long story."

She took a cushion and Steve explained to her all that had happened since the day she disappeared. He described how Uncle Edward had been kidnapped and how the police thought it was he, Steve, who had done the kidnapping.

At several points in Steve's story, Aunt Shannon's eyes

filled with tears. Her eyes sparked with life when he talked about how he accidentally discovered a way to get to the other world and then back again.

“Why did you rescue me first, Steve?” Aunt Shannon asked.

Steve sat back for a moment. He hadn’t really thought about what he’d done. “You’re still upset with your mom, aren’t you?”

“I don’t know. I never even thought of trying her first. Besides, I don’t know what her Benu stone is.”

“I think we can get her back, Steve,” Aunt Shannon declared. “But what are we going to do about Lindsay and Uncle Edward?”

“I have a few ideas,” Steve stated. “You guessed right, from the very beginning.” He paused for a moment. “Remember when you told me that it was words, that words were the key to alchemy. That completely explains the dictionary.”

Aunt Shannon nodded. “The notebook, too,” she added.

“Yeah, right. It’s all words, isn’t it? They’re somehow connected to us,” Steve said thoughtfully.

“In one form or another,” Aunt Shannon added.

“I told you about the day the kidnappers came, right?”

“Yes, you did.”

“Did I mention the ransom note?”

“Right!” exclaimed Aunt Shannon. “Of course. That’s an excellent idea. It just might work.”

“The only question is how we will get hold of it,” Steve

sighed. "That won't be easy. Detective Garner is probably still looking for me as we speak. He tried to shoot me," he remembered suddenly, his voice rising.

"What?" Aunt Shannon demanded, eyes wide.

"Long story," Steve answered, waving his hand. "He's got the ransom note and he's not likely to let us see it, considering what happened to the pictures we took from his file. We'll never be able to get those back. The kidnappers stole the pictures, so I haven't been able to give them back to him."

"Why did the kidnappers want the pictures?" Aunt Shannon asked with a puzzled look.

"Lindsay thinks they overhead us discussing them on the phone, and they probably believed they held some secrets. They were looking for clues about how your discoveries would work. I mean this discovery is worth a lot of money to someone, wouldn't you think?"

"You're right, of course," Aunt Shannon said sheepishly. "I get so carried away with the discovery itself that I forget what it might mean to the wrong people."

"It kind of surprised me, too. It's really thrown a wrench into the whole holiday."

"My goodness," Aunt Shannon exclaimed. "I almost forgot, we only have a half a week until Christmas. My decorations have been destroyed."

"Your Halloween decorations are still on the front door," Steve reminded her, smiling.

"This feels more like Halloween than Christmas, doesn't

it?"

"It's a nightmare," Steve agreed.

"I guess we need to turn Halloween into Christmas before we bother decorating for it again."

Steve smiled at Aunt Shannon's suggestion. "Turn Halloween into Christmas." Steve repeated. "What should we do first?"

"Why don't we get Uncle Edward and Lindsay back where they belong before Christmas. You're probably a suspect in Lindsay's disappearance, too."

"We need to get a dictionary for you, Aunt Shannon. Unless you want this huge spare one I have." He pulled the hefty tome from his backpack. "That way you'll be able to get in and out of the other world if you need to. Actually, I'll take this one, you take this one." He placed the huge one back in his backpack and passed her the pocket dictionary.

"Right." Aunt Shannon pointed to his backpack. "I think I'll get a big purse out of my closet to hold it all. It works well, does it?"

"Yeah."

"I'm going to call the police station and see if I can talk Larry into letting us see the ransom note."

"I'll get your purse while you call Mr. Garner. Just don't disappear on me again," Steve quipped.

Aunt Shannon rolled her eyes. "I'll be here when you get back—I promise," she said with a grin.

Steve nodded and scooted down the hallway, sliding some of the big piles of debris out of the way to make a path. Aunt Shannon stood and wove her way to the phone. She thumbed through the phone book looking for the number and then dialed.

"Hello, may I speak with Detective Garner, please?" Aunt Shannon asked pleasantly. A voice on the other end chirped a reply. "Oh, I'm sorry to hear that. Oh, that's terrible. Is he at home right now? I'll try him there, thanks. Goodbye."

Steve returned with a cavernous neon-colored purse. He put Richard, her notebook, and the dictionary in Aunt Shannon's purse and set it beside her near the phone.

"Steve, we have a small problem. Larry isn't working on the police force at the moment. He's been suspended."

"What for?"

"I'm not sure. We need to talk to him, though." She pulled a phone book out of a kitchen drawer and returned to the phone. "Let me find his home phone number." Her fingers scrambled through the pages. Aunt Shannon dialed the number and waited for a response.

"Hello, is this Detective Garner?...This is Shannon Pankratz-Bacon calling...No, no, I'm fine. No, Steve had nothing to do with me disappearing. Wherever did you get such a story?...I don't have the time to discuss that right now. I'm calling because I need your help. Can I drop by and talk with you? What's your address? All right, I'll see you in a half hour or so." She hung up the phone. "Let's get moving."

The two of them bundled up, double-checked the

contents of the backpack and purse, and hopped into the car. As she started it, she looked quickly at Steve with a furrowed brow.

"How did my car end up here?" Aunt Shannon asked. "Uncle Edward wouldn't have driven it, and you're too young to drive."

Steve smiled. "Are you sure you want to know?"

"Try me," she replied.

"Uncle Edward told me to drive it back to your house," Steve reported. "He insisted."

"Really?" Aunt Shannon sounded amazed. "What a wonderful surprise—absolutely wonderful. That's so unlike him. My disappearance must have really rattled him. And my lovely car." She patted the dashboard tenderly. "You didn't dent her either."

Larry's house was a half hour away from Aunt Shannon's place. She drove carefully over the snowy pavement and parked in front of the detective's house. She and Steve walked up to the front door and rang the bell. A tired, haggard-looking man opened the door wrapped in a wrinkled housecoat. When he saw Steve, his eyes opened wide with surprise—then narrowed in anger.

"You...You... You're the whole reason I'm here right now. I'm going to call the station and turn you in." He wheeled from the door to find the phone.

"Wait!" Aunt Shannon ordered. Larry froze at the strength of her voice, and turned around. "You're the reason you are in this situation," Aunt Shannon reasoned.

"Steve and I tried to explain to you what was happening, and you ignored us."

Larry turned and reached towards the telephone sitting on a table in the hallway.

"If you turn us in," Aunt Shannon persisted, "you'll wreck any chance you have of solving this case properly."

Larry's hand trembled, hovering over the cradled telephone.

"We came here because we need you."

His hand grasped the phone and pulled it off its cradle towards him. A faint dial tone underlined Aunt Shannon's words.

"We can help you solve this case. You can bring it to a close, arrest the right people."

Larry turned towards Aunt Shannon, meeting her eyes. Then he slowly set the phone back in its cradle. "Can you really help me solve this case?"

"I think we can," Aunt Shannon returned. "But you need us and we need you."

Larry sighed in defeat. "OK… come in," he conceded.

The three of them took seats in the living room. Larry began, his eyes on the floor. "I don't know what happened that day when we were in the interrogation room, Steve. And I'm not sure I want to know. But whatever happened there, I ended up here, on the brink of losing my job—suspended without pay." His voice choked through the words. "You disappeared and I took a couple of shots at you. The guards opened the door and found me lying on the floor with a few bullets in the wall and the case file scattered around the room. They thought I'd gone nuts. They accused me of letting you go, aiding and abetting a criminal, unlawful discharging of a firearm, and a few other things." He paused and looked away from them towards the floor. "They don't believe the story I told them. They don't know what to do with me—let a psychiatrist examine me or prosecute me as a criminal."

"Would they think differently of you if you solved part of the case?" Aunt Shannon asked.

"I think there is no question about it. If I could come up with something, they'd at least have to admit that I'm half sane."

"Plus you might live down that awful nickname. What do they call you—'Clueless'?"

Larry winced and crossed his arms.

Aunt Shannon continued. "Uncle Edward and Lindsay were kidnapped by a group of alchemists who want to exploit our discoveries and make lots of money," Aunt Shannon stated.

"Lindsay? Who's Lindsay?" Larry asked as he tightened his housecoat belt.

Steve took a few minutes to clue Larry in on the relevant parts of what happened to Lindsay, and the attempts made to capture him at the bus terminal. "We don't know who they are, but we think we can find them, and we need your help," Steve said.

"What can I do?"

"We need the ransom note," Steve declared.

"I can't do that," Larry said flatly.

"We have a way of locating them once we have the ransom note," Steve insisted. "We thought we could find the place where they're being held, and then phone you so you can make the arrest or call in the information."

"You wouldn't be able to arrest them for stealing alchemical secrets, which is what they're really after, but you could arrest them for kidnapping." Aunt Shannon's voice rose and settled firmly on her last word.

"I see what you're getting at, Mrs. Pankratz-Bacon," Larry said and he drifted into thought. "You didn't bring the pictures from the case file, by any chance, did you?"

"Ah, no. No, we didn't," Steve said sheepishly. "They were stolen when Uncle Edward was kidnapped. That's why the house is a mess. I think they tapped our phone line, and I happened to mention the pictures to Lindsay in a phone call."

"She's a neighbor who is an alchemist, like we are," Aunt Shannon answered.

"And she's been kidnapped, too."

"She has?" One of Larry's eyebrows raised as he asked the question. "I don't think anyone reported her missing."

"Call her father. He'll tell you that she wasn't at home last night. If he even noticed," Steve added to himself.

"What's her last name?" Larry asked.

"Locket."

Larry fingered through the phone book until he found

the right name and address and then dialed a number.

"Hello, Mr. Locket? This is the Police Department calling." Larry stared at the floor as he concentrated. "Was your daughter at home last night?" He paused. "No, eh? I didn't think so… I think you should file a report with our department today. No, you should fill out a report right away." He paused to listen to the voice on the other end. "I'm sorry, but I don't have the time to explain the details. Your daughter is involved in an investigation, and the fact that she's missing is important and needs to be reported." He listened again. "Yes, the main office, right on King Street. Thank you. Bye."

Larry looked up at Steve as he replaced the phone in its cradle. "Hmm. Your story makes some sense. I'm almost inclined to believe you. Why steal the pictures?"

"We thought the pictures would help us figure out how my mother disappeared. They tore Aunt Shannon's house apart hoping to catch Uncle Edward and me at home. I hid, and so they left with the pictures and Uncle Edward. I found the ransom note and read it. That's why my fingerprints were on it."

"I'm not sure…" Larry said, shaking his head.

"I'm the one who took the pictures from that file," Aunt Shannon announced. "It was my doing entirely." She took a breath and tried again. "I don't think you'd be any worse off if you trusted us. The most we could do is steal the ransom note. You're already in so much trouble that even if we did that, I don't think it could get much worse."

"You have a point," Larry sighed.

"One of us can stay with you, too," Steve suggested. "That way, if something doesn't work out, you can at least turn one of us in."

Larry almost managed a grin. "Now you're talking my language," Larry said. "I can check out parts of your story, too. If the phone was tapped, I'll be able to tell."

"And if you help this case come to a close, you might just look good to your superiors again," Aunt Shannon added.

"Right. Wait right here and I'll get dressed."

Larry emerged from a back room dressed for business. He still looked as if he'd showered with his clothes on and put himself in the dryer for forty minutes—he hadn't shaved or combed his hair—but he had clothes on at least.

He dialed the station. "Hello, Jeff, Larry here. Listen, I have some evidence that should go in the Best file. I'm going to drop by and add it to the file. Is that all right? Good. I'll see you in a few minutes." He hung up the phone.

"You two might want to wait here. I'll go and get the stuff and come right back." Aunt Shannon nodded and continued sitting in the chair. Steve continued sitting as well. Larry strode from the room and out the front door.

As soon as Larry left, Steve turned to Aunt Shannon. "What are we going to do about Mom?"

Aunt Shannon smiled weakly, trying to hide her discouragement. "I'm not sure, Steve. Your mom, well, um, she's going to be difficult."

"That's true," Steve admitted. "Do you think I should try the same thing to get her back, or do you think there is another way?"

She shook her head. "I don't think there is another way. If there is, I have no clue what it would be."

"I don't know what her Benu stone is either," Steve added. "I knew yours, so I was able to bring you back."

"Hmm."

Steve's thoughtful sigh led them both into a contemplative silence. The quiet quickly numbed his body. In a minute he had nodded to sleep, sitting upright.

Aunt Shannon let him sleep for three-quarters of an hour, until Larry returned. The detective jogged into the house and quickly closed the door. Steve's eyes blinked open just long enough to notice Larry's broad smile.

Aunt Shannon shook Steve's shoulder to return him completely from his slumber. Larry began to arrange equipment on the coffee table in front of the couch where he sat.

"Before we get going here," Larry began. "How does this traveling thing work?"

"It's a little strange, but this is how it goes, as far as I know," Steve replied groggily. For the next few minutes he recounted what he knew of how traveling with a Benu stone worked. Aunt Shannon added detail as Steve talked. Gradually, a troubled look of insight filled Larry's face.

"I think I understand what you're saying. I just have

trouble believing it. I did get the note," he continued. "I also got a little bit of detecting equipment." He held up a small black button, about the size of a quarter, and a small device with a TV screen on it.

"Who's going to travel to the kidnapper's base?" Larry asked.

Steve and Aunt Shannon looked at each other.

There is no other choice, Steve thought. And, his mind plunged into pools of panic as he contemplated the idea.

Duck Boy. Duck Boy.

But his mouth spoke before his mind objected. And he surprised himself with his own words. "I'll go."

"All right, Steve," Larry said appreciatively. "Though I'm not sure there's much choice."

"What are you talking about, young man?" barked Aunt Shannon, rebuking him. "I can go, and I am perfectly able to manage myself." Larry suddenly looked sheepish. She turned to Steve. "Are you sure you want to go?" Aunt Shannon asked, probing Steve's resolve.

"I have to, and I want to," Steve declared as forcefully as he could.

"All right, Steve," Aunt Shannon answered.

Larry held the small black button towards Steve. "This will find you wherever you go. You can take this with you, right? You can disappear with things in your bag." Steve nodded. "So, this tracking device will sit in your backpack."

"What's the range on it?" Aunt Shannon asked.

"I think it's about 25 miles."

"I hope that's enough," she stated. "Steve could end up anywhere in the world."

"Really?" Larry asked in disbelief. "That's some form of transportation. But he could end up within the 25-mile range, too, couldn't he?"

"Yes, he could," Aunt Shannon agreed.

Maybe we'll have some luck," Larry said hopefully. "I think things are looking up right now."

"Where is this ransom note going to take you Steve?"

"It'll transport me to the kidnappers' world—wherever that is, I think," Steve replied. "Remember, we're still experimenting. It's just a good guess."

"Try not to wrinkle it or damage it in any way." He held up a plastic evidence bag. Inside was the note.

"I'm afraid I'll have to touch the note directly," Steve said.

Larry sighed. "I'll accept that risk. Your fingerprints are on this anyhow." A tormented smile wavered on his lips. Larry turned to some other things he'd brought with him. "I have a few other tools I'd like you to take with you. Here's a cell phone." He passed the phone to Steve. "Some pepper spray. A bulletproof vest. A helmet with a riot mask. And a couple pairs of handcuffs." Steve stood as Larry placed the vest over his head and the riot helmet on his head. Steve tried to walk around the living room. "I can't give you a gun, of course. I did get you a stun gun. They're pretty safe." Larry looked up from his pile of equipment. "Let's try this stuff on you."

After several minutes of struggle, Steve stood before the two adults smothered behind the layers of equipment hanging off of his thin frame. "Ack," was all he managed to say.

"What? What's the matter?" Larry asked as he velcroed a voice-activated microphone to the SWAT helmet Steve was wearing.

"I don't think this stuff will work for me. Look at me. I can't move. It's meant for someone your size, not mine." Steve began to remove the bulletproof vest.

"What are you doing?" Larry asked.

"I'm going to leave everything here except your cell phone. I'll take your phone in case I end up out of the range of your tracking device."

"Are you sure you don't want these other things?"

"Absolutely. This stuff works for you because you've used it before. It won't work for me. But I do know how to use a telephone." Steve studied the face of the phone. "This is a weapon I know."

Larry sighed. "All right. You do need to feel comfortable with what you're taking." He tossed the handcuffs on the couch and began to remove the stun gun and holster from Steve's shoulder. Once all of the equipment was off, Steve picked up the cell phone.

"Can you tell that phone what number to dial so Steve can just push a button to reach you, Larry?" Aunt Shannon asked.

"Do you mean pre-program the telephone number?"

Larry asked. Aunt Shannon nodded. "Good idea." Larry pulled the phone from Steve's hand. He pushed a few buttons on the phone. "There. That should do it."

"Let's see if it works." Steve pushed the first button on the phone, and Larry's home phone number rang loudly.

"Actually, give it back for a second," Larry asked. "I should put in a long-distance version of this number, just in case." He punched the touch screen, and passed the phone back.

"Good," Larry said. "You're ready."

Steve nodded nervously. He slid the phone into his bag and picked out the underwear, setting it on the couch. Larry squinted at him oddly.

"They're clean," Steve offered.

Then he held the backpack up, and opened its mouth to take a visual inventory. "Dictionary, notebooks, clock, phone, plaque, and the tracking thing." Steve looked up. "I am ready."

"As soon as you get wherever you're going, dial the phone immediately," Larry suggested. "Let's check the tracking device to make sure it works." He pushed a key on the small TV screen and the machine gave a loud, long beep. "It's working." Larry looked up from his machine towards Steve. "You know there's danger involved. This could go badly."

"I know," Steve said quietly. "But it's the best chance we have. I have to do this, or I won't get from Halloween to Christmas." Steve crossed the room and hugged Aunt

Shannon.

“You play it safe, Steve. If it gets dangerous, give them what they want and we will find you eventually,” Larry suggested. “And you can get out of there, right?”

“I’ll play it as safe as I can. May I have the ransom note, please?”

Larry pulled it carefully out of its plastic envelope and handed it to Steve. Steve slipped it into his bag and held onto it just in case he might drop it as he transported. With his other hand he touched the plaque in his backpack. The room began to flatten into a picture.

“Whoa,” Larry yelled as the transformation began. “I’m not used to that.”

“Spectacular,” yelled Aunt Shannon with a look of awe on her face. Steve watched as their figures flattened into a photograph and drifted to the ground, through the dark air of the new space. When the photo hit the floor, it vaporized in a burp of light.

Chapter Nineteen

A WAREHOUSE. IT FEELS LIKE a warehouse.

Steve felt dark, dusty space above him and around him. He stood motionless and listened. He watched his breath cauliflower into dark clouds as the winter wind sighed quietly. He noticed a set of industrial windows glowing with daylight three or four stories above him. Beyond the moans and creaks of the building, he heard nothing. Satisfied that no human was within a reasonable distance, he pulled the phone out of the bag. The touch screen face glowed back.

I guess the trip didn't hurt the phone.

He pushed the first speed-dial number. The sounds of dialing echoed quietly through the warehouse space. Steve covered the phone with his hand to muffle the noise. After it had finished he put the phone up to his ear.

A flat, tinny, monotone voice echoed in his head. "The number you have dialed is long distance. Please dial one and the area code before the number you are dialing."

Steve pounded the off button with his finger.

Crap. I'm out of the area code.

He pushed the second speed-dial button with his forefinger. The number rang once and someone picked up the phone quickly.

"Steve?" It was Larry's voice.

"I'm here," Steve whispered.

"You're not on the tracking screen."

"I know. I had to use the long distance number."

"Uh oh. That means you're out of the county."

"I think so," Steve whispered as he looked around the blackness. His eyes began to adjust slowly to the dim light from the overhead windows. "I'm in some kind of warehouse. I don't recognize anything… it looks… um… empty."

"Really?" Larry stopped talking as Aunt Shannon's muffled voice spoke. "Your aunt thinks they may not be there any more. They might have written the note there and then moved elsewhere, she says."

"Great," Steve whispered in disgust. "We'll need to start over again."

"It's still an important find, Steve. Don't touch the stuff you find around you. It's a potential crime scene and possibly filled with clues. Try to get outside the building—there may be a landmark of some sort you could identify for us. Once we know where you are, you can come back here and we'll send in the crime unit. Do you see any equipment in the warehouse?"

"Not really. It has a bare dirt floor. There's a few old things stored here and stuff around, but that's all." Steve scanned the room for a door that looked like it might lead outside. There was a door behind him. He walked towards it. There was a heavy lock and a deadbolt to make sure the door never opened.

"The door is locked." Steve whispered hoarsely. "And I can't see another door. I can't get out."

"Don't panic, Steve. If you're locked in, you're locked in. I want you to find your way out and get to safety," Larry said soothingly. Steve listened as Aunt Shannon and Larry conferred for a couple of minutes before the detective returned to the phone. "OK Steve, are you there?"

"I'm here."

"Your Aunt Shannon says to try turning the locks into clocks. I don't know what she means by that, but she says you'll know."

"I'll try it," Steve whispered. He set the phone down on the ground and put one hand into the backpack where his plaque sat. He put another hand on the dead bolt lock. "Lock-lock-lock-lock-lock-lock-lock-clock-clock-clock-clock-clock-clock-clock," he whispered. In a burst of light the deadbolt changed to an industrial-looking clock. Steve dropped his hand to the handle on the door and repeated the process. The locked door handle turned into a little clock with a steel face and heavy-looking hands.

Steve waited to see if anyone came. Only the sounds of winter filled his ears.

He picked up the phone again. "It worked," he yelled in a whisper. "I'm out."

"Great, Steve," Larry exclaimed.

Steve pushed opened the door slightly and looked outside. Big banks of snow ridged the ground. "I'm outside now."

"Good," Larry said. "Watch the windows, Steve. Walk close to the building, and be sure you walk under any windows you see. If someone is looking out, you don't want to be seen."

"Gotcha."

Steve slogged through the snow close to the side of the building, along the wall of corrugated steel. Wind swept the snow across a large parking lot and piled it into heaps as it passed through a chain link fence. The wind whistled as it whipped passed the crags and cracks of the warehouse.

He stopped as he approached the corner of the warehouse, moving his head slowly beyond its edge until one eye could scan the world around the corner of the building. The parking lot took up most of this side of the warehouse. It sprawled over the landscape. There was a main road at the far end of the parking lot, but Steve hadn't seen a single vehicle on it yet, nor could he hear any. Up towards the road the warehouse flattened from a three- or four-story corrugated steel structure into a low, one-story brick administrative complex with offices and windows. Steve surveyed the front of the warehouse for a few minutes, looking for signs of life.

"What do you see?" crackled Larry's voice through the cell phone.

"The warehouse has some offices attached to the front of the building," Steve said. "I can't see much else. The warehouse seems deserted." He froze suddenly. As soon as he had spoken, a figure strolled in front of one of the windows of the office complex, close to the road.

The figure scanned the parking lot, and then retreated from the window back inside. "There is someone in the front part of the building," Steve whispered.

"Good. Maybe," Larry corrected himself. "Where are you?" he repeated.

"I don't know."

"Can you see any signs at all, anywhere?"

"None. This warehouse seems to be out in the country somewhere."

"Are there any hills or mountains around you?"

Steve scanned the horizon, the part of it that wasn't blocked by buildings. "There is a single mountain, a few miles off. It's more of a big hill than a mountain."

"What direction is the hill from you? North, south, what?"

"I dunno," Steve said defensively.

"Don't worry, Steve," Larry said again. "We'll figure this out."

"Can you see any cars anywhere?"

"Nope."

"OK, this isn't going to work, Steve," Larry said. "Let's

go back inside the warehouse."

"I'm on my way."

Steve retraced his steps back inside the warehouse. "This is long distance," Larry moaned. "Roaming charges. My phone bill will bankrupt me."

Steve pulled open the warehouse door and stepped inside, vaguely hearing the detective's tinny complaints. "What do I do now?" he whispered into the cell phone.

"Come home," Larry said firmly. "It's too dangerous for you now."

"I'm not coming."

"Yes you are."

"I'm not, and you really can't make me do anything. I want to know what I should do next."

"I don't think it's safe," Larry insisted.

"I don't think I have a life until this gets sorted out. So I'm not coming home until we get somewhere."

Steve heard a heavy sigh on the other end of the phone. "You guys don't listen to anything I say." Steve smiled to himself, pleased to have held his ground. "If you're going to stay, look for some kind of clue in the warehouse area—a piece of paper or something that has an address on it."

Steve's eyes surfed thc inside of the warehouse, looking for likely spots for paper. He spotted an office-like square in the side of the warehouse and began to move cautiously towards it. He shuffled through the dusty wasteland of the warehouse and arrived outside the office. A sign on the door read "Shipping Office."

"It's a shipping office," Steve muttered into the phone.

"Excellent, Steve. There'll probably be something in there. That's a good place."

He tried the door but it was locked. "The door is locked. I'm going to open it Aunt Shannon's way," he reported. Steve gripped the door handle and instead of speaking the words he thought them.

Lock-lock-lock-lock-lock-lock-lock-clock-clock-clock-clock-clock-clock-clock.

Bright light stabbed the dim warehouse air; the door handle turned into an odd-shaped clock. Steve stepped into the dark office. His latest discovery warmed his cold body—he was learning a little more about his stone's power every time he used it.

Inside the shipping office, old binders and reams of paper covered the floor. He walked behind a service counter into a small office area where an old desk sat, covered with magazines, with paper cuttings littering the floor. Steve pawed through the papers on the floor and the scraps, looking for something that might give him a hint as to his location.

"I'm looking for something with an address on it." He scanned the room looking for something, anything. There were old computer printouts of some kind of inventory, there was information listed on paper, but there was nothing that seemed to speak clearly as to where he was. He spied a trashcan, tipped over in an opposite corner behind the counter. Steve crossed the sea of paper, righted the can, and picked through the contents. Most of the paper was balled, so he set about flattening each piece carefully and holding it to a small patch of light coming through one of the dusty overhead windows in the roof of the warehouse.

"This one has an address on it." Steve adjusted his stance to give the crumpled paper more light. "It says J.C. Steel Ltd., 118 Millarville Road, Turner Valley."

"What about the other papers?" Larry asked. "That could be a note from another company."

Steve unfolded several more. Most of the sheets of paper had the J.C. Steel logo on them.

"Most of the paper says the same thing," Steve said.

"Then that's probably exactly where you are. Just a second, Steve." He heard the phone clunk heavily. Suddenly Larry's out of breath voice returned. "You're at least a hundred miles away," said the detective in an amazed tone of voice. "Let me Google you again to be sure. Just a second." The phone popped again as Larry set it down. "Let me see." Steve could hear the clack of the keys as Larry typed. "You're over here. Hmm."

Steve heard a bumping sound from somewhere in the warehouse. He dropped silently where he stood, scanning what he could see of the warehouse through the bottom of the dusty windows.

"OK, J.C. Steel is out in the country. It has open fields across from it. It looks abandoned. I think we've found you. The front of the building is brick, right? The back is a steel warehouse." Steve didn't reply. "Steve, are you still on the line?"

"I'm here," Steve replied with a faint whisper. "That sounds like the building. I just heard a noise and I'm checking it out." Steve sat and waited in silence for a few minutes.

"OK. I think the coast is clear," Steve whispered.

"It's time to come home. You can check out of there now. You've done a great job."

"I'm not coming," Steve replied firmly. "What do you want me to do next?"

"Steve, if you saw what you saw, and if the gang is really still in the building, you're probably in grave danger."

"You're going to head out this way, aren't you?"

"Well, yeah. I've got to get the people here going and chat with the police force where you are…but it's going to take a few hours before we show up."

"I'm going to stay here until you come and pick me up," Steve insisted. "So give me something else to do. Do you hear me?"

"Gotcha," Larry said in a low voice. "You stubborn guy. I'll give you something else to do, but just realize that you're doing it at your own risk. I suggested you return, and you refused. You're both my witnesses."

"Agreed," Steve muttered, scanning the warehouse carefully again.

"Now that we think we've found them, it'd be nice to confirm they're there. Plus, it'd be good to know whether Lindsay and your Uncle Edward are with them." There was a pause and Steve heard Aunt Shannon mutter some unintelligible words. "Your Aunt Shannon just discovered that J.C. Steel has been defunct for the past few years—the number is out of service and has been for a long time. She also mentioned that it might not be the place where Lindsay and Uncle Edward are being kept. The ransom note would take you to the heart of the kidnappers' world, she said. Edward and Lindsay might be confined somewhere else."

Steve tried to swallow the lump in his throat. "I'm not liking the sound of what you're saying. You want me to get into the other part of the building and try and find Uncle Edward and Lindsay?"

"You're the one who wants to stay. What needs to be done should be done by professionals, so quit and come home."

Steve sighed and thought for a moment. "I'm going to do it. I need to do this."

"You're insane. Don't do this."

"I've got to. I'm staying," Steve declared quietly.

Silence as Larry fumbled around for a moment. "The other difficulty we have is this: we have to muster a group of police officers to swoop in and back you up. That means I need to make a few phone calls and drive up there myself. So I've got to hang up for a while. I can reach you on that cell phone you have, and I'll contact you when we're all ready to go. It'll probably be a couple of hours to get everything together. I'll give you a call and you can tell me what's going on inside the building. We'll work out a plan from there. Got it?"

"Got it," Steve whispered.

"Please do me a favor, do yourself a favor. Just hide and take it easy until I get back to you, all right?"

"Sure." Steve listened to the phone on the other end click and go dead. As the sound died away in the cell phone's speaker, Steve's heart floundered.

These next few hours are going to be agony.

His ears hummed with silence as he listened for sounds of a human presence.

That bumping sound must have been a mouse or a rat or something.

For a few minutes, Steve weighed the pros and cons of waiting against a little exploration. But his backpack brought him some confidence.

Even if they catch me, I could always disappear with my stone.

And with this thought, he felt the grip of fear loosen a little.

He scanned the warehouse through the dirt-caked windows again. He couldn't see anyone or anything. He waited, just to be safe. Nothing.

After another fifteen-minute eternity, he decided to explore the warehouse.

I can't handle waiting around like this.

He stood and tiptoed to the shipping office's door, opened it, and scanned the space. His breath wafted like little ghosts around his head.

The door to the rest of the building—I need to find it.

He worked his way up the side of the warehouse closest to the office wing he had seen outside. He loosened his coat, as nerves warmed his body to a near boil.

There has to be some kind of entrance or some kind of sign to help me find it.

As he walked towards a far door he heard a burst of sound, like footsteps running towards him just to his right side. Steve froze in his shoes and forced himself to turn and look. A frightened pigeon clacked away from a small cloud of frozen dust on the floor, to find the safer heights of the warehouse.

Steve let out a white, smoky breath and continued.

As for an entrance into the administrative wing of the building, there was one solid possibility. A set of heavy metal double doors with small glass windows, located in the middle of the warehouse's inside wall, seemed to guard the entrance to some kind of a hallway.

He stalled for a minute as he remembered the two small clocks joined by a chain in his backpack. He slid the bag partway off his back, and put one hand in carefully and fished around carefully for the alarm clock. When he found it he pulled it out, and put it into his other hand. Then he put his hand back into his bag, pawing around for his plaque. When he found it, he thought the transformative words, and the clock burst into a ball of light, falling from his hand to the floor. A small tornado of dust pulled from the floor circled him. And in the settling dust, he reached down and pulled a shimmering set of handcuffs from the dirt. He placed them in the backpack carefully, so as not to damage his plaque. Then he gently swung the pack onto his shoulders.

The cuffs might come in handy.

Steve crept close to the doors. The windows were dark. For a minute or two he balled up his courage, then used it to take a look through the small pane of glass in the left door.

The hallway was dark, so Steve couldn't tell if it led into the other part of the building. It didn't look promising. He stepped back and looked around the warehouse carefully again. Towards the far end of the warehouse there was a sign that read "Manager," with an arrow underneath pointing to a single metal door blocking the entrance to another hallway. The door had a long narrow window, but he couldn't see through it.

He looked around the walls of the warehouse for any other doors that seemed as though they might do the job. The double doors seemed like a more likely entrance to the rest of the building. Steve retraced his path to the double doors. His eyes raked over the ground nearest the door looking for fresh footprints. The arc of a door inscribed in the dust indicated that one of the doors had been opened fairly recently. Clusters of footprints surrounded the entrance, but it was difficult to tell if they were recent. As he toured another possible entrance, a single door at the far end of the same wall, he noted fewer footprints around the door's foot and a sheen of dust resting on the surface of the door, something he hadn't seen on the other door. The set of double doors looked like the best option, so he took up his position next to them again.

Steve took a breath and forced himself to look again through the small glass window in the door. No one seemed to be in the hallway.

With the heel of his hand, Steve scrubbed the glass in one of the windows and stared through the door-glass one more time. No one. He slid his hand across the door lock and thought the transforming words while he touched the plaque with his other hand. Bright light focused in the door lock and radiated into a fierce blast of light that shot through the warehouse and up the hallway.

Once Steve recognized the face of a clock where the lock had been, he ducked around the corner and hid in a crevice in the warehouse wall, waiting for some kind of reaction. The light was so bright that anyone wandering close by would have noticed the flash.

Steve waited another while, listening carefully for any kind of sound. Cautiously, Steve returned to the double doors, opened one, and slipped inside. The hallway before him looked deserted. Fresh footprints dotted the thick layer of dust.

No heat.

Maybe the entire place is empty except for a security guard. Maybe I saw a security guard.

Steve glanced towards the door. He thought for a moment, and then touched the lock that had transformed into a clock. He touched the plaque in his pack and thought the transforming sequence again. The clock in the door looked rather odd and would arouse suspicion, so Steve changed it back in case someone came down this way looking for things out of order.

About thirty feet beyond Steve, the hallway veered to the left. Steve crept up the hallway to a darkened door, and sank into the door's recess. He waited, listening. He heard nothing for several minutes. And then a gentle thumping sound.

It seemed remote, so Steve stepped back into the hallway and continued up to the corner of the building.

Then he heard voices, the voices of men talking as they walked. The voices were faint and their feet tick-tacked over the floor in some far-off place. The voices seemed to be getting closer. Steve retreated to the darkened doorway and listened. The voices and steps grew louder.

Steve tried the door latch. It opened easily. Darkness greeted him.

He stepped through and closed it behind him. A musty, odd scent irritated his nostrils. He pressed his ear to the door and listened as a muddy slur of voices and tick-tacking footsteps approached. Steve couldn't make out the words; whatever they were saying sounded like another language. He heard the voices pass and walk around the corner. The two jabbered as they completed some task, then passed Steve's hiding spot again. He waited until the silence returned.

Weird smell.

The smell, though, seemed somehow familiar. As the smell wafted into his thoughts, he remembered smelling the same thing at school in his biology class.

Formaldehyde.

His inquisitive nature got the best of him, and he switched on the light. Fluorescent lights flickered before they buzzed into a solid white.

The room was used for storage. Jars filled with liquid lined every shelf, covering every wall. Two huge rows of shelves divided the interior of the room into thirds. He stifled the simultaneous urge to scream and throw up.

The jars contained pieces of human bodies. A human heart, pickled in a jar above him. A brain floating in a large glass jar. He turned to scan the room. His eye caught a particularly gruesome jar displaying a head severed just below the neck, eyes removed. Another jar held a hand with no skin covering the bone and muscle. The jar beside that one housed a human fetus. Steve stopped looking so closely and scanned the rest of the room. Spare parts.

Got to get out of here.

He switched the light off. Cracked the door. Listening. Silence. He stepped through the door and closed it silently behind him. He edged along the wall of the hallway, until he met another set of double doors with big windows. This time the windows were clean, and so was the floor on the other side. The hallway empty.

He didn't want to step through those doors, but he knew he had to. He thumbed the latch on the handle—it opened easily. He pulled the door open and stepped onto the clean, checkered linoleum.

CHAPTER TWENTY

THE HALLWAY ON THE other side of the doors was heated. Steve instantly felt as though he had caught fire.

He crept along the wall of the hallway looking for an open door. He tried the door and found his way into a huge meeting room. A giant table took up most of the room, leaving space for only a few chairs around its edge.

Not much of a place to hide.

He closed the door and slunk further up the hall. He found another unlocked door. The inside was dark, but with the hallway lights he could make out some shelving loaded with stores. A janitor closet, walls of shelves, filled with cleaning supplies and equipment. Approaching steps. He closed the door behind him and dug in behind a couple of large boxes on a bottom shelf.

A hand tried the doorknob, opened the door, and knuckled the light on. A large, stubby pair of hands reached for a mop and bucket.

A man.

The hands guided the bucket out in front of a sink and dropped a hose into it. The man muttered under his breath bitterly, in another language. He poured some kind of liquid into the bucket and turned a tap, splashing water into the mop bucket. A few pine-scented minutes later, he turned the tap off and guided the mop and bucket out of the closet. Light off. Off, down the hall. Steve watched the man leave without closing the door.

He waited until the sound of the rolling mop bucket wheels had faded. He moved the boxes aside carefully and slipped into the hallway. Following the direction that the man and the mop had taken, he moved further up the hallway. He crinkled his nose as a waft of some strange chemical drifted past. He could hear sounds of activity behind some of the walls and doors he passed.

A door on his left looked unused. A big sign beside the door read "Sterile Laboratory." The room was dark, but he could still make out beakers, test tubes, tubing, and funnels. Steve cupped his hand to his ear and pressed it against the door glass. Silence. He tried to open the door. Locked. He touched the lock and grabbed his stone.

The lock burst into a ball of light as it transformed into a clock. Steve pushed open the door. Once he was inside, he touched the clock, transforming it back into a lock. Inside the first door there was a second door. The door read "Warning: Sterile Area. Scrub down and change to proper attire before entering." Steve pushed open the second door and entered the room. Beakers, test tubes, and machines lay around workbenches, as if someone had just gone for a lunch break, laying down his or her tools, leaving the work still spread out. Plastic covered everything. One bench had several ceramic dishes that looked as though they'd been heated to an unearthly temperature. The material inside the dishes was burnt beyond all recognition.

The contents of the ceramic dishes looked similar to the pictures he had seen in Aunt Shannon's alchemy book. Someone was trying to make a Benu stone the old-fashioned way—by burning substances until they were completely pure. Steve walked around the lab, being careful not to disturb any of the work-in-progress.

Sounds of a key being pushed into the lock of the lab door made him duck behind a workbench. The door to the lab opened, and several people walked in wearing sterile clothing—hairnets, facemasks, uniforms, and special cloth footwear. They were discussing something in great detail. The lights in the lab flickered on.

Cupboard.

Steve opened a set of cupboard doors under the worktable. The space was completely jammed with equipment. Now on his belly, Steve slithered across the floor to the next cupboard door. He opened it. A little room.

Enough for me.

He flattened himself and wormed inside. He slid the glassware toward the front, moving his body to the back. With the cupboard door closed, he sat in complete darkness except for the light straining though a venting grate just above the cupboard doors. The muffled noises of the workers became sharp and clear through the vent.

As Steve quietly adjusted his body to the cupboard, the mouth of his backpack gaped on the bottom of the cupboard, and his plaque—his Benu stone—slipped to the floor of the cupboard near the back.

"We're definitely into the second stage," said the first woman, her voice muffled by a sterile facemask. "We've got eight different batches of potential prima materia. And they've been properly blackened."

"This looks promising," said another woman.

"We're definitely on the way," the first woman stated. "Have you extracted any information from the girl and the man?"

"The man doesn't know anything," said one of the men. "The girl knows something, but won't talk."

"Make her. We've all invested heavily in this project. And I don't think we should move on from where we are until we get something out of her."

"Frank has some kind of drug that will make her talk. He's getting it from one of his contacts. It should be here anytime."

Sounds like Uncle Edward and Lindsay are here.

The woman instructed her staff to process the blackened dishes into sterile storage. Steve could hear the clink of the dishes as they were moved around. Then the voices exited the room. But Steve never heard the lock of the first door open, so they had probably moved to another room in this lab.

This is my chance.

The cupboard door opened noiselessly as Steve pushed it.

He stepped cautiously into the room. He hunched so his body stayed below the tops of the workbenches and scrambled closer to the door, listening for voices and footsteps.

He pushed open the first door leading to the hallway. Then he pressed his ear to the second door—the door that opened into the hallway—listening for sounds of life. Nothing. Steve pushed down the latch and opened the heavy door slightly so he could check the hallway for people. No one. After he slipped through the door, he nursed the door closed until he heard the mammoth clunk as the door locked.

He wandered carefully up the hallway, stopping outside of any doors he could find, listening. At an intersection of two main hallways, he found a room with windows that would let him keep both hallways in view.

Voices and footsteps echoed up the intersecting hallway. The sounds of activity crisscrossed around him. He peered through the bottom corner of one window—the room loomed, dark and empty. Steve tried the door and found it open. At the back of the room there was a large, metal storage cabinet.

Cabinet.

Steve opened it and found he could stand inside with the door slightly ajar.

How long until Larry gets here?

He checked the phone. There was an hour left, at least, before Steve could expect Aunt Shannon and Larry.

He watched for several minutes and saw a few people he didn't recognize exit from one room and walk up the hallway into other rooms.

How will I figure out where Lindsay and Uncle Edward are?

He observed the room as he tried to think up some possibilities. His eyes focused on a sprinkler head poking through the ceiling into the room he was hiding in.

There's my plan.

Steve recognized the sprinkler head from his dad's enthusiastic instruction on fire equipment.. It was an ancient sprinkler system.

If I trip this sprinkler, every sprinkler in the building will go.

The impending mayhem brought a chuckle to Steve's throat. He removed his coat, letting it fall to the bottom of the metal closet and sliding it out of the way. He freed his backpack from one of the sleeves and hung it on his back. Both hallways seemed clear. Ducking low, he stepped into the room.

There was a dusty old chair in the corner, and Steve brought it over and set it underneath the sprinkler head.

He stood on the chair and mentally measured the space between his outstretched hand and the head. He needed something two feet longer to help him reach the sprinkler head. There wasn't much in the room except an old garbage can. Steve retrieved it, turning it upside down on the chair.

He heard a door open close by. Back in the storage cabinet again.

A lone figure crossed the hall and entered another room. And Steve made his move. He scaled the chair and garbage can, easily reaching the sprinkler head. With both hands he snapped the lead trigger from its place; the sprinkler sprouted a flower of water, soaking him. He was down in a flash, disassembled the chair and garbage can, and closed himself in the storage cabinet again.

By setting off the one fire sprinkler, other sprinklers in the remainder of the building began to jet water. He smiled.

Everyone is getting wet.

Steve watched the sprinklers kick in, one by one up the hallway. It was a perfect indoor rainstorm.

Thank you, Dad.

Steve kept the door open a crack, just enough to monitor what was going on as water fountained from ceilings everywhere.

A thunder of activity. Angry voices shouted and called up and down the hallway. Soon he saw several drenched people running up and down the hallway, frantically yelling orders and trying to find the shut-off valve for the sprinkler system. He worked hard to keep track of which doors opened and which doors didn't, and to try to identify any familiar figures.

People were running in and out of rooms for several minutes, slamming doors. One or two slipped and skated down the slick of water in the hallway. Others, bewildered, found the driest spots they could and waited.

As he scanned the hallways through the darkened windows, he saw Lindsay and Uncle Edward emerging out of a room at the far end of the hallway, drenched from head to toe. A couple of heavyset men prodded them forward with the barrels of guns. The two men herded the hostages down the hallway until they found another room kitty-corner from where Steve was hiding. They unlocked the door with a key and pushed both of their victims into the room. Uncle Edward fell. One of the men kicked Uncle Edward's legs inside the room far enough that the door could swing closed.

With the door closed behind them, the men stood in the hallway as the sprinkler system spouted water into the building. A few minutes later, the sprinkler's lively spray of water began to droop, until it was a mere drip from the sprinkler heads.

They found the water-supply tap.

Steve relaxed in his hiding spot. Now he needed to wait for the cleanup to begin and for things to calm down so he could work his way to Lindsay and Uncle Edward.

Confused and angry voices shot up and down the

hallway. Steve smiled at the commotion, satisfied with all of the results.

"Our experiments are ruined!" shouted an angry voice. Another voice responded, but in another language. "Where's Rudy? He needs to know that the experiments are over. We're done here. If the hostages don't give us some answers in fifteen minutes, we'll kill them and leave," said a voice Steve recognized.

Mr. Gold.

Mr. Gold halted in front of the windows of Steve's hiding spot. "Come on," he said to a man who stood against a wall. "Get things together. We're leaving." He whipped his head towards the guards in front of the room housing Lindsay and Uncle Edward. "We don't need both of you guys guarding the door. Carl, give us a hand with the cleanup." Mr. Gold turned toward the remaining guard and lowered his voice. "Don't tell the prisoners what we're doing. They may get desperate." Mr. Gold gave an ugly laugh. He turned and stormed up the hallway.

The hallways were humming with activity. Steve wasn't sure how he was going to get over to Uncle Edward and Lindsay—until he noticed the ceiling tiles.

That could work. I just need to get above the ceiling without anyone noticing me.

The only cover in this room was a short section of wall, behind the door.

Slowly, people seemed to regain control after the confusion. Steve watched the guard across the hall. When the guard turned to one end of the hallway to chat briefly with someone, Steve opened the door to his hiding spot, hunched down, and scuttled into the dark behind the door, taking the soaked chair and garbage can with him.

As he glanced at the door's handle, he noticed that it could be locked with a button from his side. For extra safety, he locked the door. The chair and garbage can gave him enough height to reach the ceiling. He lifted the tile above him and slid it quietly to one side, raising his head into the space above.

In the dim, dusty light above the tile, he saw a clear path to the other room.

This will work.

Without hesitation, he pulled himself up into the space above the ceiling.

Steve carefully examined the metal bars between the ceiling tiles, checking each piece of the ceiling system before he moved to see if it would support his weight.

He set his foot gently on the center of a ceiling tile and slowly transferred his weight to the tile. The ceiling tile bent easily, and would have broken if he'd continued.

Steve pulled his weight back from the tile and stood on the metal brackets supporting the ceiling tiles; the support brackets were strapped to the building's roof with strong cables.

Step on the support brackets.

The noise below was perfect cover for any mistakes he might make. He stepped from bracket to bracket, carefully but quickly. The ceiling shivered a little as he shifted from support to support. In two minutes he sat above the room where Uncle Edward and Lindsay were being kept. He knelt down on a slat and carefully pried up a corner of a ceiling tile. The room below was in darkness.

"Lindsay?" Steve whispered hoarsely into the darkness. "Uncle Edward?"

"Who is it?" It was Lindsay's voice in a whispered reply.

"Lindsay, it's Steve."

"Really?" she said in a regular speaking voice.

"Ssssh!" Steve ordered. "Whisper!"

"I'm glad you're here."

"I'm glad I found you, too. But you need to get out of this room right away."

These guys are planning to hurt you.

"Are you sure?"

"Yes, I am," Steve replied. "You need to come with me."

"OK, Steve, we'll try."

"Do you have any furniture in the room?"

"I think so," Lindsay replied. "But it's dark down here. Let me check." She spoke some quiet words to Uncle Edward then set about exploring the darkness of the room. "Steve?"

"Yes?" he replied.

"There's a table and a chair."

"Put the chair on the table and you can both climb up here," Steve suggested.

"Steve, I don't know if it will work. Uncle Edward is

really weak."

"He has to escape."

"OK. We'll get him out," Lindsay responded.

Steve heard some shuffling below as she moved furniture and explained to Uncle Edward what needed to happen. The noise from all corners of the building helped them work undetected.

A few minutes passed and Uncle Edward's head popped above the ceiling tile.

"Hi, Steve." Uncle Edward smiled weakly.

"Hi," Steve replied. Warmth flooded him as he saw his great uncle's face again. "It's good to see you. Let's get you up here."

Steve stood carefully and positioned himself just above Uncle Edward.

"Give me your hand."

"I don't know if I can make it."

"Give me your hand," Steve ordered. Uncle Edward lifted a shaking, wrinkled hand to Steve. Steve grabbed it firmly.

"Lindsay, can you push from underneath?"

"Yes."

"Let's go." Steve pulled as hard as he could. Uncle Edward's body rose slowly into the space above the ceiling. Steve waited until about half of Uncle Edward's body rose above the ceiling level, and then he pulled the old man so that he flopped onto the ceiling tile. Guiding Uncle Edward's hands to a support bracket, Steve whispered,

"Hold on to this." The ceiling quivered as it adjusted to the new weight. "Uncle Edward, I'm going to get the rest of you up here."

"I'll be fine, Steve."

"Lindsay, can you get through the tile here? Then, we can both help Uncle Edward get up here."

"I'm coming." Lindsay's face popped through the opening in the ceiling, and she hopped lightly into the opening and pulled herself in.

"We can't walk on the tiles," Steve whispered to both of them. "If you step on a tile with your whole weight, you'll fall through. You can only walk on the metal frame around the tiles—it'll support our weight."

"Gotcha," Lindsay replied.

"Uncle Edward, you're safe the way you are because most of your weight is resting on the brackets," Steve said quietly. Once we get you standing up, you'll need to keep your feet on the brackets, too."

"I think I know what to do," he said.

"Lindsay and I are going to pull the rest of your body up, all right?"

"Sure," Uncle Edward replied in a weak voice.

Lindsay hopped around Uncle Edward on the ceiling frame so she could hold one of Uncle Edward's arms. Steve did the same.

"Ready?" Lindsay asked.

"One. Two. Three," Steve counted.

The two of them heaved Uncle Edward's arms until his

entire body lay on the ceiling tiles. The tiles bowed with his weight, but they held.

"Uncle Edward," Lindsay called in a soft voice. "Now we're going to help you stand." She looked towards Steve. "Ready?"

"Ready."

The two of them slowly hoisted Uncle Edward to his feet, making sure his feet rested on the metal frames around the ceiling tiles.

"Lindsay, you take Uncle Edward and carefully begin to work your way towards the front of the building." He pointed out the right direction. "The police are on their way but it's going to take a few more minutes. I'm going to clean up this room so they can't tell how you escaped."

"We'll see you at the front of the building," Lindsay said, and Steve thought he could hear her smile.

Steve hopped into the opening in the ceiling and lowered his feet into the room. He wiggled his feet around looking for the back of the chair. When he found it, he slid the toes of his shoes through a space in the back of the chair to grip it and pulled his body upwards back into the ceiling cavity. He lifted his feet behind him and slid the trunk of his body sideways, dragging the chair into the space between the roof and the ceiling tiles.

He replaced the ceiling tile and began walking towards the front of the building to catch up with Lindsay and Uncle Edward, stepping carefully on the ceiling tile's metal framework.

As he began to catch up to the escaping pair, he heard a muffled, angry yell filter through the ceiling behind him.

Lindsay and Uncle Edward had made good progress. They had already disappeared into the dim light of the ceiling cavity and were partially concealed behind some ductwork. He turned towards the room they'd just escaped from and scanned the scene. Lindsay's and Uncle Edward's wet bodies left a trail of water, tracing a dark path, marking their escape route. Steve scooted over the ceiling tiles to catch up to them.

"We're going to have to alter our escape route," Steve whispered hoarsely to Lindsay. "They'll follow our trail of water drips to where we are now. Let's stick to the front of the building and make our way to the far corner, over there." Steve pointed towards a deep corner in the building. "Once we're in that corner, we can make our way to the back of the building and into the warehouse."

"Gotcha," Lindsay replied. Uncle Edward gazed at Steve with puzzled, tired eyes as he clung to a ceiling support. "We have to keep moving, Uncle Edward," Lindsay urged.

Lindsay positioned herself beside Uncle Edward again, and helped him turn and move slowly towards the dark corner. The activity in the rooms below still seemed loud enough to cover the noise of their progress. But then someone started yelling at people, commanding them to be quiet. Voices traveled to various parts of the building until the noise from below dwindled into silence.

Lindsay heard the silence grow in the building and

stopped moving. She leaned over to Steve and whispered, "I think they know we're in the ceiling and they're listening for where we might be." Steve nodded his agreement. Lindsay held her finger to her lips as Uncle Edward looked at her with a questioning look. The old man nodded uncertainly.

They listened, waiting to hear a sound of what might be happening. There were sounds of doors opening and closing quietly. The sounds grew closer.

Suddenly the cell phone in Steve's backpack gave a loud ring. Steve grabbed his pack and fumbled inside for the phone as it trilled loudly again. Steve grabbed the phone and answered it as a man shouted from the room below them.

"Let's move," Lindsay said in a hoarse whisper. Uncle Edward took a firm hold of Lindsay's arm and they began to move. Several gunshots rang out, peppering the ceiling tile with small dots of light.

"Steve, you sound like you're in trouble," came a hollow-sounding voice from the cell phone. Steve held the phone to his ear as he moved with Lindsay and Uncle Edward.

"Are you here?" Steve asked in a panicked whisper.

"We're here," Larry replied.

"Get in here," Steve whispered hoarsely into the phone. "Get in here now. I have Lindsay and Uncle Edward with me. They're OK. But we're being shot at right now."

"We're ten minutes away," Larry said.

"Get here, now!" Steve pleaded quietly. "And you're going to need back up. This place is crawling with people."

"I'm calling for back up, right now," Larry replied.

A ceiling tile behind them opened up and a burly man climbed into the space. He lowered a gun towards them. Steve took the cell phone and hurled it at the man. The man tried to duck and stepped backwards onto the middle of the ceiling tile, which split in two with his weight, sending him crashing through the ceiling. He landed heavily on the floor below. No one came up into the ceiling area after the man had fallen, but Steve could hear sounds of more people approaching the scene.

Steve turned and caught up with Lindsay.

"I can't go on," Uncle Edward muttered weakly. "I can't go any further."

"You have to," Lindsay said.

"I can't," Uncle Edward said as his legs buckled under him. Steve caught his other arm and fought gravity to keep Uncle Edward on his feet.

"Why don't we drop you two down into the room below," Steve suggested. "We'll find a safe place to hide until the police come."

He pulled a tile up quickly, scanning the room below. It seemed like some sort of storage room with all kinds of storerooms boxed in with chain-link fence. Steve dropped into the room and found a couple of empty crates. He slid them underneath the opening and stood on each of them to test their strength. Once he was sure they'd hold Uncle Edward's weight, he motioned to Lindsay to help Uncle Edward lower himself into the opening. Uncle Edward's frail legs dropped into Steve's view; he grabbed them in a bear hug. Then slowly, with Lindsay guiding Uncle Edward's upper body, Steve lowered his uncle's legs to the crates. Uncle Edward stood unsteadily on the crates, while Steve piled junk in front of him to form a makeshift set of stairs.

He helped Uncle Edward to the floor as Lindsay dropped lightly onto the crates. None of the chain link storage gates were closed. The three could hear sounds of people approaching.

Lindsay pointed towards the back of the room. "There's a window. Maybe we can make it outside."

Steve measured the time it would take to get out the window against the sounds of approaching footsteps. He knew Uncle Edward wouldn't be able to move fast enough to get to the window in time.

Steve suddenly had an idea.

The chain-link gates would take a padlock. The handcuffs.

Into his backpack he flew, fishing for the handcuffs. He stuck one of the cuffs through the padlock holes and cinched it tightly locked.

He threw his hand into the bag to look for his stone. It wasn't there.

Where's my Benu stone?

"Lindsay, do you still have your Benu stone?" he demanded urgently.

"Yes. Good thinking," Lindsay noted quietly.

"I've lost mine. I've got to go back."

"Are you insane?"

Steve and Lindsay half-carried, half-dragged Uncle Edward into another chain link cubicle with an unlocked gate. In this storage compartment, however, there was a window.

"Lock yourselves in here," Steve ordered. "Turn Uncle Edward's watch into a lock. I'm going to create a distraction, so they don't come looking for you."

"Clock-clock-clock-clock-clock-clock-clock-lock-lock-lock-lock-lock-lock-lock." The watch flattened into a single dimension and in a flash of light with a violent wind, it became a padlock.

Steve climbed one of the chain link walls of a storage area, pushed a ceiling tile out of the way, and hopped into the ceiling opening. He fit the ceiling tile back into place and began to make loud noises with his feet as he crossed the ceiling on the ceiling's support brackets. As Steve stomped through the ceiling cavity, a couple of heads popped through the tiles. Steve went for it, swinging wildly from support to support. The ruse seemed to work. The men hopped into the ceiling space and began to lumber carefully over the ceiling frame towards him.

Several more figures poured through the ceiling's opening, several ceiling tiles around the building popped upwards, and several squares of light shot into the darkness above the ceiling.

Steve knew he wouldn't last very long where he was, and he needed to find his lost stone. He heard sirens approaching the building, which seemed to throw the faces and figures in the ceiling space into mass confusion.

In the far end of the building a bright orange light licked through one of the ceiling panels. It was a flame. The building, despite being soaked with water, had somehow caught fire.

The fire alarm bells clanged into the confusion all over the building. Steve heard a dull thud as an orange ball of flame shot through the back half of the ceiling tile, throwing him backwards. The tile broke, and he plummeted through the opening to the floor below.

CHAPTER TWENTY-ONE

"I THINK WE'RE ALMOST OUT," Lindsay murmured happily. Just when they were close to making their exit, a man waving a gun entered the storage room. He saw them and gave a triumphant shout.

"I've got 'em." He screamed against the confusion in the building. "They're in here." He took his gun, steadying it with his other hand, and leveled it at Lindsay. He squeezed the trigger. The loud explosion from the barrel of the gun screamed in Lindsay's ears. She thought she had been hit, but she couldn't feel any pain.

She quickly checked her body—there was no visible wound. She realized quickly that his bullet had probably hit the chain-link fencing and deflected somewhere into the room. The man took aim again and squeezed the trigger.

An click replaced the explosion. The man examined his gun, then pulled the trigger again. Click. He squeezed the trigger several more times—empty.

In anger, the man thrashed against the locked storage gate with all of his might, then threw his gun across the room.

There was only one gate between Lindsay and Uncle Edward and a big, angry man.

Lindsay and Uncle Edward backed through one last gate. She stopped and removed her own watch, and threaded the soft leather strap through the padlock clasps. She watched as the angry man threw his weight against the first storage gate.

She waited until he was completely involved in trying to break the lock and then she whispered the words. A burst of light and wind cut through the room. The angry man stopped for a moment, gazing around the room, trying to assess what had caused the wind and light. On the last gate there hung a stylish, delicate, feminine-looking lock. When he couldn't find the source of the disturbance, he threw his weight against the gate. The lock exploded into a cloud of parts. He was through the gate!

He growled at the escaping pair and hurled himself against the last gate. Lindsay helped Uncle Edward back towards the outside wall, near the window. Lindsay took a piece of pipe she found on the floor and bashed the glass of the window, showering shards of glass through the storage room. The winter air belched into the room. She forced the bar along the bottom edge of the window to knock out the sharp pieces of glass that stubbornly clung to the bottom of the window frame. She dropped the bar outside of the building when she was finished.

"The outside is clear," she yelled to Edward. "Let's get out there." She led a confused Uncle Edward to the window, grabbed him around the waist, and hoisted him into the opening. His body drooped over the window frame.

The burly beast threw himself at the last gate with another roar. But the gate held.

Lindsay pushed Uncle Edward's legs through the window, and leapt out after him.

The man lunged at the gate again, This time the hinges gave way and the gate swung aside. He threw open the gate and ran towards the window, diving through the opening after Lindsay and Edward, but his progress stopped abruptly as his head met a metal bar—a bar that Lindsay held in her hands. The man's body dropped back inside the building like a rag doll. Lindsay turned to Uncle Edward.

"We've got to keep moving," she said.

She squatted behind Uncle Edward's seated body and hugged it. His legs dangled uselessly between hers as she stood. Undaunted, she began to move very slowly towards the sound and light of the sirens.

Suddenly an explosion ripped through the back of the building, and people began to run from various entrances and exits. Those who were jumping through the windows frightened Lindsay at first, until she realized they were trying to escape, not recapture the two of them.

She and Uncle Edward moved very slowly as people

ran helter-skelter around them. Uncle Edward's weight grew in Lindsay's arms. She knew what it meant. They needed medical help.

A long line of police officers blanketed the outside of the building, collecting each of the escapees, rounding them up into the backs of several waiting paddy wagons. An officer, with her gun drawn, approached Lindsay as she hugged Uncle Edward.

"Put your hands where I can see them," the officer ordered.

"We were the hostages," Lindsay explained.

"I said, put your hands where I can see them," the policewoman repeated.

Lindsay slowly released Uncle Edward and he slipped to the ground in a heap. She raised her hands in the air.

The policewoman called another recruit over to carry Uncle Edward. The second officer scooped Uncle Edward's wilted frame from the ground. The two officers escorted the both of them toward the vans.

Lindsay studied the burning building and remembered the man she had hit with the bar, lying inside the building still. She turned towards the policewoman. "There's a man inside that room there. He's unconscious." The policewoman called another officer over who was approaching the scene.

"You wanna check out that window over there? This girl says there's a guy inside and he's unconscious." He gave a nod and headed towards the broken window.

"Let's keep moving," the policewoman said to Lindsay.

Aunt Shannon spotted Lindsay and Uncle Edward.

"Lindsay, dear," Aunt Shannon squealed. "You're all right." She was weeping, as she spoke. She grabbed Lindsay in a fierce, boney embrace.

"Edward, you old dog," she said tenderly, putting her hand to his forehead. "I'm so glad to see you."

"Excuse me, ma'am," the police officer said. "I have to take these two over to Detective Garner. I need to make sure they're OK with him."

Larry was in his element. He barked orders left and right. One by one, each of the kidnappers was brought to him. He scribbled some information and had them put into several paddy wagons waiting in the building's parking lot.

"We'll sort this out back at the office," he said to a handcuffed woman, who was pleading with him. The policewoman escorting her hauled her away.

Larry saw Aunt Shannon with Lindsay and Edward and walked towards them, waving.

"These folks are OK. You can let them go," he said to the officers standing by. Aunt Shannon held Uncle Edward's hand awkwardly; Lindsay hovered next to the two of them. "You must be Lindsay," Larry said. Lindsay nodded.

Larry scanned the trio from head to toe. "Let's get Edward to an ambulance." He turned to survey the building again. "We'll talk when this is over," he said as he headed back to his command post.

Lindsay and Aunt Shannon followed Uncle Edward

to an ambulance, where they lay him on a stretcher and covered him with a blanket. The ambulance attendants checked his vitals.

"This guy should go now," the head attendant announced.

Aunt Shannon face turned gray.

"It's just a precaution," the attendant added, noticing Aunt Shannon's reaction. "Nothing life-threatening."

Aunt Shannon put a hand to her chest. "I'm relieved to hear that." She bent over her husband of nearly forty-seven years, and smooched him on the lips. "I'm sorry, Edward, but you deserved that one."

Uncle Edward turned very, very red, but beamed.

Aunt Shannon looked towards Lindsay.

"Your dad is desperate to see you," Aunt Shannon said.

"Sure," Lindsay replied, in a distracted tone.

The ambulance driver wanted to leave, but Uncle Edward stopped him from doing so. He asked the driver to keep the doors open and prop him up in the stretcher.

"I'm going to wait for Steve," he said to the driver. "He saved our lives."

The three of them watched as the fire gorged on the building. Another wild explosion blew through the back end of the building, and the building's fate was sealed. A firefighter held a megaphone up to his mouth and shouted to the fighters around the building.

"It's too far gone," said the firefighter, "let her burn. Make sure vehicles and equipment are clear, and spray the fire to contain it."

Aunt Shannon, Uncle Edward, and Lindsay huddled in the back of the ambulance, holding on to each other as police officers and paddy wagons slowly cleared the scene. Larry finally left his command post and wandered over to the group in the ambulance, huddled in blankets.

"Where's Steve?" he asked.

"He lost his stone. He went back to look for it. Isn't he out here somewhere?" Lindsay replied, concerned.

"Not me." Larry whipped through several sheets of scribbles on his notepad. "I thought he was with you." He looked up from his pad and shouted to a constable who was coordinating the arrest efforts. "Hey, Cassandra," Larry shouted. She nodded, quit her conversation with a firefighter, and strode over to where he was standing. "Have you seen anyone outside of the building since our last batch?"

Cassandra shook her head. "We've got everyone, haven't we? Except for John Dee, the ringleader. We've identified all of the gang, except him."

Larry's face turned gray. "We're missing someone. We're missing a teenager named Steve. Is there anyone else wandering around, someone we've missed?"

Cassandra shook her head. "Nope."

"Can we get someone to check the inside of the building again?" Larry pleaded.

"Not a chance. The fire-chief just told me that they're just going to let the building burn. The fire is too far gone—it's too dangerous to go back in there."

"He lost his stone?" A look of panic twisted Aunt Shannon's face. "He can't get out without his stone! You can't let him die. He has to be around here somewhere!"

"We've covered the ground completely. I don't think a single person escaped from here on foot. Anyone we haven't found has to be inside the building. I'm sorry," Larry said quietly, his eyes focused on the ground. "Look at the building. There isn't much more we can do." As he spoke, a large section of the building collapsed into the flames.

Lindsay looked towards the flames. "Let's look for him around the building. He might have got out from somewhere else—you might have missed him!" she said to Larry. He dropped his head.

"I'm sorry. I don't think that's possible," he said quietly. "We keep careful counts of everyone in situations like this. If he wasn't with you, and he's not on my list, I'm certain he's still inside the building."

Lindsay nodded slowly.

"You mean he's probably dead," Lindsay said, as tears began to well in the rims of her eyes.

"I'm sorry," Larry replied. "I wish there was something I could do."

Aunt Shannon stood and began to take strong strides towards the building. "If you're not going to do anything, Larry, I will," she growled. Larry grabbed Aunt Shannon's wrist. He held on to her hand until she collapsed on the ground, in tears. Then he helped her up and placed her in the back of the ambulance. Lindsay got in beside her and slid her arm around Aunt Shannon's shoulders. Uncle Edward, strapped in his stretcher, let the tears roll freely down his dirty, tired face.

After several minutes of silence, Aunt Shannon spoke. "You're right, Edward; alchemy is too dangerous. I hurt another person. I quit." She sunk her head into her hands, as the fire raged in front of her.

CHAPTER TWENTY-TWO

A WEEK AND A FEW days later, once the firefighters had gone through most of the remains of the building, the police department issued a report saying that they had found human remains in the fire. The remains were burnt beyond recognition. The report concluded that Steve and John Dee had died in the fire.

Mr. Best flew back from his business trip to arrange a memorial service for his son. The only time available was in the afternoon of December 24th, Christmas Eve. Doug Best was nothing more than a ghost—shelled, empty, vacant.

"The body is sown in dishonor; it is raised in honor and glory," said the pastor, quoting from the Bible. "It is sown in infirmity and weakness; it is resurrected in strength and endowed with power. It is sown a natural body, it is raised a supernatural body."

The pastor paused and gazed around the room. The chapel was packed with students, friends, and family. This case had caused the biggest ruckus the town had seen for quite some time. The local paper told the story of Steve's daring and courage, calling him a hero. Many turned out to pay tribute.

The chapel was decorated in a minimal way. In front of the pulpit, on a small table, stood a small vase. The vase contained a single red rose. The rose and the vase together represented Steve's life, replacing Steve's body—no one had found a trace of it in the charred remains of the building. They found human remains, but none that clearly belonged to Steve.

The pastor hovered over the vase as she spoke. "And when this perishable body puts on the imperishable, then shall be fulfilled the Scripture that says, Death is swallowed up in victory."

The pastor's words sounded hollow to most people in the room. After all, once a person dies, what are the chances of a person coming back to life? The service felt heavy and final.

The service concluded, and Lindsay, Aunt Shannon, Uncle Edward, and Mr. Best returned to the Best house to eat supper. No one spoke. Though the weather was bright and cheery, despair smothered the whole house.

No one realized that events during the fire had taken Steve on a much different course.

Chapter Twenty-Three

As the fire raged, and Steve attempted to lead any pursuers away from Lindsay and Uncle Edward, he found himself deep inside the building. A huge explosion burst through a part of the building, throwing him back several feet. He landed heavily on his back in the middle of ceiling tile, broke through the tile, and fell towards the floor. He landed on his heels and toppled backward against the wall, smashing a huge hole in it. Surprised to have survived the fall, he stood up and began to retrace his steps, looking for his Benu stone.

He returned to his most recent hiding spot, the room with the metal cabinet overlooking the hallway. People ran helter skelter through the hallway looking for escape routes. A layer of smoke floated below the ceiling tile. Screams and shouts. He scoured the metal closet where he'd been hiding. Nothing. He rifled through the coat pockets and threw his coat into the room in case he'd left the plaque underneath it.

He fought against a growing sense of panic as he tried to remember where he'd last used his Benu stone. He hopped onto the table, popped out the ceiling tile and scanned the tiles in case it had fallen out while he'd been in the ceiling system. The hallways of the building were empty now. Smoke billowed up the hallway. Steve barely noticed. His mind retraced his steps.

Steve followed his pathway back to the janitor's closet and scoured his hiding spot there. He shoved cleaning supplies out of his way to get a good look. Nothing.

The lab!

As he hurried back to the lab, flames licked the bottoms and corners of several walls.

He tried the lab door. It was locked.

I used my stone on this lock!

He peered into the window. The room was filled with smoke. He couldn't see anyone. Pulling a fire extinguisher from its place on the wall, he drove the bottom of it through the door's glass. He had to bash the window several times to break through the fine wires embedded in the glass before he could put his arm through and open the first door. A whoosh of air blew past Steve towards the hungry fire. He stepped between the doors.

The smoke in the lab thickened. Across the hallway, behind him, a portion of a wall fell over and belched a ball of flame across the hallway. Steve saw the flame moving towards him and ducked. The flame poured through the door's smashed window and over him. He stood and stepped through the room's inner door and moved through the lab, scouring the floor for the stone. He opened a few cupboards, because he'd forgotten exactly where he'd hidden when he was in the lab room. Then a flash of memory.

Over here.

He rounded the corner, crouching to stay below the smoke. He pulled back the cupboard door and stuck his head inside, feeling the back of the cupboard with his hand. His frantic fingers found a smooth flat surface at the back of the cupboard. Steve scraped the object to the front of the cupboard with his fingers—it was his Benu stone.

The smoke in the lab began to flicker into flame. He pulled up his backpack and prepared to flee to the World of Pieces. He heard the ceiling and structure around him groan. He pulled his bag in front of him and gripped his stone.

"Ah, you little rat," yelled a voice from behind the closed cupboard door. The sound of a human voice almost scared Steve senseless. A sneering, angry face met him nearly nose to nose. Mr. Gold. "I knew you were up to something, you stupid punk." Mr. Gold stepped towards him. "You ruined everything." Emotion choked most of the words from Mr. Gold's sentence.

Steve quickly pushed his Benu stone into his backpack, holding it with one hand and clutching anything he could find inside with the other. His hand happened to grasp the dictionary. Mr. Gold leapt towards him and grabbed his head in a headlock. Steve watched his body envelop in bright, bluish white light against the flames. He watched as his world of fire flattened, the roaring flames and searing heat fading as Steve moved to the World of Pieces. As he watched the warehouse turn into a picture, he saw the ceiling collapse, crushing the cupboard he had been sitting in. The picture grew small, fluttered to the ground in front of his feet, and disappeared in a burst of light.

But Steve still felt the heavy hands of Mr. Gold holding him firmly.

"You have returned, Whole One. You have come to pay your debt," said a dark and formidable voice that sounded like it was coming from everywhere and nowhere all at once. "And who have you brought with you?"

Steve felt the grip loosen on his head, so he straightened up and stepped away from Mr. Gold. Steve immediately wanted to run.

"You promised us your life, and you must pay the price for stealing from our world, for corrupting that which we had made perfect."

Mr. Gold looked around, amazed and confused. "Where are we?" he asked, looking at Steve. Steve shrugged. The mask suddenly whooshed together before Mr. Gold.

"Do you not know where this is?" the mask demanded of Mr. Gold.

"I don't think I do," he replied. He tried to sound brave, but his, "Who are you?" came out in a wavering, fearful voice.

"I am the representative of this world, the world of possibility, the world of perfection, the World of Pieces."

"This is where?" Mr. Gold asked again.

"This is everywhere; this is nowhere," the mask answered. "And what have you come here to seek?"

"I don't know," Mr. Gold replied flatly. "What can I get?"

"Do you want gold?" asked the Mask.

"Yes, I do," he replied carefully.

"Are you an alchemist, too?" asked the mask.

"Is that what this world is?" Mr. Gold asked again, in disbelief. "This is the world of Alchemy?"

"It is if you say it is," the mask answered in a warmer tone. "I can show you what this world can give you. Would you like to see it?"

"Why, yes, I think I would," Mr. Gold replied, looking cautiously at Steve with a sly smile. "Is this what you and your great aunt have discovered, Steve?" he asked with a twisted grin. "I have stumbled onto your secret, haven't I?" He laughed greedily. "This adventure has turned out much better than I planned." As Mr. Gold talked, his voice began to sound confident—smug—again.

"I wouldn't listen to the mask, Mr. Gold," Steve suggested. "It will lead you to your own death." Steve felt sick to his stomach. He hated to help Mr. Gold, but the man didn't understand the danger.

"My name is not Mr. Gold, you fool," snarled the man.

"I wasn't going to tell you my real name, now was I? You can call me Mr. Dee, John Dee."

John looked carefully at the mask's blank expression. "Steve, you wouldn't be lying, would you?"

"I'm trying to save you," Steve replied in disbelief, verging on anger. "I'm trying to help. Don't listen to the mask," he said earnestly.

Mr. Dee laughed loudly. "A convincing act, Steve, but you'll have to do better than that." He turned to the mask. "Let's see what you have to offer."

Steve couldn't believe his ears, and anger burned across his brow as he watched the mask lead Mr. Gold away. He listened to their discussion.

"Would you like to eat?" asked the mask, sweetly.

"I wouldn't mind," John replied. "I am rather hungry."

Steve studied his left hand, touching the stub where his finger had once been. He looked up and the mask and Mr. Gold had disappeared over a shiny black hill. He waited for a while, trying to decide what to do. Then he remembered his mother—she still needed his help. He turned in the direction of the Ocean of Pieces.

"You belong to us," said a voice. There was no mask to speak those words. The voice surrounded Steve. "You must be perfected."

"Perfected is just another word for dead," Steve replied furiously. "Why would I want to die?" His voice became flat as he fought his anger.

"This is your new home," replied the voice. An explosion

of light tore through the world from behind him. He turned to find that a copy of his house had materialized behind him. It looked just like his house at home, copied exactly to the smallest detail. The shiny black ground underneath the house wrinkled and whitened, mocking the winter snow that surrounded his real house in the real world. It looked quite out of place to see his house in the World of Pieces.

Steve stepped towards the house. He reached for the door handle on the front door and his hand ghosted through the handle. He walked through the front door—literally.

I have to be touching my stone.

When he stepped into the house, an eerie silence greeted him. Perfect silence. He swung his backpack to where he could reach inside it, grabbed his stone, and reached for a wall.

Intruders hadn't destroyed this version of the house. Everything was in its perfect place. Steve noticed immediately that this version of his house was clean and neat —impeccably clean and disturbingly neat.

He moved into the living room. His mother's chair sat underneath her lamp, just like it had the night she disappeared. There was no broken mug or coffee splattered on the floor. Steve approached his mother's chair. The chair's leather was worn and slightly grayed. He wandered through the house to his own bedroom. He scanned the room. On the wall hung the plaque his mother had given him—his Benu stone. He couldn't read the words on the plaque.

The two rows of letter-like shapes shimmered on the plaque, but didn't form words. He lifted his hand to touch the plaque and his hand moved through it, even though he was touching his real plaque with his other hand. He reversed his hand and dragged his fingers like a paintbrush over the house's wall. It felt solid.

I wonder why everything else is solid except for my Benu stone.

He stopped his hands, picked a point on the wall and punched through the drywall. The drywall crushed inwardly with his forceful fist, but the broken edges sparked as if the walls were electrified. A grid of zeros crisscrossed the hole in the wall. The numbers clicked through the digits, as if they were looking for a combination. Several of the numbers seemed to stop finally, settling on a particular sequence. The drywall slowly repaired itself until the wall looked as if Steve had never punched it. He touched the wall and it felt as good as new.

"Where's my mom?" Steve called out. There was no response. But minuscule pieces of her began to appear. The small pieces came together and halted in proper position, waiting for the other bits of her to arrive. After all the pieces of her had arrived, each piece hovering in its place, the pieces seemed to melt together into a whole body.

She stood motionless. Steve waited for her to move. Nothing. She was somehow empty of some essential part, just as Aunt Shannon had been. He stared at her expressionless face, trying to record those features in his memory. He felt a warm glow burn into his heart, bathing his insides with light.

"She's here!" he shrieked. The lingering shadows in Steve's world burned away instantly. "She's here," he sighed.

She looks better, more rested than before she disappeared.

The circles under her eyes were gone, and so were her glasses. Her face wasn't wrinkled with the care she used to wear constantly. Instead of its usual tousled and unkempt appearance, her hair was perfectly neat—every hair was in its proper place.

I need her Benu stone to wake her up.

Steve wondered how he was going to find his mother's stone and bring her back. He thought of his own stone, how it had ended up just being a ghostly image on the wall. His mother's chair might have the answer. He looked for anything around her seat, anything out of place or out of the ordinary. He tried to remember what was around the chair the night she disappeared.

Everything was in its place. Steve compared this new version of his home, the one with everything in place, with what he remembered of the earthly version. The lamp stood at attention beside the chair, but the dents in the brass weren't there anymore. Steve scanned the bookshelf behind his mom's chair. All the books stood in perfect, attentive rows, waiting to be pulled off the shelf. Keeping one hand on his stone, Steve slid the dictionary off the shelf and popped it open.

There were letters all in neat rows, but the words, if they came together at all, didn't mean anything to Steve. He dropped the book to the floor and returned to his place in front of his mother's chair.

Under the chair on the floor sat a book. Steve remembered that book. At home it was tattered and worn, held together by tape. It was often under her chair, along with her notebook. He whirled around to face the body of his mother as she stood there, empty, behind him.

After he glanced at her expressionless face, he turned back to the book under her chair.

Her Benu stone.

That tiny, ragged book—the pieces of the book held together with tape. It had been her mother's book before her, and her mother's mother's book, too.

It was missing, too.

Steve wasn't sure what that book was, or what it meant to his mother. He reached out to pick up his mother's ancient book and his hand breezed through it, just like his hand had with his own plaque.

This must be it. But I don't know enough about it to call it out of the ocean.

His mother stood behind him, motionless.

"I like this place," she said in a robotic voice. "It is quiet here. It is clean here." Her face remained expressionless.

The sound of her voice shocked Steve for a few moments. He hadn't heard that voice for a long, long time. It sounded like her voice, but those certainly weren't her words. A fresh wave of sadness swept over him. He reminded himself that he wasn't talking to his mom, he was talking to this World of Pieces—they were using his mom's body and voice.

"You aren't talking like my mom," Steve shouted at his mother's expressionless face. "And this isn't my house. Don't think you can fool me." Steve stomped through the house to the front door, stepped through, and slammed the door as hard as he could. The door closed with a big bang and as the door met the doorframe, the house exploded into nothingness, leaving Steve's mom standing where the house had been.

The shell of his mother began to follow him as he made his way towards the Ocean of Pieces.

Steve remembered roughly where the ocean had been, so he struck out in that general direction. He heard a voice, the voice of the mask over a small hill of polished glass. He walked to the crest of the hill.

At the bottom of the hill, on the other side, John Dee hovered near the edge of the ocean. John Dee's body stood at effortless attention. Steve descended the hill to the ocean's edge. John's face stared sleepily toward Steve, almost empty of life. The mask hovered before John, gently instructing him.

"Raise your arm," the mask said. John raised his arm automatically above him. "Now, give your finger to us, we'll make it perfect." John nodded his agreement vacantly.

Steve watched as John's little finger popped off his hand and separated into infinitesimally small pieces that dove into the Ocean of Pieces.

"John, stop! They're killing you—you're going to die."

The mask turned towards Steve. "You too will be made perfect," he said. "Mr. Dee has already decided that he wants to join us here. Nothing you can say now will make him change his mind. He is us." John smiled as if he were dreaming something wonderful.

The mask returned to giving instructions to John's body. John gave up each of his fingers, his hand, and the entire arm to the Ocean of Pieces. The mask had him raise his other arm, dismembering it in the same simple, slow way.

"Now," said the mask, "I want your head." John nodded. Steve watched as John's head lifted away from his shoulders, turned into something that looked like sand, and then, like a swarm of flies, the cloud of fragments flew towards the ocean and dove into the depths. Steve turned away, unable to watch. A wave of nausea squeezed his stomach. He despised "Mr. Gold" and all he stood for, but he did not deserve to die this way. The clinical commands of the mask continued until it dismantled the rest of the hoodlum. Then silence.

When he turned around, both the mask and John were gone. The ocean boiled hungrily as if John had been an appetizer before the main course.

I'm dinner. I should have been dinner a long time ago.

The ocean boiled and bubbled, burping small bits of

recognizable things to its surface: cars, furniture, and clothes, mingled with human parts. Steve saw his mother approaching him like a robot.

"Mother, I want to save you," Steve said through his tears. "I must save you."

"You cannot do this!" she said with a snarl. She moved her hands towards the ocean as if to summon something from within it. A storm of demonic faces swept over him, howling and eating his breath.

Steve was tired and angry. He closed his eyes to try and block them out, but the demons and ghosts poured towards him in his thoughts. Steve opened his eyes and shouted into them.

"Mom, Mom!" Steve shouted. No response. She needed a breath of life from her stone. Steve turned back towards the ocean, to the torrent of apparitions pouring over and through him. "Bring me the sacred book of Mrs. Susan Best, the book that belonged to Mrs. May Pankratz before her. Bring it to me, now!"

The book materialized on the shores beside Mrs. Best's feet. Several demonic images attempted to pick up the book, but pulled their hands away quickly as if the book burned their fingers. Steve touched his stone, knelt down, and picked up the book carefully. This book was ragged, and nearly in pieces, just as he remembered.

The body of Mrs. Best seemed to see what Steve was doing and tried to disassemble itself quickly before Steve was able to save her.

Steve stepped towards her. Mrs. Best had begun to disintegrate into a cloud of fragments. He tagged the cloud of pieces with his mother's book. The pieces of her body hesitated for a moment, as if they didn't know whether to stay or leave.

Steve stared at her, holding the sacred book to her disintegrated body as best he could. Suddenly, the pieces seemed to melt together. Her body returned to its whole self. The vacancy in the core of her being suddenly looked occupied, and a gentle, familiar flame returned to her eyes.

The flow of demon ghosts stopped abruptly. She blinked several times as if she were waking up from a long nap. She turned her head slowly, scanning the surroundings with a puzzled look on her face—the wrinkled, tired look of her eyes reappeared, and her hair flopped into a disorganized lump on the side of her head.

"Where am I?" she asked in a tired, confused voice. She noticed Steve standing in front of her. "Steve! What are you doing here?"

Steve hadn't heard the question. He had grabbed his mother in a ferocious hug. "How did you get here, Steve?" she asked, returning his embrace.

"It's a long story." The ground underneath them started to tremble and growl, the ocean snarled and snapped before him. The two of them released each other, both of them realizing there was much more work to be done before any celebration. "Here's your notebook," Steve said to his mom, with tears in his eyes. In his hand he held her notepad that he'd pulled out from his bag. Steve suddenly felt awkward, and he didn't know what to do, so he handed the notebook to her.

Steve held her Benu stone. "When I give you your Benu stone, you'll be transported back to our house," he declared, his eyes fixed on his mother's glowing face. "Just touch your stone with one hand and your notebook with the other, and you'll end up back at home," he repeated to be sure she understood. "You know how you got here with the dictionary and your Benu stone? Well, your notebook and your stone will take you back home," Steve said, tears streaming down his face. He slipped her Benu stone into the pocket of her sweater. "I'll see you there once I'm done here."

He walked towards the edge of the ocean, leaving his mother some distance back, when the mask materialized in front of Steve. "You cannot leave this world," thundered the mask. "You are ours. You promised yourself to us. We have categories, files, and places to put each piece of you. You have violated our world twice, too. You are thrice ours."

Steve plunged one hand into his backpack. He pulled out his stone and held it in one hand while he fumbled to find his notebook with the other.

Get out of here now. Get out before anything else happens.

As he juggled his Benu stone, fumbling inside his bag, he lost his grip and watched the stone tumble—spinning from his hands into the Ocean of Pieces.

Duck Boy. Duck Boy.

As it touched the surface of the ocean, it puffed into a blue cloud of fragments and added itself to the ocean of pieces. Steve opened his mouth to yell, but nothing came out.

Duck Boy. Duck Boy. I'm dead.

Steve stood there waiting for something to happen. Nothing. There was nothing else to do but pay the price.

"Show me what price I must pay and I will pay it," Steve shouted angrily at the mask.

"We must put you into the ocean of fragments, one piece at time," the mask said.

"You are only a scrap-yard of molecules," Steve yelled at the mask.

"You must enter the ocean," said the mask. "Stand still and we will give you the gift of sleep," said the mask with a sweet smile.

Steve walked towards the ocean.

"Stop," the mask ordered. "I will disassemble you before you enter the Ocean of Pieces."

But the thought of standing there was too agonizing.

Let's get this over with.

Without another thought to stop him, Steve dove into the Ocean of Pieces.

He felt nothing, at first, as he floated down through the globs and bits of things.

I wonder if this is how Richard died.

His mind conjured a picture of Richard, wet, drowned, lying on the bedroom floor.

As he sank deeper into the airy muck, he felt as if he'd fallen into acid. His skin began to burn. It felt like the liquid in this ocean was trying to dissolve his body. He remembered how this world had dissolved the parts of his finger.

It's probably trying to break me apart, Steve thought. I'm going to end up in pieces.

But from somewhere inside of Steve, a new strength found its wings: he found something inside of him that wanted to fight back.

I am whole.

And then he had a thought that almost made him laugh.

I am Duck Boy. Duck Boy floats.

His thoughts became fuzzy, like a TV that lost its signal. Words became strings of sounds in his head. He thought of his hands and feet as himself. And as he thought about himself, the burning sensation left his skin. He thought of his own body as it might appear in a mirror. The picture of himself, with his arms and legs dissolved into fuzzy blobs of color. The color lifted from the image and mixed with the light of his mind, until Steve gave up thinking for a moment, slipping into nothingness.

The image of his Benu stone floated into his thoughts. Its blue oval shape jolted him as it jumped into his consciousness. As it touched his thoughts, shock waves shot from his head to his toes, and a new thought shouted down the corridors of his brain.

I don't need to pretend I'm whole. I AM whole.

The airy muck he was floating in suddenly felt wet. He realized he couldn't breathe. Immediately, he surged upwards, kicking towards the surface. He thrashed upward towards that dim gray light of the dawn. With a final push, he broke through the surface, gasping for air.

The mask hovered near the edge of the ocean, not moving towards Steve. Steve flailed and splashed to the edge of the ocean and stepped out near the mask, drenched by the water. He walked over to the mask. It seemed to be having difficulty holding itself together. It trembled and twisted as if it was fighting with itself.

"You shouldn't have done that," the mask said in a horrible raspy voice. "You shouldn't have done that," it repeated, but its voice sounded odd, as if its voice had speeded up. "You shouldn't have done that," it repeated a third time; this time the voice seemed unusually slow.

Steve watched the mask, its pieces pulling apart, and then together, like it was arguing with itself.

"I am not pieces. I am whole. There is nothing you can do to change that except to kill me. But you can't even do that unless I agree. Your world is made of nothing—images, letters, atoms. How can you even exist? You're snippets of things from here and there—garbage and glue. I alone recognize what you are. You are pieces held together by nothing." He dripped with the wetness of the ocean on the shore.

The mask trembled and twisted, though expressionless.

It tried to hold itself together. Part of it fell away into a powdery cloud of fragments—swarming like gnats. Part of it burst into flames. Part of it crumbled to dust, and dropped to the ground and disappeared. And the mask was gone.

Steve knew something about this world had changed, though he wasn't sure just what it was. He sat down on the shiny black surface to catch his breath and think about how he might get home again.

Mom's home.

Though he hadn't slept for a long time, he felt the blaze of new life energizing him.

The mask was gone. The mask was in charge of this world, and had disintegrated. The World of Pieces seemed to have stabilized, resting as he rested.

Who is in charge of this world now?

Steve yelled hello several times in every direction, trying to summon any other thing that might be in charge of this world. Someone has to be around somewhere, he thought. Nothing. Steve cupped his hands and shouted as loud as he could, "What am I supposed to do now?" He repeated this to himself several times trying to make something, or someone, help him and give him some direction. Nothing.

As he pondered what had just occurred, he was suddenly struck by an odd and exhilarating thought.

Maybe I'm the master of this world.

Steve decided to put his thought to a test, so he turned to face the ocean. "Listen to me, ocean," he said.

Steve focused on the ocean. "Fire," he said and the ocean exploded into an inferno of intense heat. Steve backed away from the edge of the burning ocean. "Water," he said to the ocean, and the ocean flattened into a bed of calm water. Steve ran his hand through the ocean, and his hand was wet. "Grapes," he said quietly. And a cluster of the most succulent grapes he had ever seen appeared in front of him. He reached out towards them and plucked a grape and ate it. A superb, succulent grape flavor exploded in his mouth.

"Give me my Benu stone."

Steve watched as the ocean rushed to push the fragments of his Benu stone together on the edge of the shore. Steve turned to pick up his backpack, which still sat on the shore. He picked up his stone and placed it in the bag.

It's mine. This is my world now.

Steve had once belonged to it, now it belonged to him.

"You are my world now," Steve said to everything and nothing. "You will listen to me. I am a Whole One: I am the Duck Boy."

"Hello, Steve," yelled a voice. Steve nearly jumped out of his skin, shocked that anyone was around at all. He scanned the horizon—at the top of a polished glass hill stood his mother. She had seen the whole thing.

"Mom?" Steve broke into a run towards her. She didn't return his call, but simply held her arms open wide. Steve met her open arms in a crushing bear hug.

"You waited for me," he declared in a joyful voice. "You waited for me."

"What did you think I'd do?" his mom asked. "I'm not going to leave you here all alone."

Steve hugged her tighter.

"You were gone for a very, very long time, Son. I was really worried about you. Let's go home," Mrs. Best suggested. Steve nodded without speaking. He pulled his stone out of his backpack and placed it in his pocket. Then he grabbed his notebook.

"Are you ready, Mom?" She nodded and grinned.

Steve swung his backpack over his shoulder and grabbed his plaque and notepad. He kept his eye on his mom, who did the same thing with her stone and notebook. The two of them burst into spirals of bright light.

CHAPTER TWENTY-FOUR

TO BREAK THE DEATH-GRIP of silence hovering in the Best house, Lindsay walked to the window and looked up at the sky. She studied the stars as they burned their way through the dark night sky.

"Beautiful night," she said absently, hoping someone might want to notice along with her. Then, as she watched, a streak of light flashed across the sky.

Uncle Edward sat on the couch holding Aunt Shannon's hand, both looking lost and helpless. Aunt Shannon held her head with her other hand and wept silently. Mr. Best slouched in Mrs. Best's chair, dark and speechless.

Death's pall, dull and leaden, strangled the air in the room. But then, suddenly, there was a wink of light and the air tore open above them. A huge burst of light hovered above Mr. Best, slowly spinning down upon him. Mr. Best was thrown across the floor and landed in a mound in front of the couch. Mrs. Best materialized in the chair she'd disappeared from.

The others froze in their seats, and Mr. Best lay paralyzed with terror on the floor.

"Silent Night!" Uncle Edward exclaimed. "It's Susan, come home."

"Hello, everyone," Mrs. Best chirped cheerily. "I'm back."

No one moved. Each person was too stunned by what had happened even to make a comment. They just stared at Mrs. Best.

"What's everyone doing here?" Steve asked as he rounded a corner and entered the living room. He'd materialized back in his bedroom and walked to the living room. Everyone in the room turned their frozen stares toward Steve, without uttering a single word—stunned back into silence.

"What? What's the matter?" Steve asked, as he noticed the deep lines of grief and shock on the faces in the room. "What's going on? What have I done now?"

"Mary and the Blessed Baby! Steve's returned, too!" Uncle Edward exclaimed with a triumphant shout. Uncle Edward's words seemed to free everyone from the staring trance that had held them motionless, and the room exploded into pandemonium. Mr. Best leapt from his spot on the floor into his wife's waiting arms as she sat on the chair, and they showered each other with affection.

The two of them opened their arms as Steve joined them in a huge hug. It wasn't a time for words. All the people in the room flooded around the Best family, forming a huge mob of joy. Once the initial shock of the moment was over, the emotion in the room gave way to a torrent of questions.

Lindsay hugged Steve and then held him at arm's length, inspecting him with a puzzled look. "I thought for sure you were dead. What happened?"

"And what happened to your hand?" asked Mr. Best, pointing to Steve's missing finger.

The hubbub in the rest of the room settled down as he asked the question. Steve flopped onto the floor as the group began to share their stories and perceptions of all that had happened.

Partway through the festivities, the doorbell rang. It was Larry, in uniform. He stepped inside to address the family.

"I'm here to convey my official condolences to the family on the passing of Steve Best," he said somberly. His eyebrows showed his confusion as he noticed the giddy people milling around the room.

When he saw Steve sitting on the couch, Larry fainted.

Steve and Mr. Best lifted the detective onto the couch, and the group continued their conversations until he reawakened.

Larry was initially quite uncomfortable with the idea that Steve was still alive and Mrs. Best had returned.

But after a few minutes he recovered most of his composure.

"You won't believe how much paperwork I'll have to do." Though he smiled. "It's great to have you back. Now we've really got a complicated mess on our hands," he said, shaking his head. "I'm here on a matter of utmost urgency. And with you two alive, it gets much more knotted." He thought for a moment before attempting to explain.

"The criminals we captured are an experimenting group of alchemists who are after any alchemical secrets. They want to make themselves rich. You and your family have obviously managed to find and use several methods that would make you targets for the rest of your lives. That's why we must keep everything that has happened a secret. No one but the people in this room must ever know what went on in this case—ever."

He paused for a moment. "I am going to have to explain how Steve managed to survive the fire, and how Mrs. Best managed to return home. This isn't going to be easy." He thought for a few moments. "How would everybody feel if I reported things like this: I'll say that Mrs. Best went on a trip to California. I know you have a sister there. I'd like to say, um… that it was… um… well, that you were having marriage difficulties—if that's OK with you." Larry eyed Mr. and Mrs. Best carefully, waiting for their agreement.

After looking at each other, they both nodded slowly.

"Most people would believe that. Um… could we say she left a note somewhere, but that the note was lost somehow?" Larry looked around the room, making sure people agreed with him. "Mrs. Best, you're going to have to invent a clear story about where you went and what you did. Mr. and Mrs. Best, you need to invent a marriage problem. Make sure your story is straight, all right?" Larry paused for a moment and turned to Steve. "I'm going to have to say something about how you got out of the fire, Steve."

Steve thought with Larry and made his own suggestion. "Why don't you say I was hit on the head, wandered away from the scene, and was found later?"

"That's not bad. I think I'll use it. How will I explain how you lost your finger?"

"Maybe, while I was lost, one of my fingers was frostbitten and had to be amputated."

"That's not too bad," Larry said, thumbing his chin. "We'll have to create some medical records somewhere to back this story up. It's got to be perfect."

"You're not a group of alchemists, OK?" Larry insisted as he looked around the room. "You're just ordinary people who were mistakenly victimized by this gang, all right?" He scanned the room making sure everyone was in agreement. "By the way, I got my job back because of this case," he pointed to Aunt Shannon and Steve. "I owe it all to you guys. Although I lost my job because of you, too." He replaced his hat after scratching his head and staring at Steve and Mrs. Best. "Merry Christmas, everyone."

Larry headed out to his car under the clear night air, brooding over the tsunami of paper work now waiting for him.

Inside Steve's house, around the warm light of a fire, the group recounted their various experiences, and how their lives had been changed by all of it. But it was Steve's story that inspired them all, the story of how he had transformed from a frightened, frozen Duck Boy into the Lord of the Pond.

Epilogue

At the place in between, the twilight did not change, nor did the deep solitude. No soul walked the shoreline. No boat sailed the sea. The dark, hungry water raged as things below moved to the surface and dropped below again. Waiting.

Bill Bunn

teaches English at Mt. Royal University in Calgary, Alberta, Canada. He lives out in the country where he has numerous dogs and cats and three teenagers, and keeps bees. He is the author, along with his wife, of an illustrated children's book, *Canoë Lune*, and a columnist. His columns have appeared in *Salon, The Globe and Mail,* and elsewhere. *Duck Boy* is his first novel.

The chapter vignettes in this book were made using the Tombats series of fonts by Tom Murphy VII (Tom 7), freely available on the web. Thanks to Tom for making these and other designs accessible to all.